Misbegotten

W. James Richardson

8/20/01

Pamela,

It is indeed my hope that the members of Ebony Eyes Book Club will endorse my book.

W. James Richardson

Misbegotten

W. James Richardson

Pittsbrugh, PA

ISBN 1-56315-169-3

Paperback Fiction
© Copyright 1999 W. James Richardson
All rights reserved
First Printing—2000
Library of Congress #98-87020

Request for information should be addressed to:

SterlingHouse Publisher, Inc.
The Sterling Building
440 Friday Road
Pittsburgh, PA 15209
www.sterlinghousepublisher.com

Cover design and typesetting: AJ Rodgers - SterlingHouse Publisher
Cover art: Untitled abstract, by Cynthia Shore-Sterling, from the
private collection of Thomas S. Sterling

This is a work of Fiction. Names, characters, places, and
incidents either are the product of the author's imagination or
are used fictitiously. Any resemblance to actual events or per-
sons, living or dead is entirely coincidental.

Printed in Canada

Dedication

Dedicated to my departed siblings: Graylin, Joyce, Sandra, and Ronnie. They're missed and forever loved.

Acknowledgement

Gratitude is extended to Michelle Burton-Brown for her early encouragement, as well as her guidance. And appreciation to Vickey Dugan for her interest and review, which assisted with appropos content in this novel. Also, I'm indeed grateful for the great editorial assistance provided.

Chapter One

He hated this damn precinct; hated it with a royal passion because of the type of people who hung out here. They were all over the place—like pigeons in a park. And as far as he was concerned, he couldn't any better distinguish one nigger from another than tell apart pigeons. He loathed the fact that he had been forced to come here. He had no other choice, it was the closest precinct to the Renaissance Center and time was of the essence. Hugo exploded through the entrance of the Beaubein Street Police Precinct with the exigency of a firefighter off to a six-alarm fire. His appearance was a cross between a lumberjack and a cowboy. His red and black checkered shirt draped sloppily outside his well-worn jeans that hung low beneath his ample belly. His scuffed, black cowboy boots pounded against the hardwood floor as he rushed to the counter, producing a trail of water dripping from the umbrella in his hand. He figured he looked out of place—like Hank Williams at the African-American Music Festival.

It was a typical frantic Friday night at the Beaubein Street Precinct: handcuffed painted-face women in short skirts and dresses, wearing high heel shoes and cursing adeptly; slovenly attired drunks on wobbly legs, using speech as intelligible as a deaf mute; crying mothers with ragtag children; swaggering young punks with cocksure attitudes, wearing baggy low-riding pants that appeared to have ten pounds of shit inside them, causing them to sag low in the crotch and seat. A freak show is how Hugo assessed it all, while taking pleasure in the thought that when he was on the police force he'd had a chance to bust a lot of those foul-mouthed whores and young punks. He even kicked some of their asses. And kicked their asses good, too, Hugo remembered. He kicked a lot of their asses; no question about it. The stench of sweaty flesh, cheap perfume, and alcohol would have made Hugo puke if it hadn't been such an important mission he was on. Hugo caught the eye of one of two white officers who was working behind the counter. The harried-face white officer with short brown hair, who looked to be in his mid-thirties, detected the urgency on Hugo's face. He had a frazzled look. They both did. "Good evening, sir," the officer said. "Can I help you?" Hugo whispered (not wanting the niggers inside the precinct to know his business), "I wanna file a missin' person report." "A relative?" the officer asked. "My daughter," Hugo whispered.

"How long has she been missing"? "About two and a half hours; close to three." "Your daughter really hasn't been gone long enough to be considered missing," the officer said with a hint of empathy in his voice. "Why do you think she's missing? And missing from where?" Hugo felt agitated, thinking that too much time had already passed. It wasn't as though his daughter had gone off somewhere in the suburbs. His daughter was missing in Detroit. He'd been a cop in this goddamn city for two decades, and with so many blacks living here, he felt it could be fatal for his daughter to be missing as long as she had. Hugo unbuttoned his shirt pocket and showed the gold shield he'd received from the Detroit P.D. when he retired. The officer smiled, showing his nicotine-stained teeth and said, "Useta be one of us, huh?" "Yeah," Hugo said, "for twenty years. Can I talk to a detective?" "All the detectives are busy, but let me talk to the shift sergeant; maybe he can help." The officer left and entered an office about twenty feet behind the counter. Through the glass Hugo could see the officer talking to a middle-age, dark-complected black man with a medium build, wearing wire-rim spectacles. The officer returned after a short period and said, "Like I said, all the detectives are tied up, but Sergeant Washington will talk to you."

Hugo was thinking that he didn't want to confide in the black sergeant; not about his precious Emily. But, what choice did he have? He remembered a time when the city didn't have so many blacks on the force. Since Mayor Cavanaugh left office and that cocky-ass nigger took his place, the city started going to hell. Blacks everywhere; in places they'd never been. Blacks in charge of departments where you once hardly ever saw them. The damn police chief black. Blacks everywhere. Hugo felt that he'd seen enough; too much, in fact. After twenty years he just couldn't put up with it any longer. Now it'd come to the point where he had to discuss his daughter with the black sergeant, sitting behind the desk where white men used to sit. Goddamn niggers done took over the city. Ain't hardly no justice anymore in America for white men, Hugo muddled. Hugo's intense need to find his daughter made him swallow his Herculean pride in chunks as he approached Sergeant Washington's office.

Sergeant Washington motioned for Hugo to enter and have a seat in one of the two hardwood chairs in front of his black metallic desk. Hugo sat on the edge of the chair, letting the sergeant know that he wasn't intent on being in his office long. Neither man extended his hand to the other in greeting. Neither man smiled. Both were questionable of the other: Hugo suspicious as to whether or not the sergeant would help a white man; the sergeant leery as to why this honkie chose to come to the Beaubein Street Precinct this time of night—especially a former Detroit P.D. officer. "Understand you were once on our force," said Sergeant Washington. "And didn't catch the full name. What is it?" "Hugo Heiderberg." Sergeant Washington made a triangle below his chin with his index fingers and squinted his eyes as though he was attempting to glean something from his mind's computer. "Heiderberg," Sergeant Washington said. "Hugo Heiderberg. Ain't you one of those guys that Internal Affairs investigated after some citizens complained about police brutality?" Sergeant Washington's question aggravated Hugo, but he knew that he had to be cordial with the sergeant for his daughter's sake. "Yeah, I was one of them, but I was found not guilty. Sergeant, out of due respect (damn, it hurt him to say that), I came here because of my daughter. Can we talk about her?" Sergeant Washington leaned back in his black, padded, swivel chair. He unloosened his tie and shirt collar. "Yeah, I remember," he said, "they called you guys the Dirty Dozen." Now the sergeant was really annoying Hugo. "Damn, Sergeant," Hugo uttered, "are we gonna talk history, or can we discuss my daughter. My daughter's missing for God's sake!"

Hugo wiped beads of sweat from his forehead with the handkerchief he retrieved from his back pocket. He squirmed in the chair and said, "Didn't mean to get upset, but I'm here to talk about my daughter. She disappeared. We looked everywhere. She's nowhere to be found." Sergeant Washington bent forward and rested his arms on top of his desk. "How long your daughter been missing?" the sergeant asked. "About three hours," Hugo answered. "Not long enough to file a missing person report, you know," said Sergeant Washington. "I know," Hugo replied, "but thought a former, fellow officer could get some special consideration." Sergeant Washington leaned fully back in his chair, ran his hand backward across the top of his head and said, "Special consideration. That's what you're looking for?" Hugo fashioned in his mind that the sergeant wasn't going to make him beg. No way was he going to beg his black ass. He'd tell the black son-of-a-bitch to kiss his lily white ass. Goddamn it! What in the hell was he thinking? His precious Emily was missing. Missing somewhere in this goddamn, god-forsaken city; and the only person who could immediately help him was this pompous-ass nigger, sitting behind a desk where white men used to sit. Hugo said, "I'd appreciate it, Sergeant Washington. I really would, sir." (Goddamn if it didn't hurt to use "sir".)

Sergeant Washington flashed a canny smile, generated by the regard that Hugo had just paid him. That's what he wanted from the honkie—some respect. Respect with a capital R; nothing less. Some Aretha Franklin type of respect: R-E-S-P-E-C-T. He remembered the mean-ass bastard; part of the Dirty Dozen: White-ass cops who abused and beat black people for the sport of it. Half the bastards got off; found not guilty only because some black citizens were scared to testify, and there wasn't enough evidence to convict them without their testimony. His ass should've been suspended from the force; instead, he got his twenty years in and retired. Now look at the honkie bastard, the sergeant was thinking, his ass asking a black man for some consideration. Bet it's killing him to be at this precinct and asking a black man for a favor. His precious daughter's missing, he says. Probably afraid some black folks done did something to her. That's how his kind thinks. The racist bastard!

Chapter Two

"**D**amn, Juice, yah coulda wiped yer mess offa her. Where's the rag? Now I gotta clean yer stuff offa her 'fore doin' my thang." "You stupid-ass fool, why yah call my goddamn name! I'm gonna have to waste the bitch now. I should make your ass waste her. Yah old drunk-ass fool!" "I ain't gonna kill nobody. I ain't no killa. Ain't gonna kill nobody. Ain't no killa. And why yah talkin' 'bout killin'? Juice ain't yer real name, anyhow." "Old stupid-ass fool, shut the hell up and go 'head and do your little bit of business. All your old drunk-ass got in yah is a couple of humps, anyways." "Yeah, think so, huh? Well, I'll show yo' young-ass what an ol' man can do."

She had run out of tears, but not hate. She never possessed so much hate. She wished she had a bomb inside of her that would explode and kill these animals who were treating her like meat in a snare. And no matter if she killed herself; she was convinced that they were going to kill her anyway after their feast was over. "Yah a purty, lil thang. Yah gonna love what I got fir yah, baby. Yah gonna love it. I knows what a woman likes. How do it feel? Feel good, don't it? I bet if I took that tape offa yer mouth you'd tell me how yah lovin' it. Now, won't yah, sweet thang? I know yah would." She sensed that he was smaller in size than her first assailant. He felt slender and appeared to be a lot shorter. His voice was deep and raspy. He was adding insult on top of injury with his prattle. She thought he smelled like manure. His beard felt like a Brillo pad against her face. She just wanted to die. He kept pounding and grinding. His pounding and grinding suddenly halted. But she hadn't felt his discharge inside of her. Then she heard a distinguishing sound: the sound of an umbrella opening. The other voice, the younger-sounding and mean voice; the voice that was Juice's said, "What the hell is yah doin'? Why yah got that damn umbrella up?" "Makin' love in the rain! I'm doin' a Gene Kelly wif the lil, sweet thang." "A what, yah crazy ass fool?"

"A Gene Kelly, young boy. He danced in the rain. You don't know nothin' 'bout him. 'Fore yo' time. But I'm makin' love in the rain. And this sweet thang here is my partner. Come on lil mama, flow wif daddy. Show daddy some rhythm." "Old crazy ass fool," the younger voice said. The voice that was Juice's. She could hear them whispering in the front of the van. The younger-sounding voice got louder. There was agitation in his voice. She heard, "You old, dumb son-of-a-bitch...," then his voice tapered off, but the agitation in his voice hung in the air like dust in the ensuing silence. The smell of marijuana grew stronger. She could detect the rustling sound of anxious feet scraping across the floor and restless butts twisting incessantly in the squeaky seats. The engine started. A dog began yelping. The van began to move. She prayed. The faces of her mother, father, and siblings flashed in her mind's eye. She was preparing for her death. He told him to take the wheel. He told him to drive slow. He told him to keep his old-ass eyes on the road. So who in the hell did he think he wuz, anyway? Orderin' him 'round like he wuz some kinda kid or somethin'. Hell, he wuz twice his age. The young boy wuz bigger and stronger and probably the reason he always tried to order him 'round. But he didn't care how big and strong he wuz, he wuzn't gonna kill that white girl. Saw enough killin' in Vietnam. Damn near drove him crazy. Wuz sent home on disability. Got a check every month from Uncle Sam like clockwork. The young boy knew it too, and always showed up at his apartment the first of the month like a damn landlord. Stayed 'round 'til the money wuz gone, which most the time wuz eight to ten days. Be buyin' lots of weed and booze. The young boy thought he be usin' him; but he be usin' the young boy, too. The young boy knew how to git some women, which wuz why he put up wif his ornery ass. But when his money ran out he never saw the young boy 'til the followin' month when he showed up again—like a damn landlord.

This month he won in the lottery. Played 1940, the year he wuz born. Played a whole dollar on it, straight. They paid him $5,000. Gave him a check. He didn't have no account at the bank, so couldn't cash it. Didn't want no damn bank account, either. Took it to the dope house; they gave him $4,000 for the check. The young boy couldn't understand why he had so much money this month. Couldn't understand how he could still buy weed, whiskey, and malt liquor past September tenth. Told the young boy he'd won $500 in the lottery. The young boy's eyes lit up like 150 watts light bulbs. The young boy hung 'round 'til after the tenth and showed him some more good times wif the ladies. He always gave the young boy $50 to git him a woman to entertain him in bed. Told the young boy that for $50 he didn't want no ugly broad. The young boy never disappointed him. Just so happened that white girl wuz in the wrong place at the wrong time. They'd been smokin' weed and drinkin' all day. Left Belle Isle and decided to cruise down by the Renaissance Center. The young boy saw that white girl runnin' wif a undabrella over her head. She by herself. Told him to git behind the wheel. Next thang he knew, the young boy wuz back at the van wif that white girl. Wasn't givin' that white girl a break. Back there now on the floor doin' his business wif her again. Could see his naked ass in the rearview mirror bouncin' like a beach ball. "Aw, shit! What the hell!" Scared the shit almost outta him. Henry's rumination ended. He ran over something. Nothing small, either. The van bounced; cans rattled. Henry damn near fell out of the driver's seat. He struggled hard with the steering wheel, trying to bring the van back under control. He heard the loud sound of rubber flapping against the asphalt and van. He managed to bring the van back under control and stopped it on the side of the expressway. "What the hell happened?" "I ran over somethin'!" "Yah dumb-ass fucker, I told yah to keep your goddamn eyes on the road. Now the tires are fucked up. We can't go nowhere in this goddamn van, now. Shit! Goddamn! A car is pullin' up behind us! Let's get the hell outta here!" The two of them were befuddled seeing the two guys struggle up the muddy embankment in the rain. The bigger guy in front was struggling to secure his pants. The smaller one in the rear was doing more crawling than running. They approached the van cautiously: one on the driver's side and the other on the passenger side. They couldn't see anyone else inside the van. "Let's open it," one of them said. And just as they did, they saw the flashing lights of a police cruiser approaching.

Chapter Three

Hugo Heiderberg's complexion had turned tomato-red. He'd been at the Beaubein Street Precinct for an hour and Sergeant Washington had yet to communicate if he'd provide assistance. Kept asking Hugo questions. Kept saying, "The police need information to do its job, you know." Sergeant Washington was thoroughly enjoying himself with Hugo. He pretended he was concerned; but there was nothing about the racist bastard that could really concern him. Hell, his daughter probably ran off with one of those hillbillies. Hundreds of them down there at Hart Plaza for the Country and Western Jamboree. And with so many policemen assigned down there, how in the hell could someone have abducted his daughter? The city council and the mayor wanted those white folks down there safe and protected. Got police all over the damn place: from Hart Plaza to Greektown. Hell, his daughter's probably up in a room at the Westin Hotel screwing her a cowboy. Missing! Missing his ass! Sergeant Washington thought.

Officer Zemanski came to the door and beckoned for Sergeant Washington. He rose from his chair in the middle of a question he was asking Hugo. Hugo's eyes followed the sergeant. His complexion was now fire engine-red. He was seething; damn near ready to explode. And no telling what he would say or do if he did. Sergeant Washington left his office door open. Hugo could again smell the odor of the humanity gathered in the lobby. The stench made him frown harder. Hugo watched as Sergeant Washington spoke to two burly white police officers. The officers were about the same height: One was considerably younger than the other. The older officer looked familiar to Hugo, but he couldn't quite make him out. The two officers came behind the counter and followed Sergeant Washington into his office. "Hey, Hugo," the older white officer said. Hugo recognized that it was Sergeant Charlie Wolffiel; a good ol' German guy like himself. They'd drunk a few beers together. Hell, ol' Charlie had more than twenty years on the force.

Must be thinking about retiring himself, Hugo thought. "Hey, Charlie," Hugo responded. "Apparently you two guys know one another," Sergeant Washington said. He motioned at the younger officer and said, "This is Officer Cunningham."

Officer Cunningham and Hugo nodded at each other. Officer Cunningham had a compassionate look on his face; the same as with Sergeant Wolffiel. Probably feeling sorry for him having to be at Beaubein with all the niggers, Hugo figured. "We think we found your daughter," Sergeant Washington said. But this time his voice was softer and temperate. "You think? Why? Why don't you know for sure?" said Hugo as he stood up from the chair he was sitting in. Hugo looked Sergeant Wolffiel in the face, then Officer Cunninghan, then back to the white sergeant. He ignored Sergeant Washington. As far as he was concerned, now that the two white officers were present, Sergeant Washington didn't exist. Sergeant Wolffiel said, "We found a young white girl in a van, but she didn't have any I.D. on her. We found this wallet inside the van. It apparently belongs to you. Got your driver's license in it and some other I.D. Of course, the money and credit cards are gone." He displayed the black wallet that was inside a plastic bag. "Didn't you ask her?" Hugo said. "She'd told you she was my daughter." Hugo thought for a moment, then said," Is she alive? Please tell me she's alive! She ain't dead is she? Please God, tell me she ain't dead!" Hugo had a strong grip on Sergeant Wolffiel's arm. "She's alive," Sergeant Wolffiel said. "We took her to Henry Ford Hospital. She's in shock. We couldn't get anything outta her. She had a real bad ordeal. She was raped."

No! Not his daughter! Not Emily! He always kept her safe. He always saw to it that no harm would come to her. He sent her to good schools. He'd moved his family to the suburb away from niggers. This was all just a bad nightmare, Hugo was thinking. He sat back down in the chair. He used his handkerchief to wipe away the tears—big tears. Tears the size of butter beans. Hugo's eyes roamed the room. He saw a large, framed photo of Dr. Martin Luther King, Jr. on the wall behind Sergeant Washington's desk. He sneered at the photo. Hugo got angry at himself for having allowed his daughter to go alone to the car to retrieve his wallet from the trunk. But she'd insisted. She'd handed her purse to her mother and took off. That was the last time they'd seen her is what Hugo was recalling. Sergeant Washington asked, "How solid are the suspects?" "Don't know," Sergeant Wolffiel said, "they were at the van when we pulled up, but claimed they stopped to help the occu- pants after seeing the van hit something in the road and go outta control. Said they'd just walked up to the van before we arrived. Said two black guys ran from the van up the embankment and dis- appeared down by Wayne State University. Neither one has a rap sheet. Both are students at the University of Michigan. Said they'd gone to a concert at the Fox Theater and then hung out with some friends. Said they were headed back to Ann Arbor when they saw the van in trouble. Checked the car parked behind the van; it was registered to one of the suspects. The van was stolen." "Do you wanna continue to hold 'em as suspects?" Sergeant Washington asked.

"We'd like to dust the van for prints first. We found some mar- ijuana in the van and a pile of beer cans; most empty, but a few still full." Sergeant Washington said, "We'll hold 'em for twenty-four hours and question 'em to see what more we can get from 'em. You said they claimed to have seen two guys run from the van?" "Yeah, they did," Sergeant Wolffiel said. "Two black guys," he empha- sized. "Sergeant Washington thanked the two officers. He let Hugo use his telephone to call the hospital where his daughter was taken. He admired the ring Hugo was wearing on his right hand: A gold ring with a cross in the center, with three diamonds clustered around it. Hugo left the Beubein Street Precinct faster than he'd entered it. "Shit!" Sergeant Washington exclaimed as he dropped heavily into his desk chair. "A white girl abducted and raped downtown. The press is gonna eat Detroit alive. The mayor and the city council are gonna raise holy hell. The chief is gonna kick some ass. Why couldn't his daughter have been at the Westin Hotel screwin' one of those hillbillies down there? Shit! Gotta call the chief. He ain't gonna like this shit! Sure in hell ain't! There's an army of police- men assigned to that damn Country and Western Jamboree. Goddamn! This shit ain't good! Ain't good at all." Sergeant Washington's knobby finger punched the digits on the touch-tone phone.

Chapter Four

ROMULUS, MICHIGAN SEPTEMBER 23, 1992

About fifty enraged white men assembled inside the barn on a remote farm—all proud Anglo Saxons. They referred to each other as "Brothers" and used code names. Prodigious and majestic mountains of Europe (the Alps, Balkon, Caucasus, and Pyrences) were code names reserved for their exalted leaders, who were looked upon to be as lofty as the mountains of Europe. The other Brothers took on the names of rivers of Europe (the Volga, Rhine, Danube, Belarus, Oder, Thames, Dnepr, etcetera) which flow perpetually throughout Europe and serve as receptacles for the immaculate rain that the Almighty gives the earth for nourishment and growth. It was a Code III situation—a very serious matter. It's written in the code. The language is as clear as glass. It's stated:

...The rape of an immediate family member by a nigger, Jew, or person of Third World origin is a capital offense and punishment for such a crime is to be dispensed by the sacred hands of members of the Society.

Language in regards to Code III also stated: ...

When what's deemed to be a capital offense is exacted against a member of the Society, or any person of a Brother's immediate family, the punishment is to be dispensed in accordance to the trilogy: God, Europe, and the white race; meaning that for each capital offense, three executions must be carried out.

Grand Superior Alps well understood it to be a Code III situation, and the second Code III meeting the Society had had in its fifteen-year history. The first Code III situation and meeting occurred seven years ago when two Korean thugs car-jacked Brother Belarus' car in Hazel Park and shot him to death, leaving behind his wife of ten years and two children. When the retribution was carried out three Orientals were executed; but not all of them were

Koreans as the grand superior recalled. The revengers couldn't distinguish, so in the end one Korean guy, a Chinese fellow, and a Jap were executed—all gooks, nonetheless.

Now this: damn niggers done raped a white girl. And not just any white girl. But the precious daughter of one of the Brothers. Brother Elbe's daughter. A young, beautiful girl with good white features. Two coons having their smutty way with her was too goddamn hard to swallow; like trying to digest filthy garbage. And the Society wasn't going to stand for it. The vicious rape happened to Brother Elbe's daughter, but could've easily been another Brother's daughter, or some other white man's daughter or wife, the grand superior thought. A lot of decent white folks—including several of the Brothers—had been down there in nigger town for the Country and Western Jamboree. Several of the Brothers had attended the jamboree since it started. Thought it was safe because a lot of police officers were assigned to downtown. It made decent white folks feel as safe as one could in a city with so many niggers. This was just too damn much; a decent white girl raped and treated like that. The pretty thing's body defiled. Never will be right. Hope she doesn't get pregnant. That would tear Brother Elbe's heart totally apart. He's just hanging on by a thread as it is. Gotta do something about this. God-fearing white men gotta step forward. Niggers done gone crazy; out of control. White people gotta be protected. White people got rights, too. Got the right to protect their families. Goddamn it, white men built this country; and ain't no fucking spooks gonna take this country away from them by running over white people and fucking their daughters. White men gotta protect and defend what's theirs.

After contemplating the situation for awhile, Grand Superior Alps stood and brushed the seat of his pants with his hands as he rose from the bale of hay he was sitting on. He was relatively short in stature, but, as the Society's highest ranking officer, he was lofty in status. The Brothers' voices were clamorous and echoed in the rafters of the barn. A Boeing 747 landing at Detroit Metropolitan Airport could be heard over the voices. The grand superior was very pleased by what his eyes saw: proud white men of the Euro-

Brothers Defense Society, uniformly dressed from head-to-toe in brown flattop hats with black shiny bills; white long sleeve shirts with epaulettes and a circular patch stitched on the left arm with the Society's emblem embossed on it; dark brown military-type pants with a brown thick leather belt woven through the large belt loops; and tall spit-shined, black leather boots. The grand superior had three different colored braided cords through the epaulette on his left shoulder: a blue one symbolizing the sky and God's domicile; a green one betokening the motherland of Europe; and a white cord denoting the purity of the white race. The other officers wore a colored cord according to rank, plus a white cord. The white cord, alone, was worn by all other members. "Brothers," Grand Superior Alps shouted over a crescendo of wrathful voices, "it's time to call the meeting to order. Brothers, please take your seats. Brother Volga, prepare to call the roll." As the members' names were called, a chorus of "present" rolled off the Brothers' lips with the cadence of tumbling rows of dominoes.

"Forty-six present," Brother Volga reported. The grand superior nodded his head approvingly and gestured for the Brothers to stand by raising both his hands, palms up, from his waist to shoulder height. The members rose from the three rows of pew-like wooden benches. The grand superior waited for the noise of a 737 to diminish and said, "Brothers, let us now cite our pledge." All cited in unison: "We, the members of the Euro-Brothers Defense Society, pledge to honor our God, who gives us wisdom and glory; to glorify Europe, the land of our origin; and to preserve the purity of the white race, the supreme Homo sapiens. We pledge to honor and defend God, Europe, and the white race for all the days of our lives; and we swear this to be our sacred pledge for all the days of our lives; for all the days of our lives; for all the days of our lives. This we do solemnly pledge."

The grand superior lowered his hands, palms down, from shoulder height to his waist, which signaled the Brothers to be seated. The Brothers sat in unison. "Brothers," the grand superior said, "we live in a society with heathens. Black heathens; animals that should've remained in the darkest jungles of Africa. The animals have attacked one of our own, the lovely daughter of Brother Elbe. And as is the tradition, I'll give Brother Elbe time to speak after I've finished and before we decide on how we're to avenge the dastardly act that has brought us to a Code III situation. And be assured, Brothers, we are, in the name of God, Europe and the white race gonna avenge this crime." As though it'd been rehearsed, loud voices shouted, "Avenge the crime! Avenge the crime! Avenge the crime!" The Brothers extended their right arms high above their heads with clenched fists each time they said the words. Their voices echoed and then dissipated. Their voices returned to a hush. An airplane could be heard and then the sound of a cat rustling in the barn.

The grand superior said, "Some would say we're unlawful; that we're only vigilantes; that we are taking the law into our own hands. Some bleeding-heart white people would criticize us. No, Brothers, let me take that back; let me rephrase that; some nigger-loving, kiss-ass whites would talk against us. It seems that we've always had that kind; probably always will, but we, the members of the Euro-Brothers Defense Society, know better; and the reason we started this Society fifteen years ago is because this nation is causing God-fearing white men to lose their God-given rights and place in society and in the world. Too many minorities have been allowed to come into this country, a country built by the honest sweat and supreme intelligence of white men. Men like our fathers; our fathers' fathers; and their fathers before them. Generations of white men built this nation and made it great. Intelligent white men from the soil of Europe with supreme intelligence and armed with the blessing of God built this country. If God hadn't wanted white men to inhabit this land and become masters of it, they wouldn't have succeeded. There were too many obstacles to overcome if it hadn't been the divine will of God. It was white men who liberated this country from a bunch of savages and enabled it to grow and flourish to become the greatest nation in the world." A thundering 747 could be heard. The grand superior temporarily halted his speech; looked up in the rafters; took a swig from the canteen laying on the bale of hay next to him. All the Brothers had canteens; some contained water; but most contained a more potent beverage.

It was known that the grand superior's beverage of choice was vodka. This was also an opportunity for all the Brothers to drink from their canteens. The grand superior's virulent words had stirred their emotions and caused their throats to become parched. The grand superior screwed the cap back on the canteen, laid it back on the bale of hay and said, "The airplanes that fly above our heads, planes with powerful engines, capable of flying people all over the world; who gave the world such a miraculous machine? The white man, the supreme Homo sapiens!" In unison all the members shouted, "The supreme Homo sapiens! The supreme Homo sapiens! The supreme Homo sapiens!" They lowered their right arms and placed them again in their laps and sat erect on the benches with their feet flat on the makeshift, plywood floor.

The grand superior continued, "Today, my Brothers, we have a Code III situation, because heathens are still in our presence; heathens that prey upon innocent victims. Heathens that don't have any rightful place in a civilized society and among decent, God-fearing white people. We're beleaguered, my brothers. The NAACP has worked to lessen and sometimes destroy the white man's power. Then, we got a black Muslim nigger like Louis FarraCoon going around bad mouthing the white race and in particular white men. Now, I don't care what FarraCoon says about Jews, but whenever you got someone like him going all over berating white men, then such a coon is dangerous. He and his kind have to be stopped! Make no mistake about it, Louis FarraCoon is the most dangerous nigger in America; much like that Martin Luther Coon nigger used to be. We need to put FarraCoon where Luther Coon is! It's their kind who stir up the blacks; make them think they're equal to the white race and the white man; and make nigger men desire white women and cause them to rape white women when they can't find white trash to voluntarily lie down with them. We cannot and will not tolerate our women being sullied. Hail to the white race! Hail to white men! Hail to the supreme Homo sapiens!" "Hail to the supreme Homo sapiens! Hail to the supreme Homo sapiens! Hail to the supreme Homo sapiens!" all the

Brothers bellowed so loudly that the 737 overhead couldn't be heard. "Now, Brothers," Grand Superior Alps said, "I want Brother Elbe to come forward and address the congregation."

The grand superior sat back on the bale of hay, unscrewed the cap of his canteen and took a hefty drink. Some of the other Brothers followed suit and swallowed from their canteens. Brother Elbe rose slowly from one of the juxtaposed front row benches. He laboriously moved to the position on the floor vacated by the grand superior. The Brothers thought Brother Elbe appeared to be smaller in stature than his six-four height normally displayed. He wasn't as erect as the Brothers remembered—in fact, his shoulders seemed to have drooped. But they didn't have to discuss it among themselves. Each of them knew with certainty what had happened. The rape of Brother Elbe's daughter had diminished him as a father, protector of the family, and as a white man. That's what those nigger rapists had done to Brother Elbe; they had diminished him. And there wasn't a single member of the Society who was going to let niggers get away with what they'd done to one of their own. They all knew that this was a Code III situation if ever there was or would ever be. Brother Elbe turned slowly around to face the Brothers. Pain and sadness were etched on his pale, alabaster face. He looked out at the Brothers. He saw somber expressions. It was like being at a wake. He looked down at the scuffed plywood floor, then up into the rafters, then back into the hard and frozen faces of the Brothers. He said (with the words oozing out like catsup out of a bottle), "Brothers, I stand before you as a wounded man. I'm in pain; lots of pain. I've been scarred; deeply scarred."

Brother Elbe's cracking, baritone voice increased in volume. Bitter words ensued. "My entire family's in pain," he muttered. "My family has been deeply scarred—not by men—but by animals. Predators! My daughter will never be the same. She's been defiled and adulterated. She's a prisoner in herself: afraid to venture out of the house; afraid to return to school in her senior year of college; and, of course, worried that no decent white man will ever have anything to do with her if they find out that she—." The words got stuck in Brother Elbe's throat. Tears streamed down his sorrowful-looking face. He looked down at the floor again, then back up into the rafters. He was searching for strength to go on. He looked down to the floor again, then back into the enraged faces of the Brothers. He gathered his composure and said, "I don't know if my daughter will ever be able to find a decent white man; and God forbid if she becomes pregnant with a nigger baby." Tears gushed from Brother Elbe's eyes and rushed down his contorted face. He trembled and stood there looking more like a seedling than the image of a towering oak that the Brothers were more accustomed to. All the Brothers—with the exception of the grand superior—rose to their feet and shouted, "Vengeance is ours! Vengeance is ours! Vengeance is ours!"

The grand superior rose from the bale of hay and placed a hand of comfort on the shoulder of Brother Elbe. He urged Brother Elbe to take his seat and motioned for the Brothers to be seated. They obeyed without further comment and sat down in unison: bodies erect, feet flat on the floor, all proud members of the Euro-Brothers Defense Society. The grand superior said, "In light of this Code III situation and in accordance with the duties and responsibilities vested with the Superior Board, the Board has chosen three options of retribution which represent the trilogy: God, Europe, and the white race. Brother Rhine, do you have the envelopes?" "Yes, grand superior!" Brother Rhine barked. "All rise," the grand superior instructed. Everyone rose from their seats, except for Brother Rhine and the grand superior, who were already standing. "Brothers," the grand superior said, "the three options of retribution are printed on the outside of the envelopes that Brother Rhine is about to pass out. As soon as each Brother has an envelope we will vote, then the nature of the retribution will be manifested. Distribute the envelopes, Brother Rhine." The sealed white envelopes were inside a black attache case that Brother Rhine opened upon command. Starting with the front rows, Brother Rhine approached each Brother in a ceremonious fashion, allowing each member to seize an envelope. In accordance to the Society's ritual, the last envelope was left for the Code III victim, which Brother Elbe took.

"How ye vote, Brothers?" the grand superior queried. He stat-

ed each option of retribution and called for a show of hands. When
the vote was finished, the grand superior said, "The Brothers have
chosen the first option of retribution. It shall be carried out in the
name of God, Europe, and the white race, according to the code.
Each Brother has a key inside his envelope. Only three Brothers
possess keys that fit the lock of the weapons vault." The grand superior asked Brother Rhine, Brother Vistula, Brother Thames, and
Brother Dvina for assistance. They removed a section from the plywood floor and raised a wooden vault from a hole in the ground by
hoisting the vault by rope handles. Starting with the front row of
benches, each Brother walked to the wooden vault behind a white
curtain and tried his key in the lock. Three of the Brothers' keys fit,
but only they knew. Written instructions were left inside the vault,
which were to be memorized and destroyed when the three
revengers returned to secure their weapons and other trappings
needed to carry out the retribution. The Brothers shouted,
"Vengeance is ours! Vengeance is ours! Vengeance is ours!" The
grand superior bellowed, "In the name of God, Europe, and the
white race, we leave here in brotherhood and with the sacred vow
to be loyal to one another and to not reveal anything directly or indirectly associated with the Society to others."

The Brothers all said in unison, "This we vow! This we vow!
This we vow! In the name of God, Europe, and the white race."

Chapter Five

Toto led Henry into her bedroom. She threw the clothes that were scattered across her rumpled bed on the soiled, green velvet, lumpy chair in the corner of the room next to the beat up dresser with the spiderweb-cracked mirror. A partially used bottle of Gorgio Red (imitation) perfume sat on the dresser amongst assorted tubes of Wet N' Wild glossy lipstick. A faded red bra dangled from the dusty, smudged mirror. An unopened box of Spring Mountain douche sat tilted on top of a crumbled Kool Mild cigarette pack.

Toto fluffed the thin pillows on the bed and turned back the tattered covers. Henry stared admiringly at her as she undressed. He stood back close to the bedroom's entrance to get a broader view as he puffed on a joint. Toto was his favorite whore. No question about it. He wuz as happy as he ever remembered when Juice talked Toto into lettin' him have sex wif her. At first she hadn't wanted anythang to do wif him. Juice told him that for twenty-five more dollars he might be able to talk Toto into it. He looked at those big long legs, cantaloupe-like tits, and ass that could stuff a bushel basket and gave Juice seventy-five dollars. But he could only 'ford her once a month; 'round the first of the month when he got his government money like clockwork. Damn thankful to Tommy, too. That young boy knew how to find the pussy—good pussy, too. But Toto had the best as far as he wuz concerned. He wuz partial to her; thought she liked him a little bit, too. The third time this month he'd been wif her. A damn lucky month. Won big in the lottery, so he could 'ford to be wif her more than one time this month. And bought her a bottle of that perfume she likes—called Gorgio. Hell, he could've bought some more pussy fir what that shit cost—had no idea. Then when he gave it to her, she said, "Uh, ain't imitation either." Didn't know what the hell she wuz talkin' 'bout. As far as Toto was concerned, this was gonna be some easy money, again. Easiest money she ever made: forty dollars for less than twenty minutes. She could make him cum before she could finish a cigarette. And he thinks his ass be doing something on top of me with his worm-size peter, she thought.

Henry stepped over a pair of Toto's yesterday-panties and a pair of scoffed red high heel shoes resting on a frayed, multi-colored throw-rug. He was butt-naked by now. His slender penis was throbbing. He crawled into the bed on top the grayish sheet that was once white. He folded his narrow body in between Toto's generous chocolate thighs. The burning incense helped tame the smelly odor in the cramped slovenly kept room. Toto turned her head away in order to avoid the stench of Henry's foul breath. She lit a cigarette. She was going to let Henry play inside of her for a few moments before she squeezed him between her large thighs and made his peter shrivel and go limp. She listened to the rain rapping against the pane of the bedroom window that was covered with faded newspaper and thin, pink curtains that hung from a lopsided rod. Tommy Williams (a.k.a. Juice) sat alone in the dim light at the end of the Jefferson Street Bar with the temperament of a rattlesnake. The regulars knew well enough to leave him alone when he was in the mood he was—irritable as hell. He had a lot weighing on his mind. He turned up the bottle of malt liquor and guzzled from it. He sat the bottle back down on the bar and twirled his index finger in the glass of whiskey on the rocks in front of him. He knew the police were looking for him and that stupid-ass Henry. They'd had to leave the van in a hurry and left their fingerprints all over the goddamn van because of Henry's stupid ass. He told Henry to keep his eyes on the road. But, no, he couldn't do that. He had to look in the rearview mirror to see what he was doin' with that white girl. He would've wasted the bitch like he'd planned if it hadn't been for Henry's stupid ass. Yeah, he knew it was his nickname that Henry called, but, as far as he was concerned, it was somethin' that the police could use. Henry was too damn stupid to know that, Tommy was thinking. Ain't goin' back to prison, Tommy vowed to himself. Tommy wasn't even thirty years old yet, but had spent more than half his life incarcerated for something or other since he was fourteen years old. The last time for unarmed robbery. He knew what prison was like and it wasn't no place he wanted to be again. And he wasn't goin'. He had to get out of town. Had to leave fast. But he needed some money. He drank from the glass containing the whiskey and then guzzled from the bottle of malt liquor. He noisily thumped the bottom of the beer bottle on the bar a few times to get the bartender's attention. The bartender looked down to the shadowy end of the bar and saw it was Tommy making the racket. He didn't like that shit: someone banging on the bar or the table to get his attention. But he didn't dare say anything to Tommy. Everybody knew that Tommy had a temper and most of the time he was high on something and wasn't functioning on all his mental cylinders. So, you best not say nothing to a six-four over two hundred pounds dope-head who had the disposition of a grizzly bear. The bartender opened the cooler, uncapped a bottle ofmalt liquor and took it to Tommy. Tommy pushed two dollars toward him without uttering a word. He sipped the whiskey and guzzled the malt liquor.

Sho' ain't goin' back to prison. Need to get my hands on some money. Gotta get the fuck outta Detroit. Gotta leave Mich'gan. Gotta leave in a hurry. Need some money right away. Bet that fuckin' Henry got some money. Told me that he only won $500 in the lottery. Probably won more than that. If his ass told me he won $500 he probably won more. Bet his ass did. Know he did. He'll be back in here in a few minutes. Toto will have his old ass limp in no more than fifteen minutes, Tommy thought. Toto thought Henry felt like a skinny rail with a bump between her legs. "Where's yo' undabrella?" Henry asked. "My umbrella? Fool, wha'cha talkin' about? Just do your little business." "N'all, Toto, I want a undabrella so I can pretend I'm makin' love in the rain, just like I did wif that white girl. Juice never heard of Gene Kelly; 'fore his time. Probably yose, too." "What white girl?" Toto asked. "That white girl me and Juice picked up the other night." "Did you pay that white bitch more than you pay me? I bet your ass did." "No I didn't, Toto. Didn't pay her nothin'. The white girl gave the pussy to us." "To both of y'all?" "Yeah. Yah ain't jealous is yah?" Toto pushed Henry off of her and sat up in the bed. Henry said, "What yah doin'? I ain't finished doin' my thang wif yah yet." "Where did y'all pick up this white girl?" Toto asked.

"Down by the Renaissance Center. Yah jealous! Yah jealous! Can tell yah jealous. Don't worry, though, that white girl ain't got nothin' on yah." Toto laid back. Henry's worm had turned limp. She touched it like she knew how to touch it and made it erect again. Short, but erect, anyway. He entered her. Shallow. She maneuvered him; bundling him just right between her log-size thighs. Henry moaned in pleasure. He was through in a matter of seconds. Toto said, "Get up Henry; get dressed. I wanna hurry up and get back to the bar." Henry and Toto came into the bar together. Tommy thought they looked like a scarecrow and a young Patti LaBelle with a raveled wig. Toto went swiftly to the pay phone by the front door. Henry walked down to the end of the bar where Tommy was sitting. Henry had a panorama smile on his scraggly bearded, narrow, sunken face. "Damn if I didn't make Toto jealous," Henry said. "Told her I had a white girl and made Toto sit up in the bed. Thought she wuzn't gonna let me finish my business wif her." Tommy turned cat-quick around on the barstool and grabbed Henry by the shirt collar with such force that it damn near caused Henry to suffer whiplash.

Tommy rose from the barstool and towered over Henry, still holding Henry's shirt collar in a death grip with both his hands. Henry was choking. His eyes were as large as saucers, as though he was looking into the face of the devil. "What did yah tell that ho'?" Tommy said with a look so menacing that it made Henry literally piss on himself. Henry attempted to speak, but only a hoarse, gurgling sound came from his mouth. Tommy loosened the grip on his shirt collar. Henry coughed and sucked air into his mouth. "What yah mean, Juice?" Henry gurgled. "Why yah mad at me? Ain't told Toto nothin'." Tommy tightened his grip on Henry's shirt collar again and said,"Yah a goddamn lie, yah dumb-ass mothafucker. Just told me yah mentioned that white girl to her." Again, a hoarse, gurgling sound came from Henry's mouth. Tommy eased the grip on his shirt collar again. Henry coughed and swallowed air. "Just told her, Juice, that we had us a white girl," Henry labored out of his mouth. Tommy looked down at the other end of the bar. Toto was hanging up the telephone receiver of the pay phone. She went to the bar, sat down, crossed her legs, and lit a cigarette. She looked down the bar to where Henry and Tommy were standing. Tommy released Henry by the shirt collar and said,"Yah follow me, mothafucker!" Henry followed closely behind Tommy like his shadow; step by step and in his very tracks. He bumped up against the back of Tommy when he stopped where Toto was sitting. Tommy said, "Toto, I need to talk to yah."

"I'm listenin'," said Toto. "I wanna talk to yah outside," Tommy replied. "I just ordered a drink," Toto responded. Tommy looked around at the dozen or so other customers in the bar: Two guys were sitting four stools down from where Toto was seated; two stools from them a man and a woman were sitting. The other customers were sitting at tables. Tommy walked over to the jukebox as the bartender brought Toto's drink. Henry was right behind him. Tommy turned around and bumped into Henry. He pushed Henry. Henry stumbled back toward the bar and caught his balance on a barstool. Tommy walked back over to Toto. Henry followed. Tommy stood by Toto without saying a word. He just stared at her. Toto tried to avoid his stare, but she could feel the heat of his glare. "What is it, Tommy? What in the hell do you want?" "I told yah, bitch!" Tommy whispered as he placed his mouth close to the side of Toto's head. "I told yah I need to talk to yah. And if yah don't get your ass off this stool and go outside with me, I'll knock your ass off this goddamn stool."

The tone of Tommy's voice made Toto feel uneasy. And he would, too. He was mean enough. He was crazy enough. He was high enough. She knew he would knock her off the barstool if she didn't go outside with him. And nobody in the place would help her; not a goddamn one of them. All scared of Tommy, each and every last one of them, and herself included. If she offered Henry free pussy for a lifetime he wasn't gonna stand up to Tommy. None of them would. Toto swivelled around on the barstool and stood up. Tommy interlocked their arms and guided Toto out the door. Henry followed them directly in Tommy's tracks. Once outside the bar, Toto opened up her umbrella and asked, "What do you want from me, Tommy?" "I wanna go to your apartment, so we can talk. You, Henry and me." "About what?" Toto asked. "I'll tell yah when we get there," Tommy said. He still had his arm interlocked with hers. Tommy guided Toto down the street, heading toward her apartment two blocks away. Henry trailed in Tommy's footsteps. Toto didn't resist. The rain was now just a drizzle. Sergeant Washington felt good about the tip. The lady told him over the phone that she might have some information about the abduction and rape of the white girl that happened down at the Renaissance Center. Said she heard that there was a reward and remembered it being $10,000. He confirmed the amount of the reward and gave her an identification number to claim the reward if the suspects were apprehended and convicted.

"Thank you, Lord! Thank you, Lord!," Sergeant Washington recalled her repeating. She sounded like one of those Sunday-going-to-church women. Had a voice as sweet as honey; a pleas-ant-sounding woman. Probably one of those nice church-going-women a little down on her luck. He wasn't going to miss this opportunity. He was going to be there when they descended on the Jefferson Street Bar. Hell, he was up to become a lieutenant. It sure wouldn't hurt to be able to catch those bastards who raped that white girl. Lieutenant Ulyssis Washington! Had a good ring to it. That sure was what he was thinking. The three of them marched up the stairs to Toto's apartment. Tommy's face was stern as a tree stump. A look of fear had crawled over Toto's Tammy Faye Baker-like made-up face. Henry had the worried look of a man about to enter a lion's den. Tommy flung Toto across her unmade bed and said, "What did yah and Henry talk about?" "I don't remember all we talked about," Toto replied as she straightened the wig on her head. Wham! The sound of flesh against flesh echoed in the small bedroom. Henry flinched and turned his head. Toto's head twisted from the force of the open-handed slap to the side of her face. "Tell me, bitch, what Henry told yah about the white girl!" Tommy raised his hand, ready to slap Toto again if she didn't give him a sat-isfactory answer. Toto pressed her hand to the side of her face, attempting to subdue the sting. The force of the slap brought tears to her eyes. Mascara trickled through the rouge of her ebony cheeks.

"Henry said you and him picked up a white girl and fucked

her!" Toto answered in pain. "Where did he say we picked her up at?" Tommy raised his hand higher and balled his large fist. "Down by the Renaissance Center," Toto said. Tommy didn't bother to waste his sight on Henry, who was standing behind him as fidgety as a person with diarrhea. Tommy knelt on the bed and straddled Toto. He placed both his hands around her slender neck. Henry was rocking nervously back and forth with his hands clasped tightly in front of his narrow chest. "Who yah call on the phone in the bar?" Tommy asked. "A friend, Tommy," Toto answered. "Yah lying, bitch! You read the goddamn newspaper. Don't yah?" "Yeah, Tommy, I read the newspaper." "And bet'cha can put two and two together, can't yah, bitch?" Toto gurgled. She was grimacing, pulling at Tommy's hands, desperately struggling to loosen his powerful grip. "Ain't goin' back to prison! Ain't goin' back to prison..." Tommy kept saying as his grip got tighter.

Toto dug her long, painted nails into Tommy's arms, face, and back, desperately fending for her life. She drew blood. "You fuckin' bitch!"

Toto felt Tommy's full strength. She fought back as best she could: clawing, twisting, and pounding her knees into Tommy's back. Her frantic clawing and twisting subsided to feeble, ineffective..... as her breathing became more shallow. She suddenly went limp. Toto stopped breathing, saliva dripping from the corners of her mouth, her body limp. Tommy was sweating and panting, blood trickling from the side of his face and arms. Henry hollered,"Juice, yah kilt her! Yah done kilt her! Have mercy, Jesus! Yah done kilt her!" Henry was in a panic, not believing what he was seeing. Just minutes ago he and Toto were screwing, now she was dead. Tommy sprang off the bed and punched Henry in the face. Henry fell back against the dresser and tumbled to the floor. Tommy was angry enough to kill again. Henry sensed it as he cowered and trembled on the floor. Tommy picked Henry off the floor by his shirt collar and said,"Mothafucker, it's all your dumb-ass fault. I need some money. How much money yah got? And don't yah goddamn lie to me 'cause I know yah got some money hid someplace." "Ain't, ain't got but, but a cou-, couple dollars, Juice. That, that's all; jest, jest a cou-, couple dollars. Ha-, have mercy, Jesus! Please don't hur-, hurt me, Juice." Henry stuttered.

Tommy let go of Henry's shirt collar with one hand and punched him. Blood squirted from Henry's mouth. The blow wasn't hard enough to make Henry go unconscious. If Tommy hadn't been holding onto Henry with one of his powerful hands, Henry surely would have hit the floor again. Tommy's large fist was raised, ready to pound Henry again. The throbbing pain and warm blood seeping out of Henry's mouth, flowing underneath his chin and down his neck made the thought of money unimportant. It was his life Henry was now more concerned about. He knew Juice wouldn't hesitate to kill him any more than he would swat a fly. Henry was petrified. He hadn't been as afraid since his first encounter with the Vietcongs in Vietnam. Tommy reached inside his jacket and pulled out a .38 revolver that was tucked in his pants at the small of his back. "Have mercy, Jesus!" Henry exclaimed. "Please don't kill me. Have mercy, Jesus!" Tommy pressed the barrel of the revolver against Henry's perspiring forehead. "How much money yah got, mothafucker?" Tommy barked. "Have mercy, Jesus! Got almost $2,500, Juice. Got almost $2,500. I give it to yah; all it, Juice. Have mercy, Jesus! Please don't kill me. Have mercy, Jesus!" Henry began crying, scared out of his wits. Tommy walked behind Henry down the stairs, his hand and the gun concealed underneath his sweat-drenched shirt. Tommy saw police cars; about a dozen. "Ain't goin' back to prison! Ain't goin' back to prison!" Tommy bellowed.

Henry tumbled like a log from being pushed down the stairs. Tommy leaped over the railing and sprinted down the alley. He ran into a garbage can, picked himself up, continued running. A police car came behind him down the alley. He ran faster. Another police car was facing him, coming down the alley in the opposite direction. Tommy jumped over a fence. He heard, "Halt or we'll shoot!" "Ain't goin' back to prison! Ain't goin' back to prison!" Tommy declared. He turned to fire his revolver. A hail of bullets penetrated his body and ripped his flesh like tissue paper. He fell to the soggy ground and laid sprawled across the lawn in a pool of blood, his revolver still clutched in his large hand. The fine rain peppered his still body. As far as anyone was concerned, the only thing that Tommy Williams (a.k.a. Juice) left behind in life was misery.

Chapter Six

Hugo was as restless as a caged animal. His insomnia had routed sleep like a bully. He sat up in bed. The clock-radio on the nightstand read 12:15. Freida was sleeping peacefully. Hugo was bewildered; he couldn't understand how Freida could sleep so serenely. He hadn't been able to sleep with hardly a microscopic degree of placidity since Emily's rape. Emily was having nightmares most every night since the rape. She woke up screaming. Piercing screams. Screams that made the hair on the back of your neck stand up. Screams of mercy. Pleading screams. It was just too much for him to take. Her nocturnal screaming and pleading wrenched his heart like a dishcloth. It made him feel impotent as a father and as a man. Some goddamn niggers done messed up his Emee's mind. His also. Why in the hell did he let her go to the car alone? Stupid him; thinking it was safe because of the police presence. It was supposed to have been safe. It had been safe all those years. Why? Why Emee? She ain't never done anything to hurt a fuckin' soul, Hugo thought. Tears clouded his eyes again, which had been happening ever since Emily's rape. And all because of what some niggers done. Niggers, Jews, wetbacks, gooks, flies and mosquitoes; he didn't have use for any of them. Hugo wiped his moist eyes with the lower sleeves of the pajamas he was wearing. The phone rang. It startled him. Hugo picked up the receiver before the second ring. Freida hadn't stirred. "Hello," Hugo said in a muted voice. It was that nigger sergeant: Sergeant Ullysis Washington. Why in the hell was he calling him? Hugo wondered. Must have something to do with Emee's rape. "Hold on, Sergeant; let me get the phone in the other room." Hugo peeled the covers off him and sat on the side of the bed. His large feet hunted for his house shoes in the shadowy bedroom. He tramped to the living room; the house shoes flopping rhythmically on his feet. Hugo picked up the phone. "Okay, Sergeant, I'm back. What is it?" Hugo accepted the sergeant's apology for calling so late, thinking

that whatever the sergeant was calling about it had to be important.
"That's okay," Hugo said, "I wasn't asleep anyway." He started to say he couldn't sleep, but that would've been too personal. It
had hurt him to his Christian heart when he had to go to the
Beaubein Street Precinct and talk to the sergeant about his daughter
being missing. He wasn't about to share something personal with
the sergeant. "Good news? What is it? "Hugo asked as he listened
intently to the sergeant's response. "You did?" Hugo responded.
"You caught the two nig-; uh, the two guys that raped Emily. That's
good. About fuckin' time. Where are the animals? I wanna look
'em in their cowardly eyes. I wanna see the animals that would do
something like this." Hugo listened, then responded, "Good! One
of 'em is dead. I wanna see the other. Where's he being held?" The
sergeant's response irritated Hugo. "How can you tell me it ain't a
good idea to see this animal. The nig—; uh, the son-of-a-bitch
raped my daughter. I wanna look the bastard in his goddamn eyes."
Sergeant Washington's rationale didn't satisfy Hugo. "Justice?"
Hugo blurted. "You think justice is being served? You really think
that, sergeant? You really believe that because one of those bastards
who raped my daughter is in jail and one is dead? No, Sergeant!
Justice ain't being served. My daughter wakes up screaming in fear
every night. She's afraid of the darkness. She constantly lives in
fear. She dropped out of college; too afraid to be around niggers."
Hugo halted his angry discourse after saying "niggers." He'd forgotten he was talking to one of them. He said, "No offense,
Sergeant. I'm just upset. You should be able to understand."
    The phone went dead. Hugo slammed down the receiver and
said,"Fuck you! The likes of you ain't seen justice yet. We're
gonna show your black asses what justice is. Soon! Very soon! In
the name of God, Europe, and the white race."
    "The racist bastard," Sergeant Washington said to himself, star-
ing at the phone. "Used the word nigger and expected me to understand because of what happened to his daughter." Tried to be nice
to the bastard, Sergeant Washington thought. Just goes to show, you
can't be nice to a honkie, especially a racist one. The bastards
always take your kindness as a sign of weakness. White boys can't

deal with a strong black man. Always want the black man to feel beneath him and that he's not as good as him. That's why I don't trust a honkie. Never have and never will.

Saturday, October 2, 1992 Westside, Detroit (12:45 P.M.) A neatly dressed young black man, known as "Brother Johnson," attired in a dark suit and wearing black, spit-shined shoes, was exuberantly peddling Black Muslims' The Final Call newspapers on the busy avenue near the I-94 expressway. The scarlet bowtie around his neck looked ablaze against his milk-white shirt.

The roaring of an ungarished black Harley-Davidson motorcycle reigned over the rumbling, clanging, humming, rattling, honking, and clanking sounds of vehicles that dotted the litter-strewn avenue. A black-clad Ninja-looking driver was nestled swaggerly in the chopper's seat. "The Final Call! The Final Call!" shouted Brother Johnson, waving one of the newspapers high above his head as he cradled a dozen or so of the weeklies in his other hand, close to his side. A stack of the weeklies lay behind him on the semi-grassy ground behind the concrete curve near a traffic light. "Minister Farrakhan speaks of the white man's transgressions against blacks. Get your special edition. The Final Call! The Final Call!" The stiff wind carried Brother Johnson's voice down the avenue. Brother Johnson handed a paper here and there to hands outstretched from car windows as he took money in exchange and sometimes made change, but always said a polite "Thank you." He was oblivious to the slowly approaching Harley-Davidson until it stopped next to him. "I'll take three," slithered from the mouth of the person on the chopper whose face was obscured behind the tinted protected shield of the helmet he wore. "Three?" Brother Johnson asked. "Three," was the response back. Brother Johnson smiled and handed the enigmatic person on the Harley-Davidson a trio of The Final Call newspapers.

"Tell me something, boy", the mysterious man on the chopper said," when are you niggers gonna learn that white women are off limits to you; and that white men don't like niggers soiling their women? Can you answer that?" Brother Johnson's eyes grew large. His smile turned into a scowl. He said, "You're one of those white devils that Minister Farrakhan warned us about. Give me back my papers, you white devil!" Brother Johnson reached out his hand. "I'm gonna pay you for them, boy!" the man said. He quickly reached inside his short, black leather jacket, then said, "Got change for a forty-five?" Three thunderous shots rang out which resounded like cannons in the brisk wind. Scattered pages of The Final Call blew across the avenue as Brother Johnson's body fell to the ground. Car tires squealed and squelched. The squalling tires were those of cars that accelerated in both directions on the avenue. The squeeching tires were the results of drivers who were in momentary shock, consumed with the horror of seeing Brother Johnson's blood-splattered body lying along the side of the avenue like a dog that was slaughtered in traffic. The Harley-Davidson jetted west down the I-94 expressway; the rider and motorcycle faded quickly into a postcard-size figure.

In Royal Oak, Michigan. "Shit!" he intoned as his revolver fell to the ground. The guy peddling the newspapers was running like a rabbit down the street. He'd dropped all the newspapers known as The Final Call. He picked up the revolver and gave chase on his motorcycle. "God-damnit!" he swore. "I can't let the nigger get away." It was crucial that he carried out the plan. Precision was outlined, but now he had fucked up by accidently dropping the revolver as the guy was about to hand him the newspapers. Brother Dishman sprinting and the Harley-Davidson motorcycle in pursuit of him attracted much attention on Lazer Road. Brother Dishman was fast, but not fast enough to outrun a Harley and the man giving chase. Brother Dishman dared not look back, fearful of losing speed. The sound of the motorcycle got louder, meaning that it was getting closer, gaining on him. He would reach the Quick Shop convenience store in four or five more strides, but he never made it. The bullets stopped him. Brother Dishman fell lifeless to the ground, felled by three shots, and witnessed by astonished onlookers, gasping, seeing the young, well-dressed man sprawled on the ground and a black-clad rider zooming down the street on his motorcycle, dodging in and out of traffic. The motorcycle rider cursed himself for his blunder as he made his getaway. He nevertheless had executed his part of the plan, albeit without the precision designed.

Inkster, Michigan The motorcycle driver was angry, thinking about how the nigger Muslim son-of-a-bitch had dropped his newspapers and spat in his face. He spat in his face before he could draw his forty-five revolver. And he almost shot his black ass more than three times. Damn almost did, but remembered that he was only supposed to shoot him three times. He started to run over him with his bike, but didn't want no blood on his Harley. The nigger sure got upset when he told him that he was just a paper boy working for some nigger pimps. That's when he dropped those The Final Call newspapers and spat in his face. Smack-dab in his face. But he was a dead nigger now and one less to be bothered with is what the driver was thinking as he drove his motorcycle into the barn. Hugo answered the phone in his den on his private line. All the Society brothers had private lines. It was required. He had been expecting the call. "Brother Elbe," he answered. "Brother Elbe, it's the grand superior. It's done! Glory be to God, Europe, and the white race!" "Glory be to God, Europe, and the white race!" Hugo responded. They hung up. Hugo muttered to himself, "Now some measure of justice has been served. That should get some niggers' attention."

Chapter Seven

A battalion of people—more like two battalions—filed into the VFW hall past uniformed and plainclothes policemen of the Detroit P.D. A plethora of footsteps trampled the scuffed, scratched hardwood floor. They were footsteps of all sounds: scurrying, plodding, heavy, soft, and shuffling. Footsteps unlike what you'd hear attending a pop, rhythm and blues, rock, or country and western concert. Footsteps contrasting to what you would hear attending church service. They were footsteps of incensed community activists, enraged militants whose minds and hearts had never advanced beyond the 60s, only-get-involved-when-there's-a-crisis-folks, and generally concerned citizens (mostly black, but with a few good-hearted whites sprinkled in) who had come to find out what was going to be done about it and when and how. That is why they came. And they came in large numbers. Their voices produced a clamorous sound that spilled outside the hall and attracted some curious passerbys who didn't have a clue as to what was going on.

Sergeant Washington removed his eyeglasses, then a handkerchief from his back pocket. He wiped smudges from his lenses. He'd been assigned to security and was going to see and hear all that was going on. It hadn't been this much fervor in the community about something since the death of Lamar Jacobs back in 1990. Four white policemen beat the living shit out of Lamar. They suspected Lamar of having drugs in his possession, clenched in his tight fist. Lamar wouldn't open his fist like they demanded. Stubborn like a mule he was, so they beat his hand with those large police-issued flashlights they carry. Lamar still wouldn't unclench his fist, no matter how hard they beat on his hand. The crack cocaine he'd ingested helped him endure the pain. They then started beating Lamar on other parts of his body, including his head. Blood splattered all over the steering wheel, dashboard, and the seat of Lamar's car. They couldn't drag Lamar outside his car. He held onto the steering wheel, clenched his fist like his life depended on it. And it did. Lamar died. They killed Lamar. He took too many hard blows to the head. Cracked his skull and caved parts of his head in. And all of that happened one year after the Dirty Dozen trial. People in the community got fed up; just fed up with all the police brutality—particularly white policemen brutalizing black citizens.

Lamar Jacobs wasn't no angel, not by a long shot. The young man had been in and out of trouble for a long time. And he had been known to deal drugs: sell and use. But it wasn't Lamar's good character that the community was up in arms about. It was about the viciousness of the beating that those white policemen administered to Lamar. Beat his ass like some wild or crazed animal, some people had said. Said if Lamar had been white, it never would've happened the way it did. "No, siree!" some people said, "never would've happened like that if Lamar Jacobs had been white." Now this, Sergeant Washington pondered. Three young black Muslims gunned down in cold blood on streets in Wayne County: one in Detroit, Royal Oak, and Inkster. It had the appearance of some kind of conspiracy. The black Muslims were calling for protection from white devils and demanding a "...thorough and complete investigation." Pastors and ministers of all denominations were demanding the same. Citizens were wondering out loud (in meetings, via newspapers, radio, and TV) as to what city hall and the police were going to do about it. The black Muslims called for the FBI's involvement but said, "They didn't want a bunch of blue-eyed agents taking charge of the investigation because they couldn't be trusted." Demanded that some black agents be sent and, hopefully, they wouldn't be "pawns of the white devil." Ain't seen no shit like this since the Lamar Jacobs affair, Sergeant Washington was thinking.

Chapter Eight

NOVEMBER 2, 1992

This was the day. The doctor at Henry Ford Hospital told Emily that it would take at least six weeks to learn if she'd been impregnated. She hoped to God the results were negative. Hadn't she suffered enough? God knows she had; so, God, a merciful God, wouldn't let her suffer any more. He just wouldn't allow it. God would understand. He would understand why she didn't want to be pregnant. Tears streamed down the side of Emily's face and onto the pillow her head was embedded in. She had cried a lot since her rape. Cried a lot and slept very little. The night light cast geometric patterns on the bedroom's walls and ceiling. It was only her crying that pierced the nocturnal silence. Sleep was difficult to come by; about as arduous as catching water in a sieve. She laboriously slow-dragged her arm off the bed in front of her face to glance at the Timex on her wrist. It was 3:18 in the morning.

They were going to be so happy together, Timothy and her. That's whose baby she'd wanted: Timothy Hankins'. They had it all planned; just perfectly planned. They'd been engaged for six months. Those bastards even stole her engagement ring. More tears flowed down Emily's face. She and Tim were going to marry after they both graduated from college in June. They'd been sweethearts since junior high. After high school Tim went to Michigan State University to study veterinarian medicine; she attended Oakland University to study journalism. She loved Tim, but she hadn't seen or talked to him since her rape. She just couldn't stand to look into his face; afraid of what she might see in his eyes and on his face. Afraid of what he might think and what images his mind would summon. Afraid he would probably visualize two men having sex with her, two niggers, and that would just be too much for him to stomach and cope with. It was enough to have to look into her father's wilted face and see gloom implanted in his indigo-colored eyes and hurt and pain adhered to his face like sap. No, she didn't want to see Tim or talk to him. She didn't want to read in his eyes and on his face what she knew she'd see: the same things she saw every day in her father's eyes and on his miserable-looking face. She continued to cry like she'd done since the night she was abducted and raped.

Now, she was thinking like her father. She'd never considered herself a racist. She knew her father was, but she really wasn't. But now "niggers" rolled off her tongue so easily. She'd never used the N-word before but her father did. He said niggers were always looking for something free; always looking for handouts. Said the government handed niggers things that white people worked hard to get. Her father said niggers couldn't be trusted and the reason you see so many of them in jails and prisons was because they were shiftless people and naturally prone to committing crimes. Her father hated them all, but she hadn't. Not until now. Not until her rape. Maybe her father had been right about them all along. She felt different about them now, a lot different. She hadn't particularly been afraid of them before, not really. Not until now; not until they'd done this to her. And she'd never be the same; she knew it. How could she? She always felt dirty and this was the reason she took a shower six to eight times a day. She just couldn't get clean enough. She itched a lot and scratched a lot. She constantly felt as though something was crawling over her body.

Her mind was all jumbled. Just too many things resonating in her head at the same time: Sounds of pelting rain, dissonant traffic, harsh voices that excreted vulgar parlance. And she couldn't sleep; at least, not well. She couldn't sleep any more than two hour intervals because she was afraid to sleep. When she did sleep, she often saw faceless men enjoying their sordid pleasure with her. And although they were faceless, she knew they were black. She woke up screaming: dreaming of faceless black men pawing her like animals. So, she resisted sleep as best she could. But sleep sometimes overpowerd her and seduced her against her will—like those niggers did. Emily pushed the bed covers off with her feet. Her hands were occupied with wiping the tears from her plastic face. She rolled out of bed with the vitality of a tortoise. She needed a shower. Her skin was itching. Her epidermis was imbued with a tactile crawling sensation. She dragged herself to the bathroom.

Hugo heard the water from the shower running, like he'd heard several times a night since Emily had come home from the hospital. Tonight her showers were longer. The water seemed more clamorous, as though gravel rather than water was pelting the shower floor. Insomnia was a bold intruder that brazenly robbed him of sleep at night and caused him to be somnolent and as irritable as an unfed rottweiler during the day. But Freida was sleeping peacefully; and, for the life of him, he couldn't understand how she could sleep so blissfully and undisturbed. It was as though she wasn't bothered by all this. But how could she not be? Hell, her flesh and blood, her own daughter, had been savagely raped; so, how could she not be troubled. It angered him that Freida could sleep so serenely while he couldn't sleep hardly at all. He assessed Freida sleeping like a baby.

Baby! "Goddamnit," Hugo uttered in a muted tone. He was reminded that this morning, in a matter of a few hours, Emily was to call her doctor to learn if she was pregnant. What if she's pregnant? he thought. What would she do? He knew what he wanted her to do. He wanted her to have an abortion if she was pregnant. There was just no way that he could live with his daughter carrying a nigger's child inside of her. He would rather burn in hell. But what would she do? he asked himself again. For years she'd been pro-life, demonstrating at abortion clinics. He supported her. He was pro-life himself. The whole family was pro-life. It was a part of their Christian belief. But this was different. It was different he thought because Emily had been raped by niggers who ain't human like white folks. They're a different breed, so it'd be okay for Emee to have an abortion. Damn right, it'd be okay. And he didn't give a fuck what nobody said. It'd be okay, because niggers ain't human like white folks. That's how he felt. But it wasn't his call. Emily had to make the decision if she was pregnant. So, what in the hell

would she do, Hugo wondered. Pro-life she was. Goddamnit!
What would she do? He wasn't certain. The uncertainty of it
caused Hugo to hyperventilate. For sure, he'd rather burn in hell
than to see Emily carry a nigger fetus to term. The very thought
was asphyxiating, as though something was sucking oxygen out of
Hugo. He began to have heart palpitations. Emily returned to bed
around 5 A.M. In about three hours she was going to call Dr.
Strodder to find out the test result. A fist-sized knot was in her
stomach. She used both her hands to depress her abdomen as she
looked around the bedroom. The cartoon characters Lucy, Linus,
Charlie Brown, and Snoopy were scenic and thematic in the colorful wallpaper that covered the walls. Stuffed animals of assorted
species, shapes, and sizes huddled together in a corner of the room;
just like they'd been since her days in elementary school, but their
population had grown until she entered high school. It was then that
she felt too old to collect stuffed animals any longer. Slender, fash-
ionably dressed Barbie dolls with neatly coiffured hair lined the
neat, alabaster dresser that matched the color of the bed, chest and
nightstand. The nightstand looked barren since she removed the
eight-by-ten, framed, colored photograph of her and Tim Hankins.
Emily commenced crying again. She used to be so happy and full
of life. There was a time when all the things in her bedroom meant
so much to her. But not now; not since her rape. Now it seemed as
though Lucy, Linus, Charlie Brown, Snoopy, the stuffed animals,
and Barbie dolls were gawking at her, all wondering what would
she do if she learned she was pregnant. Everybody, even the characters on her wall, the animals in the corner, and the dolls on top her
dresser, knew that she was pro-life and opposed to abortions of any
kind. She'd demonstrated not just against abortions for white
females, but all females, because she thought it was cruel and sin-
ful to abort a child.

Emily recalled when she once went to a rally, stood at the podium and said: "It's more than a man's seed that gets planted inside a
woman; it's also a gift from God. And all of God's gifts are intended to be delivered and exposed, because all of God's gifts are precious..." Her own words reverberated in her head. She pressed

harder on her abdomen at the growing knot in her stomach. The silence was disquieting and too accommodating to her thoughts. She picked up the remote control from the nightstand and turned on the TV. She clicked the channels to the AMC cable station that featured old, black and white movies. Gene Kelly was dancing with an umbrella held above his head. The movie was Dancing in the Rain. She clicked the remote control, blackening the TV screen, and flung the remote control across the room into the dresser's mirror. Glass shattered and the Barbie dolls fell in different directions. Hugo was still awake. He heard the noise. Sounded like somebody was breaking in. He looked quickly at Freida while jumping out of bed. She was still fast asleep and undisturbed. He removed the revolver from the drawer of the nightstand and scampered out of the bedroom in his bare feet. He went to investigate the racket.

Freida was awake. She feigned to be asleep. She hadn't yet taken a sleeping pill. Tears trickled down her face. She tried to be strong for Emily and her family, but it was a false demeanor she exhibited. Emily's rape had devastated her. The best she could do was to appear to be strong and supportive. But she wasn't as strong as she let on. She constantly agonized on the inside about it all, thinking that Emily could be pregnant and witnessing all the hatred that had consumed her husband. She wasn't the same. Their marriage wasn't the same. Their family wasn't the same. Nothing was the same in their lives. It all had suddenly changed as a result of Emily's rape, which was painful for Freida to acknowledge. They were neglecting the business of the Guardian Security Agency that her husband started after his retirement as a police officer. She wasn't as conscientious in maintaining the agency's books, and her husband had neglected several personnel matters associated with the agency. The pleasure of working in her garden had disappeared. The weeds in the garden didn't bother her, unlike the weeds in their lives. That's how Freida thought about it: there were weeds in their lives that had taken sudden root. Deep roots. Everyday was such an ordeal. Freida understood very well that her family had changed. It wasn't the same family, and never would it be again. The house was quiet, now. Not a sound. Freida knew where everybody was.

Emily in her bedroom awoke. Her other children, Brian and Johanna, in their bedrooms asleep. Her husband, Hugo, in the den sitting in his favorite chair, suffering, and probably by now crying softly and silently, just as she was doing.

Freida had hidden the pills but she would take them now: sleeping pills and Prozac. It was a secret she kept from her family because she needed to appear strong. The nightly glass of water on the nightstand wasn't really for her thirst as she'd let on. It was to wash down the pills and medicine she needed. Freida reached underneath the bed to secure the elixir and panacea for all that was troubling her. She would now sleep well and in the only manner she could.

Chapter Nine

4:00 A.M. NOVEMBER 3, 1992

Fire raced through the building with meteoric brilliance and speed as two men ran from the mosque to a dark-colored car waiting around the corner with a driver behind the steering wheel. Once inside the car they removed their dark hooded masks and looked back at the rapidly burning structure as the car took off toward Woodward Avenue. Their car sped past another vehicle headed in the opposite direction. "Where yah think those honkies goin' this time of the mornin' in this neighborhood?" one of the car's occupant asked. "And they're in a damn hurry, too". As their car entered the intersection, to their right, about two blocks down, they saw bright flames bellowing from Mosque #31. They looked at each other. Now they knew why those honkies were speeding in their Highland Park neighborhood.

"Those honkies done sat fire to the mosque!" the driver exclaimed. He made a u-turn in the intersection and accelerated his late model Ford Thunderbird in pursuit of the dark car with three suspicious white men in it. They saw the cherry-red lights of the escaping car that was heading north towards the Davison Expressway. They gave chase like two fighter pilots on a combat mission. "Let's catch those honkies," the occupant on the passenger side shouted. "Think they can come into the 'hood and set fire to shit. Let's catch 'em." Intermittent red lights slowed the hasty getaway of the car occupied by the three white occupants, allowing the red Thunderbird to get within three blocks of the fleeing vehicle. "They're gettin' on the Lodge," the passenger-side occupant in the Thunderbird blurted. "Fuck these red lights!" the Thunderbird driver said as he sped through a red light and then a yellow caution light to get on the Lodge Expressway. "I think we're being followed," the driver of the escaping car said as he glanced into his rearview mirror. The other two passengers looked back and saw the headlights of a car quickly gaining on them. "Goddamn, what are we gonna do?" the occupant in the back seat of the fleeing car wondered out loud. It wasn't really a question for anyone to answer; the three of them were wondering the same thing.

"We don't wanna speed at a high rate and get a police car on our trail," the front-seat passenger said. "Let's see what the car behind us is gonna do," said the driver. The Thunderbird caught up to the escaping vehicle and perched behind it within two to three car links. "They're two niggers," the back seat passenger said. "It looks like one of them is writing; probably our license plate number". The occupants in the escaping vehicle looked at one another. The driver said, "Gotta do it" as he pulled over in the far left lane of the three-lane expressway and decelerated to 50 miles per hour. "What the fuck you think they're doin?" the passenger-side rider in the Thunderbird said. "Don't know, but we got their license plate number. Now, let's see what these honkies look like." The Thunderbird's driver pulled over into the center lane and positioned his car abreast the black Ford Taurus that was occupied by the three white men they'd been pursuing. The occupants in the two vehicles exchanged glacier-cold stares at each other that were equally hateful and contemptuous. "What the shit!" the driver of a trailing car mumbled as he saw rapid red flashes of light emanating from the end of two arms extended outside the windows of the dark car in the far left lane ahead of him. He'd thought something was up. It'd looked pretty strange to him: two cars driving that slowly, side by side, on the expressway this time of the morning. Looked suspicious, for sure, and the reason he'd slowed down behind them. Wanted to know what in the hell were the two cars doing. Wanted to know what they were up to and why in the hell they were driving so slowly next to each other in the far left and center lanes. "The damn fools!" he mumbled to himself. Some of the scant number of vehicles on the expressway had passed cautiously in the far right lane, but not him. He wasn't taking any chances and wasn't in a hurry. And he was curious about what the fools were up to. After the flashes of red light, the dark car sped away; the car in the center lane zigzagged: right, suddenly left, suddenly right, then left, then right again. Anything and everything with wheels, though few they were this time of the morning—started screeching and squealing in order to avoid the red Thunderbird that was weaving across the road and erratically dominating all the lanes until it struck an overpass abutment and burst into flames that enveloped it. Hugo looked at the watch on his arm. It was 5:05 A.M. He'd told Grand Superior Alps that it was unnecessary to apologize for calling him so early, because he hadn't been asleep anyway. The first phase of Operation Little Black Sambo was a success," Brother Alps said. "But had to kill two more niggers in the process. They followed the car, so there was no other recourse but to kill the niggers. Just two less of them to deal with." Hugo thanked Grand Superior Alps for the call and for the information. And, of course, it didn't bother him that they'd had to kill two more coons. They started all this. Had to rape his daughter. Now she was pregnant by one of them and he'd begged Emily to have an abortion, but she'd refused. It was against her beliefs. It had been against his beliefs, too. But he never thought—not in a million years—that his own daughter would ever be raped and have to carry a black baby inside of her. The thoughts brought tears to Hugo's eyes, pain to his heart, and aches in his stomach. Whenever he thought about it, it hurt. It hurt all his waking hours. The pain was always there. Always. Just like the hate. Always there. He possessed hate for blacks like he never had. Hated them with a passion. He wished there was a way to exterminate them like vermin. Damn, he wished Emily could see that it was okay to abort a nigger baby. She just needed to look at it as cancer growing inside of her. She'd have an operation if it was cancer, but he just couldn't convince her that was the same: cancer and niggers, all the same. It was just killing Hugo to think about his own daughter carrying a black child inside of her.

Ullysis Washington attached the gold bars to the epaulettes of the commercially starched white shirt he'd just removed from the white wrapping paper. It brought a satisfying smile to his round face each time he pinned on his lieutenant bars. This morning was no exception. It made him feel proud. After fifteen hard, dedicated years he'd deserved his recent rank, he thought. He'd worked as a patrolman, a homicide detective and in vice. He earned a bachelor's degree in law enforcement at the University of Detroit, and received domestic unrest and terrorism training at the FBI Training Academy. Had been Officer of the Year three times with the Detroit P.D. He savored the thought of how he'd earned his bars. It'd been a good year. He could only see things getting better for him. His son, the son he had with his first wife, was doing well in college and was coming to visit him around Christmas. He was looking forward to it. He hadn't seen Kevin in over a year, but had spoken with him over the phone two weeks ago. They'd had a good conversation. Kevin had told him that he was going to graduate with his degree in mechanical engineering in May from Penn State University. Also, said that he'd gotten engaged and wanted him to meet his fiancee. He wanted to come to Detroit around Christmas so he could meet his future daughter-in-law. A wider smile spread across Lieutenant Ullysis Washington's face. It had been a good year; no matter about all the shit he had to put up with in his job. It was going to be a good Christmas, too. Hadn't seen that son of his in more than a year. He was proud of Kevin, who was the only good thing that materialized from his first marriage. Sure 'nough proud of Kevin, a chip off the old block, Ullysis thought.

Ullysis finished dressing and went to the kitchen. His wife, Gloria, his second wife, was in the kitchen preparing breakfast before leaving for her supervisor's job at the Detroit Medical Center. The woman was certainly a good cook and the reason he'd put on a few pounds since they'd married ten years earlier. Gloria fixed him breakfast every morning—even on the weekend and sure 'nough unlike that first wife of his who bitched about everything and hardly cooked at all. Gloria was different. He loved the shit outta her. She gave him two lovely daughters; two pretty black girls. Pretty like their mama. Just hoped his son, Kevin, got him a black woman like Gloria; and hoped the hell his fiancee wasn't like his mother, his first wife. Ullysis' rumination ended as Gloria entered the kitchen. He said "Good morning" to her and planted a

traditional morning kiss on his wife's lips. He sat at the end of the
kitchen table, where he always sat so he could see the thirteen-inch,
colored Sony TV on the kitchen's counter. He'd just begun to place
the cup of black coffee to his mouth when he heard: "Channel 7
Action News reporting some early morning breaking news. Last
night and early this morning, wanton destruction and violence
rocked the metropolitan area. Late last night fire appeared to be
deliberately set to three black churches. And early this morning a
bullet-riddled car with two charred bodies was found alongside the
Lodge Expressway. We'll have more details in a moment. Stay
tuned..."

Ullysis spilled coffee from the cup on the white linen table cloth
as his hand dropped to the table like a brick. His eyes were fixed
on the TV screen. He hadn't noticed that Gloria had occupied a
chair to his right. After watching Ullysis' reaction, Gloria's eyes
were now riveted on the TV screen.

Hugo was watching the reporter from Fox 2 News interview the
black pastor of Mt. Calvary Baptist Church. "How much damage
was done to your church, Pastor Graham?" "We don't have an official assessment of the damage yet, but as you can see it's considerable". A Fox 2 camera panned the burned structure. "Damn good
job," Hugo murmured in a reclining position on the living room
sofa. "Do you have any idea as to whom would do such a thing?"
the reporter asked. "Don't rightfully know at this time, but it's obviously the work of the devil. Only depraved minds and evil people
would destroy a house of the Lord". "Screw you, nigger," Hugo
muttered as he flipped the channel to a station where Rush
Limbaugh was spewing satirical statements regarding affirmative
action.

Acholam Asante was an early riser. And had been since the
1960s when he was a young man in his early twenties. His memories of those days brought him both joy and sadness. He recalled
how black people were together in the 60s and 70s and didn't take
shit from white folks. As a matter of fact, they had white folks
shaking at night in their beds, thinking black folks might invade the
white enclaves they'd carved out in suburbia. He loved those days:
his Black Panther days, and days of black cultural enlightenment

when he abandoned his slave name of Danny Robinson and officially changed it to Acholam Asante: Acholam meaning Do not provoke me, and Asante representing a proud people and heritage of Western Africa. But it saddened Acholam as to how things had deteriorated. The brothers and sisters done gone from Afros to Jerri curls, weaves, and processed hair, he thought. Done buried their dashikis deep in drawers or started using them as dust-cloth because white folks have made it easier for some of them to get credentialed at white schools. Done window-dressed corporate America and other white institutions with some token Negroes who think they're free and done overcome, but don't know shit about their heritage. Done brainwashed their asses with equal employment and equal opportunities propaganda bullshit that bourgeois black folks done swallowed hook, line, and sinker is how Acholam thought about it all. The news reporter on Channel 4 Eyewitness News interrupted Acholam's contemplation:

> "The charred vehicle found along the Lodge
> Expressway has been identified by authorities as
> belonging to a resident of Highland Park. The
> remains of two males were found in the vehicle.
> No names were released, pending the notification
> of next of kin. We have Sergeant Whittaker from
> the State Police post here with us..."

"Bet they're brothers," Acholam whispered, as though he was talking to the news reporter. "Wonder who they are?" he mumbled. The words rolled coarsely off Acholam's tongue and seeped through his clenched teeth. He finished drinking the V-8 juice; got up from the small, rickety, wooden table in the tiny, frugal kitchen; retrieved his short, tan, jacket from the closet; and headed down the stairs, which led from his private entrance. He drove east on Puritan Street in his 1989 Ford Bronco. By ten o'clock Acholam had found out all that had happened in Highland Park last night and early this morning. Stops at Jud's Barber Shop and the Players' Bar & Grill, as well as serendipitous street conversations in between had illuminated him. Now he knew. He knew what the deal was. He understood what was going down. It was all a white conspiracy. The burning of the mosque was not a random act. Some white sons-ofbitches had burned it down as well as the other two churches in black neighborhoods. "Damn right it's some kind of fucking conspiracy," Acholam mumbled. He knew it. He knew it if no one else knew it. Black people have to protect themselves he thought. Must fight back. Have to do like they did in the 60s and 70s. Must strike fear in the hearts and minds of white folks. The black Muslim brothers are okay, but that innocuous rhetoric of theirs ain't moving nobody to action. Down there on Moss and Hamilton where their mosque was burned, talking about petitioning city hall and the government for help and intervention. "Petition, my ass! Black people have to take action. Have to make white folks stand up and pay attention. Have to send white folks a wake up call. Fuck all the rhetoric!" Acholam exclaimed to himself. Acholam's thoughts were interrupted when Big Sam rushed through the front door of Players as quickly as his legs could carry his rotund body. "They done killed Dorag and Sonny Cool," said Big Sam, excited and panting. Acholam was sitting at the bar, close to the door. He saw Big Sam rushing in. He'd never seen Big Sam move so fast. Big Sam always walked with a shuffle, like he was too lazy to pick up his size fifteen feet. But in all probability, Acholam mused, Big Sam walked the way he did because it was easier for his feet and legs to transport the three hundred pounds on his six-six frame. "Who killed them?" Acholam asked. "Don't know yet," Big Sam replied. "Why'd you say they?" Acholam queried. "A figure of speech, but somebody killed 'em. They, or whoever it was, shot Sonny Cool's Mustang up. Had bullet holes all on the left side of the car. Shot the shit outta his car. Somebody done a job on Sonny Cool and Dorag. Their bodies were burnt to a cris'."

Blair, the bartender, said, "The news said the car was found alongside the Lodge. Why would Sonny Cool and Dorag be on the Lodge heading west that time of the morning? Don't make no sense. How you find out about all this?" "Dorag's sister told me," Big Sam said. "I been kickin' it with his sister for two months now. The whole family's upset. They can't understand why somebody would shoot Dorag and Sonny Cool like that." Joann, a slim black woman in her forties, said, "One of those reporters asked the police if they thought their killin' was gang or drug related. Police said they wasn't rulin' out nothin'." "Dorag and Sonny Cool wasn't involved with no gangs and neither sold drugs. Hell, Sonny Cool worked at the Ford plant for fifteen years and Dorag worked for the city. They wasn't associated with no gangs, and wasn't pushers, either," Big Sam declared. "Big Sam," Acholam said," didn't Dorag live off Hamilton, near where the mosque was burned?" "Yeah, he did. He lived 'bout two blocks from there. Why?" "It's all a damn conspiracy if you ask me," said Acholam. "What'cha mean?" Blair asked as he served Big Sam a draft beer.

"Who the hell yah think burned the mosque and the two churches in the city last night?" said Acholam. "It sure wasn't black people. Black people don't go around burning churches, especially their own. Even black people who don't attend church would be afraid to burn a church; be thinking God would descend from the sky or Heaven or someplace and send their asses to hell or someplace worse. So, it sure in the hell wasn't a black person who burned those churches." "Sho' you right." "No, black people ain't gonna do that." "Sho' ain't." "They ain't gonna do no shit like that." "Yah right!" The outburst of agreement in the bar surprised and pleased Acholam, producing a smile on his face. Acholam took a sip of the Truly Canadian that Blair served him in a glass. He never did drink alcohol. But he liked to smoke a joint now and then. He sensed that the people in Players were paying him some attention. They were listening to him, which made him feel good. Hell, he hadn't commanded this kind of attention since the Black Glory days — back in the 60s and 70s. But he needed a larger audience. He felt suddenly compelled to enlighten his people. He needed to help them take the shackles off their minds. Black people needed to see what was happening to them and in their community. It was all a conspiracy, white people coming into their community in the darkness of night and burning their churches. Acholam had words for his people. Words that hopefully would wake his people up and drive them to action. That's what was needed, Acholam thought, as he left Players.

"My brothers and sisters," Acholam appealed to those traipsing the sidewalk in front of Granberry's Market on Woodward Avenue in a commercial district of Highland Park, "we can't allow white people to come into our community and burn our religious institutions. What's next? Our homes? The two brothers massacred on the Lodge Expressway, Dorag and Sonny J Cool, they saw who burned the mosque on Moss and Hamilton. They followed the perpetrators and got murdered for their efforts. I don't know about you, but these two brothers' lives mean something to me and it should also mean something to every black person who lives in Highland Park." People stopped to listen to Acholam. He paused dramatically, savoring the feeling of being on stage and having an audience. He looked earnestly into the faces of the people gathered. He read the concerned expressions on their faces. He had their attention. He needed to get into their heads and touch their hearts. Acholam drove around Highland park pontificating to those who stopped to listen to what he in his heart thought to be the truth of what was happening to the community and its denizens. Telling the people about the white conspiracy against them. Telling them that they would be stupid and crazy to sit around and do nothing and take the shit that white people were dishing out to them.

Big Sam rode with Acholam around Highland Park into the night. Acholam entreated Big Sam to tell the crowds what had happened to Dorag and Sonny Cool. Acholam avowed that Sonny Cool and Dorag had been killed because they knew something and that rational people shouldn't think for a moment that somebody black killed Sonny Cool and Dorag. People listened and some got incensed. Acholam stood majestic before them: Tall, physically fit, and wearing an Afro he'd never abandoned that looked like a crown on top of his head. He felt energized and invigorated. He hadn't felt this charged and inspired since the 60s and 70s. He spoke knowledgeably and astutely of black history and culture. Acholam quoted Marcus Garvey and Malcolm X as well as passages from Richard Wright's book Native Son and Eldridge Cleaver's Soul On Ice. He spoke articulately, forcefully, and motivatingly. He beseeched his people to look around in their neighborhoods; to look at the foreigners who had come into their community as entrepreneurs. Acholam asked, "Why is it that foreigners who hardly can speak English, or any at all, are able to get bank loans to start businesses in black communities, but black people who lived in this country all their lives can't get a loan from a bank to open a hot dog stand?"

"It's all a conspiracy," Acholam exhorted, and urged the people to do something about it, for it was time to protect their community and seize control of it for the benefit of the people who lived in it. "And to paraphrase Malcolm," he said, "we must take control by any means necessary". It was then when a Purdue's Fish and Poultry delivery truck occupied by two white men stopped at a traffic light at Woodward Avenue and Sears. Two young black men, who appeared to have mutual as well as parallel thoughts, rushed toward the delivery truck, dragging the unwary driver from the cab. More young black men surged toward the truck and subdued the other passenger, beating both men unmercifully. That began the looting and rioting as many young black citizens and not-so-young black people threw rocks, stopped traffic, broke store windows, and took store merchandise for what someone was heard to describe as a "ten-finger discount." Acholam would have none of it. The sounds of impish jubilation and wanton acts of criminality in the streets disturbed him. It wasn't what he'd had in mind. Acholam took his agonizing thoughts with him to his apartment. He fell on his bed, closed his eyes, and reminisced about the 60s and 70s when black people had it more together. If only black people could be more skillfully tactical is what Acholam wished. None of the madness out there in the streets had anything to do with Dorag and Sonny Cool, or the burned mosque, or anything meaningfully related, is what Acholam was thinking. "By any means necessary!" he mumbled. "Fuck!"

Chapter Ten

DECEMBER 18, 1992

Lieutenant Washington as well as other assigned members of the Detroit PD had been working long hours, but still they had no solid leads in the cases. But what they knew with certainty was that .45 caliber revolvers were used to gun down the three black Muslims who had been peddling newspapers on the streets. They also knew the shooters were clad in all black and rode black Harleys. And because of the times and distances, it had been concluded that it had to have been three individuals who had done the shooting. Couldn't say with certainty if the shooters were white, black, or what, because their faces were hidden and they wore black gloves. For certain though, Lieutenant Washington ruminated, the executions were well planned and organized. The FBI agents thought it may be a militia group or a white supremacist group, but the undercover agents' surveillance hadn't come up with anything solid yet. And then on top of everything else, there was the firebombing of the three black churches. The damnest thing, everything in threes: Three shooters, three victims and each shot three times; and then three churches firebombed. Sure think they're related, Lieutenant Washington pondered. He also thought there was some connection between the firebombing of that mosque in Highland Park with the two guys who were killed on the Lodge. Bet they saw something and followed the car that had something to do with the firebombing, he thought. The shooters used bullets identified to .45 revolvers. A witness said he saw three white men in a dark colored Mercury or Ford. They were heading toward the Edsel Ford Expressway; just like the bikers. Heading west, too. Bet there's a connection, Lieutenant Washington was convinced. Lieutenant Washington figured that he wasn't going to concern himself anymore about all this until Monday. His son, Kevin, and his fiancee were due to arrive at the Detroit Metropolitan Airport at seven o'clock. He had an hour to get there and traffic was bad. Lieutenant Washington removed his feet, which were crossed at the ankles, from the top of his desk and walked to the three-tiered file cabinets in his office. He stored several manila folders in one of the file drawers. He removed his hat, overcoat, and scarf from the coat rack near the office door.

"Have a good weekend, ladies and gentlemen," Lieutenant Washington said to the clerks and officers in the outer office. "See you after Christmas. I'm off to pick up my son and future daughter-in-law." "How long will your son be here, Lieutenant?" someone asked. "A week!" Lieutenant Washington responded. "They'll be leaving the day after Christmas."

"I'll be damned! I'll be damned! I'll just be damned!" The words crept quietly though coursely out of Lieutenant Washington's mouth. He just couldn't believe it. He wondered why in the hell didn't Kevin tell him so he could've been prepared for this guess who's coming to dinner shit. Kevin never hinted as much. All along Lieutenant Washington thought Kevin was engaged to a black woman and not what he'd describe as some flat-ass white chick with lips so thin that it'd probably be like kissing the opening of a balloon. Lieutenant Washington was indeed surprised watching his son Kevin getting off the plane with his white mate, and it bothered him seeing Kevin smiling like he had died and gone to heaven. Lieutenant Washington observed that the young white woman was smiling right along with Kevin, like she had found herself an O.J. Simpson, was the lieutenant's assessment.

Lieutenant Washington looked over at Kevin, who was sitting in the front passenger seat. Kevin was still smiling and taking in the view along I-94. The lieutenant looked in the rearview mirror and saw Kevin's woman taking in the view and yet smiling. Lieutenant Washington mumbled under his breath, "Feel like I'm driving Miss Daisy." The fact that Kevin's pet name for the woman was Candy bothered the lieutenant as well, and he figured he knew what kind of candy she wasn't. "Damn sure ain't chocolate!" he mumbled to himself. Lieutenant Washington just couldn't stand it; he figured it was enough having a white girl in his house sleeping in the bed with his son: the only son he had in this world. He had looked forward to having grandchildren some day; some black grandchildren and not some "zebra children" who didn't know if they were black or white. And how did it look to his two daughters: Binta (whose African name meant beautiful daughter), and Nwanaka (whose name meant a child is beautiful)? Hell, he and his wife, Gloria, had been exposing their daughters to Afrocentricity so they could learn more about their culture. Wanted 'em to be proud of being black and proud of who they were. Wanted 'em to appreciate their heritage. Wanted 'em to understand that black was beautiful. Then what happened? His only son brings home a Scandinavian blond with blue eyes. Had Binta and Nwanaka asking if Kevin thought white women were more beautiful than black women and was that why he was gonna marry Candy. Binta, ten and the youngest, wanting to know what color would Kevin's and Candy's children be. And Nwanaka, twelve, wanting to know if their half-brother Kevin was one of those "confused Negroes" that he, himself, often referred to whenever he saw black men married to white women. And heard Nwanaka say, "Candy, huh? Sure ain't chocolate." The same damn thing he'd said. Lieutenant Washington was troubled by his thoughts. Everyone in the house was asleep. The lieutenant got off the sofa in the living room, turned off the Nightline program on TV that he was half watching and took his agonizing thoughts to bed with him. Everyone was surprised when Lieutenant Washington showed back up for work this morning. He had been expected to be on vacation until after Christmas. But he just couldn't tolerate being around Kevin and Candy any longer, with both of them always holding hands. Acting like their asses had discovered paradise. Everybody looking at their asses holding hands. Made him feel uncomfortable, like when they went to Greektown to Fishbones. He couldn't enjoy his meal because he felt everybody in the restaurant was looking at their table. Hell, wasn't it enough that Kevin and Candy came into the restaurant holding hands like lovestruck teenagers? But why did they have to smack each other with a kiss what seemed like every five minutes? Ullysis pondered.

He knew everybody was looking at their table. He'd sensed it. Ruined his appetite and spoiled his meal. And, hell, he'd been looking forward to going back to Fishbones and having some jambalaya.

On Christmas day they all gathered at the dining room table: Ullysis and Kevin sitting at opposite ends of the table; his wife sitting to his immediate right; and Candy sitting to Kevin's immediate right; Binta and Nwanaka sitting across from each other. Ullysis said grace and mumbled under his breath, "Thank yah, Lord, just one more day!" "The time sure went by fast," Kevin said. "It doesn't seem like we've been here a week already. Does it seem that way to anyone else?" Candy said,"The time flew." Gloria looked at Ullysis with guilt-ridden eyes, turned to look at Kevin and said,"I agree." Binta smiled but didn't say anything. Nwanaka looked at her mother and mumbled under her breath, "I know you must be jokin'." Ullysis didn't bother with the question and said, "Now, let's see. I see the ham, the duck, the collard and mustard greens, the candy yams, the sweet corn, the cornbread muffins, and the black-eyed peas and, of course, chitlings. A broad smile flared on Ullysis's face as he began to dig in. The others at the table followed suit. The chatter and merriment at the table pleased Ullysis. It even softened his temperment toward Kevin and Candy. A good meal and family, so what the hell, Ullysis thought. What the hell?

Ullysis pierced the chitlings on his plate with a fork and had the morsel to his mouth, then noticed that Kevin had only vegetables and corn bread on his plate. Ullysis lowered the fork to his plate. "What's wrong Kevin?" Ullysis asked. "Dad, I hate to disappoint you," said Kevin. I know you meant well, but I don't eat chitterlings any longer. I stopped eating that kind of food. It really isn't good for you. It contains a lot of fat and cholesterol. That's why so many black people have hypertension and health problems because of eating fatty foods." "What did you say?" Ullysis asked, not believing what he heard out of Kevin's mouth. "Dad, I don't eat chitterlings any more." "They ain't no damn chitterlings. They're chit'lins," Ullysis insisted. "Dad, they're spelled c-h-i-t-t..." "I don't need no damn spellin' lesson. I know how the damn things are spelled. But nobody goes around pronouncin' 'em chitterlings.

They say chit'lins!" Binta and Nwanaka giggled. Gloria's eyes danced from side to side as though watching a tennis match. Candy was holding Kevin's hand, but now not smiling like she had all evening. "When did you stop eatin' chit'lins?" Ullysis asked. "You used to love chit'lins. I remember a time when you couldn't get enough of 'em. Always asking, 'Are we gonna have chit'lins'? Every holiday: Thanksgiving, Christmas, and New Year's. Always asked, 'Are we gonna have chit'lins'?' Now you don't like 'em. When did you stop likin' 'em?"

"About four years ago," Kevin said. "I don't mean to hurt your feelings, Dad, but I simply don't like them any longer, for the reasons I gave you." "Don't like 'em anymore, huh?" "Yeah, Dad, I don't like them anymore. They aren't good for you." "No, I know what it is. It's soul food. You just don't like soul food any longer. Talkin' about it's bad for your health. Hell, black people been eatin' soul food for a long time and will still be eatin' it when you're buried in your grave. Hell, everybody's gonna die from somethin'. You've gotten too good to eat soul food. That's the problem; too black for you." "Dad, what's that suppose to mean?" Kevin asked. "What part didn't you understand?" Ullysis said. "I said soul food is too black for you". Ullysis picked up the bowl containing the blackeyed peas and said, "What about these blackeyed peas? Do you eat 'em anymore?" "No, I don't," Kevin said. "It's the same thing. They have fatback in them." "I bet you like white northern beans, don't you?" Ullysis said.

Ullysis was happy Kevin and Candy were gone. His son's visit hadn't turned out like he'd wanted. It hurt him, too. That damn white girl done changed his son; had him acting white and done come between them. Kevin called him a racist and claimed he was prejudiced against white people. He told Kevin that if you're black, then you can't be a racist. Impossible to be black in America and be a racist because it's white people who hold the power and use it against black people. They do it all the time. And been doing it since they brought black people to this country in shackles. That's what he'd said to Kevin, but knew he hadn't bought any of it. Kevin still insisted that he was a racist. Also said that his and

Candy's love for each other was colorblind. Colorblind his ass, Ullysis mused, for he knew the first time his son and that puny-ass white girl had a big argument, she was gonna call Kevin a nigger. Bet'cha, Ullysis meditated as he sipped on the cup of black coffee and stared down into the plate of scrambled eggs, bacon, and amply buttered grits he was going to enjoy before going to work. "Chitterlings," he mumbled to himself. "What kinda shit is that? Chitterlings!" Ullysis shook his head in disgust, thinking how that white girl had changed his son and come between Kevin and him. Done changed Kevin, Ullysis was convinced. He used to love chit'lins. Now he doesn't like 'em anymore. Done changed him. Candy put a whitewash on Kevin's ass. Ullysis finished his coffee in deep thought.

Chapter Eleven

She shook. She poked. She jostled. She pulled. But Johanna could have just as well been doing the same to a rock, for the response would have been the same. Nothing Johanna did helped to awaken her mother, who was recumbent on her back in bed, wearing a blue nightgown trimmed with white lace. Johanna rushed to the kitchen to fetch her brother. Emily was the oldest, but she wasn't going to be of much help. All Emily did was lie in bed in a comatose state. Just lie there in bed: hour after hour and day after day. Only getting up to occasionally eat and to take her frequent showers, which she had been doing for almost nine months. And during that time her stomach — with life in it — had gotten larger and larger. It seemed the larger she got the more withdrawn she became. So, Johanna didn't bother about summoning Emily.

"Brian, Brian!" Johanna shouted, "something's wrong with Mother." Johanna latched onto Brian's hand. He followed her not knowing what to expect. They entered their parents' bedroom and approached the bed, where their mother appeared to be in a tranquil slumber. Nothing seemed awry to Brian; after all, their mother had been sleeping a lot since Emily's rape. Emily's rape had changed everybody in the family. It wasn't the same household any longer. It seemed as though strangers had inhabited each of their bodies. "Mother," Brian called as he shook her: first gently, then firmly. "Mother, wake up," Johanna beseeched. "Mother!" they both shouted in unison as they feverishly shook, pulled, poked and jostled their mother's limp and unresponsive body. Brian detected that their mother wasn't breathing. He checked her pulse and his deduction caused Johanna to become hysterical.

They were all consumed with their own thoughts as they rode in the limousine from the church to the cemetery. Hugo was struggling to appear strong in front of his children, but he was hurting inside. He was hurting terribly; as though barbedwire was churning inside his intestines. He was missing Freida; missing her more than he had ever imagined. They had said a lot of good things about his dear wife of twenty-six years at her funeral, Hugo mused. A lot of good things and all true. So very true. She had been a good wife; a mighty good wife. She had been his friend and business partner. She had helped him start and then run the Guardian Security Agency. She had kept the books and knew the source of every penny and where every cent went. And she was a good mother. She stayed home and raised their three children, even though she had a degree in accounting. Tears came to Hugo's eyes, which he quickly wiped away so his children wouldn't see. But they weren't looking at him; they were consumed by their own sorrow. Why? Why? Hugo asked himself over and over. Why didn't she let him know? Why didn't she tell him. He would have understood. He would have helped her. But now he hated himself for having felt the way he did at the time: thinking that Freida had been apathetic and tolerant about Emily's rape. She didn't tell him. He just didn't know. She kept it from him. He hadn't realized that Freida had been taking sleeping pills in order to sleep. And it was the same regarding her depression. He didn't know. He hadn't detected it. And so he didn't know about the Prozac that had been prescribed for her. He prayed to God that it had been an accident and that she hadn't intended to take her life by consuming both the sleeping pills and Prozac together.

He loved her. But they hadn't been affectionate with each other since Emily's rape. Her rape managed to weaken the passion between him and Freida. It just seemed animal-like and simply dirty for them to have sex after what happened to Emily. They had become like two strangers sleeping in bed together; sleeping far apart and anxious about touching each other. He just didn't know. He didn't know about the sleeping pills. Didn't know about the depression and the Prozac. Since Emily's rape it had been difficult for him to focus on much more than his own pain and the hatred that had consumed him. He hoped Freida knew that he loved her. God, he hoped she knew. He always loved her. Tears returned to Hugo's eyes. This time he wiped the tears away with a handkerchief and wasn't solicitous about his children seeing him cry. He gently squeezed Johanna's small hand. He slumped in the limousine's cushioned seat and soliloquized: "I swear to you, Freida, I ain't gonna let no goddamn son-of-a-bitch ever harm Johanna; no son-of-a-bitch." He wrapped his heavy arm around Johanna and squeezed her close to him. Johanna rested her head against her father's shoulders. His arm around her felt comforting. She needed to be touched. She needed to be comforted and reassured. She remembered hugs; lots of hugs. But the hugs and visible showing of affection stopped after her sister Emily got sick. Everybody used to hug her except Brian after he got older, because he thought it was a sissy thing to do; but regardless, she knew he loved her by the things he would say to her and do for her. Her father hugged her and always called her his little girl, then he would smile. His smile had disappeared. She realized that the smile on her father's face disappeared after Emily got sick and went to the hospital.

Johanna remembered how her mother used to hug her every day before Emily got sick. Her mother would say to her, "Take this hug and deposit it." Then she would ask her mother, "Deposit it where?" Her mother would say, "In your hugbank and let them accumulate so that one day you'll be able to withdraw from your bank." It had been a game that she and her mother played. She hadn't understood what withdrawing hugs from her hugbank really meant until Emily got sick and the hugs stopped. She didn't know at the time that she had begun withdrawing from her hugback, but she knew it now. And now she was both sad and scared: sad about Emily's sickness; sad about losing her mother to God; and scared that one day no hugs would be left in her hugbank. Tears trickled down Johanna's face. She raked her small fingers through her platinum hair that she'd inherited from her mother. The more she thought about her mother, the more hugs she withdrew from her hugbank. Emily couldn't cry. She loved her mother. But she had no tears for death. In a way she envied her mother—after all, her mother now had peace. She had wanted to be in the same state as her mother when she was being raped. She had wanted to die. That night she could have easily taken her own life. That night she

begged death to descent upon her and take her away. She had wanted to ride off in the chariot. After awhile she just kept repeating to
herself "Sweet chariot, sweet chariot, please come and take me
home." She would've welcomed death that night. Not only that
night, but many nights since.

It seemed so ironic to Emily that death had chosen to take her
mother away rather than her. She had no tears; no tears for death.
Living had consumed her tears. The dead don't suffer. The dead
don't cry. The suffering was in the living, and she'd suffered every
day since her rape. And now the life inside her was causing her
physical pain. It was life that she never wanted, but couldn't come
to terms with aborting. And it was a life punching and struggling
inside of her, eager to enter into a cruel world. It was a life she
would be unable to care for and would have to put up for adoption.
She had no tears for death, though she loved her mother. It was the
living that provoked her tears—not death. Brian looked across at
Emily. He saw what he had been seeing since she returned home
from the hospital after being raped: A face as blank as a sponge and
eyes as distant as the horizon near sundown. She wasn't the same
Emily. He missed the old Emily: the Emily that laughed a lot, kid-
ded often, and was so full of life. She should have let him go with
her that night. Their father should have insisted. If he had gone, no
niggers would have raped Emily; not if he had been with her. He
was happy that he had graduated. His parents wanted him to attend
college, but his mind wasn't ready for college; so he had enlisted in
the Navy. He had to get away. He just couldn't stand seeing Emily
the way she was. And he couldn't tolerate seeing his family torn
apart.

Everyone had become a different person—including himself is
what Brian was thinking. He wasn't the person he used to be. He
wasn't a boy any longer. He was now a man. A man like his father.
And he hated them. He hated them just like his father hated them.
Hated niggers. Ever since he could remember his father hated niggers; said they were a low class of people who couldn't be trusted.
So, he, himself, never associated with any of them and didn't like to
be around them. And he hated them more for what they did to

Emily. They had taken her away from him, because she was no longer the same. They had caused everybody in his family to change. He wasn't a boy anymore. He now was a man. He was ready to go out into the world on his own. But before he left for the Navy he had to do something about Emily's rape. He had to make somebody pay. Somebody! He had to do something, but just didn't know what. Brian shrugged his broad shoulders—which he inherited from his father—and jerked his head backward, flinging his auburn hair out of his face. The black limousine moved slowly out of the cemetery, past groomed grassy knolls and onto the highway. Burying his dear wife had been the most heart-wrenching thing Hugo had had to do. The Heiderbergs were heading home and preoccupied with their personal thoughts, until Emily bellowed in pain. All eyes fixed on Emily, observing her hands underneath her bulging belly. Emily's eyes were shut and her teeth clenched. Hugo reached across Johanna and placed his hand on Emily's arm. "What is it Emee?" he asked.

Emily responded with groans and moans in the mantra of a person in earnest pain. "Emily's sick!" said Johanna. "I think she's having a baby!" said Brian. Hugo asked, "What is it Emee? What's the matter?" "She's having a baby!" Brian said. The limousine driver asked, "Who's havin' a baby?" "She can't be havin' a baby!" Hugo exclaimed. "Not now!" "She's sick!" said Johanna. "We better get her to the hospital! Driver, take us to the hospital!" said Brian. "What hospital?" the driver asked. "Any goddamn hospital!" Hugo responded. Emily slumped on the limousine's seat, wrenching in pain with her head cocked backward. She could hear their voices but the chatter registered as gobbledygook to her. The words she understood were "sick", "having a baby", and "hospital." It was too late for the hospital. Emily understood as much. She felt the child inside her about to be delivered, right where she was now lying. Her water broke. "It's too late!" said Brian. "She's delivering!" "She's sick!" said Johanna as she wiped perspiration from Emily's forehead with the same white handkerchief she'd used to mop tears from her eyes at the funeral and cemetery. "Move over Johanna. Get outta the way," Hugo ordered as he attempted to make

Emily as comfortable as possible on the seat. "Is the baby comin'?"
the driver asked. "Yeah! Yeah!" Brian said. "Pull over!"

   "Aw, shit!" the driver said. "Who's gonna help her deliver it?"
I see the baby's head!" Brian exclaimed. His eyes as large as tennis balls. "Put something underneath her!" the driver said. Hugo
and Brian both jerked their coats off. Hugo placed one coat behind
Emily's head and the other under her as he wiped sweat from his
brow with the back of his large, hairy hand. "It's coming; it's coming!" Brian hollered. "Somebody do somethin'!" the driver said.
"Goddamn!" Hugo shouted as he removed a pocketknife from his
pocket and severed the umbilical cord. "It's a baby!" said Johanna.
"A brown baby. A boy baby. Emily's got a brown baby boy!"
Hugo was on his knees, damn-near in shock. It had all happened so
suddenly. He was holding a little black baby in his hands, whom he
helped bring into the world. Emily cried, but not on account of any
physical pain. The physical pain had subsided. It was a different
pain that she was experiencing. She covered her face with her
hands as the tears flowed. She had no desire to look at the baby, nor
did she want to hold the child. Giving birth to a child that she had
no desire to hold or cast her sight upon is what now pained Emily.
She felt a need to triumph over her motherly instinct. It all was so
painful. Mother? Emily's body heaved uncontrollably.

Chapter Twelve

GRACE MEMORIAL HOSPITAL
FARMINGTON, MICHIGAN

The news had filtered through the hospital like water through sand. They had classified the infant as Baby John Doe, but everybody referred to the newborn as "The Limousine Baby." Brenda Morgan had heard the rumors—after all, the grapevine was extensive at Grace Memorial, especially with a thing like this. She had heard so much talk and gossip, and it had gotten to the point where she couldn't sort truth from fiction.

Brenda had heard that the young lady's father, irate because the child was fathered by her black boyfriend, forced the girl to put the child up for adoption. She'd also heard that the girl had been raped at the Country and Western Jambaree when she slipped away from her family to meet friends; and she'd even heard the girl had been gang-raped by some black men while attending the African American Music Festival. Brenda considered all the other rumors she'd heard and concluded that only one thing was factual: the black baby boy with the white mother was being put up for adoption. Brenda perceived that the poor baby was being treated like a novelty; like she'd been treated when she got hired as the first black nurse at Grace Memorial four years ago. And she still couldn't get over how naive some white folks appeared when they stared at black folks because they're black; and they stare at black folks because in white folks' minds black people appear out of place; and white folks stare at black folks like black folks don't know white folks are staring at them because they're black is what Brenda thought. Then, too, she considered, maybe white folks aren't naive. Maybe they're not naive at all. Maybe some white folks don't give a damn; don't care at all; and don't care that black folks know that they're being stared at because they're black and stick out like Reverend Jessie Jackson at a Ku Klux Klan rally.

But, then too, Brenda mused, it'd be the same thing in the neighborhood where she'd lived in Detroit before she and her husband moved to Southfield. White folks looked out of place in her westside neighborhood in Detroit. And when you saw a white person in her old neighborhood, she thought, you'd think they were lost—lost as hell. Then what do you do? You stare at them and don't care if white folks know you're staring at them because they're white in a black neighborhood and stand out like a teaspoon of whipped cream in a large bowl of fudge. Suppose the pot couldn't call the kettle black, whatever that really meant, Brenda mused, and wondered who came up with such a saying. Probably a black person, she pondered, but she didn't like it when white folks said it. It just rubbed her the wrong way when they said it. It just didn't settle well when white folks said it. It was near the end of her twelve-hour shift and things had somewhat slowed down in the respiratory unit of the hospital, so Brenda made up her mind to go to the pediatric unit on the sixth floor to see "The Limousine Baby." She understood all the commotion at Grave Memorial concerning a white woman having a black child; after all, it wasn't as though it was a frequent occurrence, particularly at Grave Memorial, which was located in a mostly all-white suburb. Brenda was sure that if the white woman, whoever she was, hadn't had the baby in the limousine she'd have had the baby somewhere outside of Farmington, someplace way outside of Farmington. She knew it had to be embarrassing to the family to have one of their relatives give birth to a black child in their own community.

Brenda punched the button to the sixth floor, catching what she thought to be the slowest elevator in town. She exited the elevator, walked to the nurses station, and greeted one of the white nurses at Grace Memorial who, from the very first day she started working there, always spoke unpretentiously to her, and with a smile which was unlike most of the white nurses who only half spoke to her, if at all, or would labor a forced smile, if they smiled at all. Brenda assessed Pam's smile as being genuine, because her eyes smiled. Brenda's grandmother, whom she missed, had told her years ago when she was a young girl that she could always tell when a smile was sincere by looking in the eyes of a person. If she saw the smile in their eyes, then the smile on their face was real because the eyes don't lie. "Hi, Pam, how's it going?" Brenda said as she approached the nurses' station. "Oh, Brenda, it's been hectic up here. A lot of traffic. Lots of people wanting to see the Limousine Baby. Even the mothers who'd given birth to their own babies have been asking to see the Limousine Baby." Pam gave Brenda a smile and said, "Well, friend, what brings you to ped? Is this a social visit, or would you just happen to be interested in seeing the Limousine Baby, too?" Brenda simpered and said, "Do you want the truth?" They both laughed. Brenda detected Pam's eyes smiling. "Now, I'm not a nosy person by no means," Brenda said, "but I have to admit that I'm a bit curious, but for reasons perhaps different than others who asked to see the baby." "I know, Brenda. I know you love children. One day you and Frank are going to have a house full of children."

"Well, I don't know, Pam. If we don't have a child sometime soon my biological clock is going to run out." "You and Frank are going to have children, I just know it." "Hope you're right, Pam. Hope you're right." "You'll see. Now, let me take you to see the baby." Pam escorted Brenda to the nursery and pointed the baby out. "I'm going back to my station, so I'll talk to you when you come out. A cute thing, isn't he?" "Yes he is," Brenda agreed. "Yes, he is." What does his chart say? Hmm, nine pounds, four ounces. Twenty-four inches long. A big fellow. Blood type O positive." Brenda crooked her index finger underneath the baby's chin and gently stroked him as she whispered, "Coochie, coochie, coo. Have they been bothering you today? Bet they have; haven't they? Precious little thing probably tired of all those people looking at you so. Bet you are. Coochie, coochie, coo. Bet you are. Calling you precious little thing the Limousine Baby. Precious little thing gotta have a better name than that, now, don't you? Yes you do. Coochie, coochie, coo. Gotta have a better name than that. What about Baby Lim? Mind if I call you Baby Lim? That's what I'm going to call you, Baby Lim. Precious little Baby Lim. Coochie, coochie, coo..."

"I'll be damned!" Lieutenant Washington shouted as he read the article in the Detroit Free Press at his desk. The bold printed headline grabbed him right away: Former Detroit P.D. Officer Buries Wife, Then Delivers A Life. Seeing Hugo Heiderberg's name in the article made Lieutenant Washington sit erect, plant his size twelve shoes firmly on the hardwood floor, scoot his chair closer to his desk, place the newspaper flat on top his desk, remove his eye-glasses to wipe away the smudges, put them back on, then bury his sight and mind back into the article. The lieutenant finished devouring the article. He was so immersed in the article that he'd actually had to read a couple of the paragraphs more than once. He shook his head in utter amazement and muddled, "Ill just be damned! Hugo delivered that baby who resulted from his daughter's rape. I'll just be damned! Now that's something. That's really something. The guy loses his wife, then is forced to deliver a baby that one of those bastards fathered. Don't too much care for Hugo with his racist ass. Matter of fact, I don't like his ass at all; but this is too much, even for somebody like Hugo. Wonder how he's takin' all this? Bet he'd not takin' it worth a shit. How could he? A white racist forced to deliver a black baby; ironic as hell. This is somethin', really somethin'."

Hugo Heiderberg had a splitting headache. He felt as though boulders were crashing together inside his head. He hadn't been long arriving home this morning. He still had on the same clothes that he'd worn to Frieda's funeral yesterday, except for the coat. The people at Grace Memorial had the nerve to ask him if he wanted his coat back after he'd spent about forty-five minutes in the lavatory washing all that sticky afterbirth shit off his hands. "Hell no!" he told them. Hell no, he didn't want his coat back. They must've been fuckin' crazy, Hugo thought. Hugo left the hospital right away. As soon as he cleaned all that sticky-ass-shit off his hands, he left. He told the limousine driver to drop him off at the very first bar he saw. He drank damn near a fifth of Old Forster Whiskey, a double shot at a time before they refused to serve him another drink. That's when he told them he wasn't driving. They told him it didn't matter, they still couldn't serve him because he was intoxicated. "Damn right I'm intoxicated!" he'd said. "You would be intoxicated too if you just buried your wife and then delivered a nigger baby in the back of a limousine. What the fuck you think?"

But he wasn't too drunk to realize that he'd caught the attention of every white person in the bar. And that's all there were in the bar was white people. And a good thing too, because if there had been a nigger in the bar at the time, no telling what else he may have said or done. Just no telling. But, there were only white people in the bar and every single face was turned toward him and all eyes were fixed on him like he was crazy, or just plain out of his ever-loving mind. He wasn't too drunk to see them looking at him like they were. And he didn't like it a bit; not in the least. That's when he'd asked, "What the fuck you all lookin' at? Ain't you ever seen a white man who'd delivered a nigger baby in the back seat of a limousine before?" That's when they asked him to leave. They said he was drunk and was disturbing the other customers. They insisted that he leave. That's when he said, "I'm a white man! How you gonna just put me out? You put niggers outta places; not a white man. I've got as much rights in here as any white person. I said I delivered a nigger; I didn't say I was a nigger. There's a difference if you're too fuckin' stupid to understand it. I'm Brother Elbe, a member of the Euro-Brothers Defense Society. It's men like me who stand up for your fuckin' rights. Stand up to niggers, Jews, and the like so they don't trample over your God-given rights as white people. Are you too fuckin' stupid to see? Niggers, Jews, and the minorities are tryin' to take over. Don't you fuckin' see it? Are you too goddamn stupid to see?

Do you know how that nigger baby got inside my daughter, a white girl? Do you wanna know? Do you fuckin' care? You should care if you don't. I'll tell you any goddamn way. I'll tell you how that nigger baby got inside my Emee. She was raped! Do you hear me? She was raped! Raped by some fuckin' niggers! Do you hear me? Do you? Now do you care? Next time it might be your own daughter or wife. Now do you care? Fuckin' right you care! And you know why you care? You care because you're white. Just like me, you're white. And you wanna feel safe—especially safe from niggers. That's why you live here, or wherever you live. You live here because you wanted to get away from niggers.

And there ain't nothin' wrong with that! Not a fuckin' thing!"
Hugo remembered the bar being quiet and then two white policemen coming into the bar to remove him. He remembered telling
them about the nigger baby he'd delivered right after burying his
wife. He showed them his gold badge, letting them know that he
used to be one of them. They offered to take him home, but he
asked them to take him to his office at the Guardian Security
Agency instead. They were accommodating. They were white men
like himself, so they understood. They understood what he was
going through; so they dropped him off at his agency where he commenced to drink some more and fell asleep until early this morning
when he called a cab to take him home. Hugo was lying on the sofa
in the family room. He still had yesterday's clothes on. He didn't
want to go to the bedroom where he and Freida slept. He didn't like
sleeping alone. No matter that he and Freida hadn't been sexually
intimate for months before she died, he still didn't relish the notion
of sleeping in the king-size bed without Freida. God, he wished she
was still alive. He wondered what he was going to do without her.
Hugo had fallen back to sleep. His monumental hangover had him
anchored to the sofa in the family room. It was as though a Sumo
wrestler was sitting on top of him. It was just after twelve o'clock
noon when his son Brian came rushing into the living room.

"Father! Father!" Brian yelled, "they're showing the house
across the street to some niggers!" "What?" Hugo replied. "They're
showing the Callihans' house to niggers!" Hugo leaped off the sofa
with more vigor than he'd shown for a long time. His hangover had
subsided. Besides, there was something of more importance and
significance now. Niggers were looking at the Callihans' house,
which had been up for sale for only a week. And he'd be god-
damned if he and his family were going to live across the street
from some niggers. "Goddamn niggers!" Hugo bellowed. "Why
don't they just live with their own kind and stop botherin' white
folks?"

Chapter Thirteen

The black Muslims hadn't forgotten. They hadn't forgotten that three of their members had been gunned-downed in cold blood on streets in and outside of Detroit. Then too, they were enraged about the torching of the mosque in Highland Park. And family members, relatives, friends, and acquaintances were asking what about Sonny Cool and Dorag, whose scorched bodies were found in the charred, bullet-riddled car alongside the Lodge Expressway? "What about all this?" the Muslims, black leaders, the black community, and even the white press were asking. They were asking: "Why haven't the culprits been apprehended? What leads do you have? How close are you to solving the crimes? What are you doing about it? Did the perpetrators just simply vanish into thin air? What's going on with the investigation?" And some—particularly the black ministers whose churches had been fire-bombed—had gone as far as to suggest that city hall, government officials, and law enforcement were foot-dragging, dilly-dallying, and pussy-footing with the investigations.

Then there was this fellow in Highland Park who went by the name of Acholam Asante, one of those black militants held over from the 60s and 70s. He was over in Highland Park stirring up the people. The FBI thought he was the catalyst for the riots several months earlier. They said he "beared watching" because he could be dangerous. Not dangerous in the sense that he, himself, would commit any violent acts; but rather dangerous because he had the smarts, intelligence, gift-for-gab, and wherewithal to inflame a sit-uation and excite people to action. And the FBI had a rather exten-sive dossier on Mr. Asante— dating back to the 60s when he was a member of the Black Panther Party. Asante had been arrested sev-eral times but never convicted. He had been arrested for suspicion of arson, breaking and entering, larceny, taunting and challenging, interference with an officer, resisting arrest, and assault upon an officer. He had also won a civil judgment against the city of Detroit for injuries he sustained in an arrest, which was one of those cases that the Dirty Dozen was involved in. It was an undisclosed settlement but the word was that Mr. Asante had gotten paid handsomely. And shortly afterward he took a medical leave of absence from his Chrysler Motor Company job in Highland Park.

As Lieutenant Washington pondered the situation, he entertained some halfway respect for Mr. Asante because he didn't have a problem with an intelligent brother, providing that he was within the law. After all, Mr. Asante had never been convicted of a crime and anytime the Dirty Dozen was involved with black people—especially black men—they couldn't be trusted. Hell, they would just fabricate shit in order to arrest black men and have excuses to beat them. He knew most of those racist bastards who had no respect for black people. Hell, they didn't get along with most of the black officers on the force, so what would you expect? But even though, Lieutenant Washington mused, he didn't hold any esteem for brothers and sisters who rioted, looted, and burned down their own neighborhoods. What kinda goddamn sense did that make? Didn't make any sense at all. Their crazy asses riot, he thought, chase businesses out of their community, can't shop close to home anymore, lose jobs in their neighborhoods, and then be looking to the white man for some damn handouts. It didn't make sense. No damn sense at all, Lieutenant Washington pondered. Stupid shit! That's all it is; just stupid shit. The mayor's office was calling. Calling like some bill collector trying to collect a debt. No small debt, either; but a large debt. And the mayor wanted some action. The word was out that the mayor had told the chief to do whatever it took and use as many people as necessary to solve the crimes so he could get the preachers, the media, and everybody else who'd been calling his office demanding results off his ass.

And he'd heard the mayor didn't like it too much; didn't like it at all when the chief reminded him that it was costing his department a lot of money for overtime. He'd heard that the mayor said, "I don't give a flying fuck about some goddamn overtime. Solve these goddamn crimes!" So now the mayor had been in the chief's ass and the chief, in turn, was in all their asses. The chief had told them, "I'll be in your asses like I own 'em until these damn crimes are solved." And damn if he hasn't, Ullysis muddled. Damn if he hasn't. In his desperation to solve the crimes, the chief had sought greater cooperation from the law enforcement agencies throughout Wayne County. After all, there had been a connection in the murders of the three black Muslims that occurred in Detroit, Royal Oak, and Inkster; all on the same day and with replicated circumstances: each biker riding a Harley-Davidson motorcycle, dressed alike and using the same caliber weapons while employing the same modus operandi. The mayor used his political muscle and some arm-twisting in order to get several of the adjoining suburbs to cooperate by forming a metropolitan task force. The mayor suggested to the media that some predominantly white cities outside Detroit were resistant about joining a metropolitan task force because, as the mayor was quoted in the newspapers as saying, "After all, it was only three black males who were slaughtered . . ." "A damn shame!" Lieutenant Washington fumed, "the mayor had to play the race card in order to get something done and create the Metropolitan Anti-Violent Task Force."

The task force was having its first meeting. Some members acted eager; some looked apprehensive; some appeared nonchalant; and some seemed resentful. But no matter their disposition, there were about twenty of them there with a couple of FBI agents in the mix. They had agreed to meet at the Wayne County Building in Detroit. Lieutenant Washington took his seat at the long table. He looked right and left of him, reading the facial expressions and checking out the body language—especially the white members' body language. He'd had lots of practice. He had been reading white folks' body language for a long time. He couldn't rightfully recall when he'd started reading white people's body language but he was good at it. He could tell without them uttering a sentence or speaking a single word when they didn't want to be bothered, especially bothered with some black shit or nigger shit. And this is exactly what it was all about as far as they were concerned: black shit; nigger shit. Three black men killed in cold blood. But the shootings had been organized. Nobody could refute that fact. The three killings all happened in Wayne County and not one agency had made an arrest. Nobody had a suspect. It was no wonder that black communities were clamoring for some arrests and some manifestation of justice. The media had begun asking questions that had become more and more difficult to answer with each passing week and then with each passing day the longer the murders and the firebombings went unsolved. He was reading their body language all right and reading it well, which caused the lieutenant to wonder if the task force was really a good idea.

"So let's discuss the common denominators in these cases," Pat Wilson, the Wayne County sheriff said. He'd been selected to head up the task force and serve as its official spokesperson. "The facts are, gentlemen," he stated, "three men were murdered and murdered with the same M.O. You all have copies of the report before you. Now, gentlemen, beyond the obvious, what can we hypothesize from the report?" "The black Muslims are sellin' less newspapers?" a white officer quipped, eliciting subdued laughter and chuckling from some of the other white task force members, including a black FBI agent sitting across from Lieutenant Washington. The sheriff said, "Now, gentlemen, this is a serious matter. There are people pushing for these murders to be solved and we need to be dutiful about our task." "Yeah. I agree," one of the white task force members said. "We need to solve these murders before they have Louis Farrakhan or someone like him coming in here and stirring things up more than they are." "You're right." "Yeah." "I agree . . ."

Most heads were nodding in agreement, that is, the heads of most of the white task force members as well as the lone black FBI agent who was wearing a dark suit. Ullysis and the other six black officers on the task force withheld any visible affirmation. And that yo's right Mr. Charlie grin on the black agent's face was beginning to irritate Lieutenant Washington. He hadn't found the agent too friendly to begin with. The other black officers had made efforts to greet and meet with each other, unlike the black FBI agent who was aloof and didn't make eye contact with the black officers on the task force. But he was a brother. The lieutenant thought perhaps the brother was preoccupied with solving the murders and maybe that was simply the persona of FBI agents inasmuch as the white FBI agent appeared just as reserved. Really sort of cocky, Lieutenant Washington thought. Lieutenant Washington said, "I believe the murders were race related." "So, Lieutenant Washington, are you speculating that the killers were white?" "I think they were," Lieutenant Washington replied. "And I think the murders of the three black Muslims are somehow tied to the torchin' of the mosque in Highland Park and the two black churches in Detroit. I think we need to look at the big picture and perhaps the notion that all this is tied together." "Jesus Christ!" a white officer said. "We came together to solve the murders, so is the lieutenant suggesting that in addition the task force should investigate the arsons of the churches? Hell, we can't be solving the city of Detroit's crimes, too."

"No one's askin' anyone to solve Detroit's crimes," Lieutenant Washington shot back. "We're capable of solvin' our own crimes just as well as any of you; maybe better. All I'm sayin' is that there might be a connection because of the pattern as well as the circumstances." "What pattern are you referring to?" the sheriff asked. "The pattern of three," Ullysis said. "Three black Muslims killed, three bullets fired into the body of each victim, and three black places of worship burned." "So, lieutenant," another white member of the task force said, "why couldn't the perpetrators be someone other than whites? Isn't it a fact that the black Muslims have been putting pressure on drug dealers? So maybe the shooters were black. Maybe they were black drug dealers retaliating and attempting to scare off the Muslims. Isn't that possible?" Before Lieutenant Washington could respond, the black FBI agent said, "That's a possibility." "Possible,"Lieutenant Washington said, "but not probable." "And why's that?" the black FBI agent asked. "Well, let me tell you why since you asked and the issue was raised," the lieutenant said. "First of all, if it had been drug dealers retaliatin', I assure you more than three shots would've been fired into the victims. Drug dealers aren't that clinical. The shooters sent a message entirely different than drug dealers would've. The drug dealers would've sprayed more shots. They wouldn't have been clinical about it, so to speak. And then, too, forty-fives ain't the weapons of choice for drug dealers, gentlemen."

The white FBI agent said, "The lieutenant makes a valid point.

The shootings do have elements of being hate crimes; so the murderers are most likely white. Perhaps a white hate group- -skinheads or the like. The FBI has been investigating this angle, but we've yet to come up with anything solid." Lieutenant Washington looked at the black FBI agent who, by the look on his face, seemed to suggest that he hadn't appreciated the fact that the white agent was concurring with the points Lieutenant Washington had made that challenged any notion that the killers were anybody other than white. Lieutenant Washington wanted to tell the black agent that he didn't have to cater to these honkies. Wanted to tell him that he was free to be black and that the Emancipation Proclamation had been signed into law in 1863 by Abraham Lincoln. So that means . . . let's see . . .that black people have been theoretically free one hundred and thirty years, Lieutenant Washington contemplated. The sheriff said, "After this discussion and exchange I think we can reasonably assume that the killers were likely white. Is there anyone who disagrees." All the black officers—except the black agent—indicated verbally or by some gesture that they believed the killers were most probably white, as did some of the white officers—including the white FBI agent. But, in any case, no one registered a sign of disagreement. "Then what about motive?" the sheriff asked. "What can we conjecture as to a motive? I heard 'hate crime', but can we explore this further and more in depth?"

"Revenge!" one of the black officers said. "It seemed to be revenge or retaliation for something." "I agree," Lieutenant Washington said. "The murders were probably revenge or retaliation by the manner the murders were carried out. But let's not forget about the church burnings. I think the torchin' of the churches was also retaliation that was racially based. And another thing I believe is that the two guys whose car got shot up on the Lodge and exploded in flames saw somethin' that night. I think they saw who firebombed the mosque in Highland Park. They lived in that area. I think they gave chase and then as a consequence lost their lives. And you know somethin' else gentlemen?" "What, lieutenant?" "What's that?" "I think you're about to tell us." "let it out..."

Lieutenant Washington said,"The shooter on the motorcycle in

Detroit was seen headin' west on I-94 and the two fellows from Highland Park who died were headin' west in their car. And I think they were in pursuit. So, gentlemen, I think our killers not only are white, but also live outside of Detroit and possibly in one or several of the communities of the people sittin' at this table." Everybody in the room looked at one another. Lieutenant Washington felt proud of himself. He had them thinking, do doubt about it. He could tell by the expressions on their faces.

Lieutenant Washington and his wife Gloria were sitting at the kitchen table eating breakfast, talking, and watching Channel 7 Action News. The announcer said, "We have some early morning breaking news. We now take you live and on site in Farmington." "Early this morning," the reporter said, "Home Estate Realty here in Farmington was firebombed around four o'clock. I have the owner Dave Richter here. Dave, how much damage was done?" "Well, looking at the building; it's unsalvageable and will have to be replaced, so I estimate that it will cost at least $250,000 to rebuild." "Will your insurance cover it?" "Yes, the building and business were completely insured." "Dave you told me something else that I think our audience should know regarding a phone call that came into your office earlier. Please share with our audience the nature of the call." "Yeah, our office did receive a message from a caller, stating that we oughta be more selective about the neighborhoods where we show houses to black people. But the caller didn't say black people, he used the n-word. Then he said, 'You'll learn after being taught a lesson.'" "So, it was a male that called?" the reporter asked. "Yes, it was."

"Do you think the caller's warning of a lesson to be learned resulted in the firebombing of your business, Home Estate Realty?" "Can't say for sure, but I suspect it is." "Well, Dave, regardless of the circumstances, I know this has got to be devastating for you. And thanks for sharing that information with us. There you have it, folks. A real estate business has been firebombed and it's suspected that race has something to do with it..."

Chapter Fourteen

Emily wanted to leave. Wanted to get out of here. She wanted to go some place far away—anywhere, but here. She was simply tired. Not so much physically tired, but rather emotionally spent and mentally drained. And she was fed up with their inquiring eyes. She was tired of the conspicuous expressions on their faces. She was tired of being treated like a freak. She loathed walking down the corridor because they all would stare, gaze, and gawk—including the janitors, nurses, doctors, and nurses' aides. They all knew her. They all knew who she was. She was known as the mother of the Limousine Baby; the white woman who gave birth to the black baby in the back of a limousine on the day of her mother's funeral. That's who she was to them. That's why they stared. That's why they gazed. And that's why they gawked. And she was fed up. They didn't know her God-given name. She could hear them whispering everywhere.

Emily realized that she was the only mother on the floor who didn't stroll down the corridor with her baby lovingly folded in her arms and indiscriminately talking baby talk to her newborn. And she was probably the only mother on the floor who never ventured into the nursery to ogle over her newborn. She hadn't asked to be the mother of that child—the black child they call the Limousine Baby. The baby was forced on her. Had any of the other mothers had a baby forced on them? She didn't know who the baby's father really was because it had been two of them: two bastards who had turned her life into a constant nightmare. All the other mothers had to do was tolerate the physical discomfort of giving birth and some pain. They didn't have to endure the mental anguish and emotional battering she, herself, had to endure; so they didn't understand. How could they? Tears formed in Emily's eyes. There she went again, crying. Crying for herself and crying for giving birth to a child who she was incapable of loving. And crying like she'd done for far too long; crying on account of the living. Emily was happy to be leaving. But not particularly happy to be going home because there was going to be sad memories there and a looming emptiness with her mother gone. She was leaving, but not with cards from well-wishers; not with flowers honoring her motherhood; and not with a bundle of joy that she would take home to love, fond over, and raise. She wasn't even taking home the person she used to be. She had changed; changed considerably.

There wasn't much for her and her father to talk about as she packed her things to leave. One would have thought they were two strangers in the room awkwardly sharing space and neither person knowing what to say to the other. Her father left to get the car. Just as well, Emily thought. Emily felt that none of the employees knew what to say to her as she was leaving, which was unlike how they would say their farewells and wellwishes to the other mothers who were discharged. Some stumbled over their words. Some said nothing. Some nodded. But the look on their faces was the same— pity. She was happy to reach the elevator and happier to reach the lobby. She wanted the attendant to push the wheelchair she was sitting in faster, but he seemed to be taking his ever-loving time. Her father had pulled his car up to the door so they could both make a quick getaway. They were finally at the car; that's when she saw him looking at her. But he wasn't really staring. He wasn't gawking. It wasn't pity, either, that she saw on his face. It was more like he was admiring her. And she had seen that look before, for that's how her boyfriend Timothy looked at her when she first met him, which seemed like so long ago. But why was this stranger looking at her the way that he was, Emily wondered. She didn't know him. She wondered if he knew who she was. He probably does, she thought. He probably does. The attendant opened the car door and assisted her inside. Emily saw the stranger still looking toward the car as they drove off.

Danny Donnell, M.D. looked at his wristwatch after having been pleasantly distracted. He'd been halted in his tracks. It was weird and never happened to him before. It was just something about the woman he'd just moments ago sat his eyes upon. She was pretty for sure; naturally pretty, for it was obvious that she wasn't wearing makeup—at least not much, if any at all. She had an angelic appearance and, at the same time, a look of forlornness. He wondered who she was. He wondered why she'd been at Grace Memorial. He pondered if she was married. He wondered a lot of things about her, but what did it matter? He'd probably never see her again. He punched the button to the third floor and rode what he and Brenda Morgan thought to be the slowest elevator in town. Brenda Morgan was in her car, heading home to Southfield after her shift at Grace Memorial. A lot was on her mind. She smiled when she thought about Danny D. That's what she began calling Dr. Donnell after he started his residency at Grace Memorial and she got to know him. Dan sounded too blase. D.D. was boring. She did like Danny, but where she'd come from it was customary to put some spice in a person's name, so she started calling him Danny D. She knew he liked it by the way he would smile and show those pearly whites of his whenever she used the moniker when addressing him on a personal level. He's a good guy, Brenda thought. She'd taken to him right away. He had a good sense of humor and was unpretentious—unlike most residents she'd met and had to deal with.

She'd never seen him the way he was today when he came in: He appeared to be mesmerized, as though he was in a hypnotic state. Spellbound was an apt description. "Angelic." He'd said this woman possessed an angelic appearance. Now if that ain't being spellbound by someone, then fat meat ain't greasy is how Brenda figured it. Baby Lim floated to the surface as thoughts swam in Brenda's mind. She'd thought a lot about that precious little thing since she first laid eyes on him. Well, she ruminated, he wasn't so little; not for a newborn, but precious, no less. So full of spirit and hardly ever cried. And talk about an appetite, he had a good one. She finally got enough nerve to hold him. She fed him a couple of times, too. She fought it; fought it as long as she could. She'd known all along that the moment she held him that she'd get attached. Babies always did that to her whenever she held them. She fought holding Baby Lim, but she found herself drawn to him like a magnet. Then what did she go and do? She knew better, but couldn't help it. It was as though she'd lost all willpower like a teenager with her first credit card. And Pam didn't help matters. Didn't help matters at all. "Go ahead, Brenda; go ahead. You know you want to hold him, so go ahead," Pam said. Brenda smiled in mid-thought. She knew it wasn't fair to blame Pam because she knew herself that sooner or later she was going to pick up Baby Lim and hold him. After all, she visited him in the nursery every day while at work and more than once on the same day.

Brenda's mind was now made up. She was going to tell Frank about Baby Lim. She was going to describe him from his head to his toes and tell Frank all about Baby Lim's infectious smile, sparkling grayish eyes, strong limbs, powerful grip, and indomitable spirit. She would tell Frank all about him. She was so excited and engrossed in thoughts that a driver behind her had to blow his horn. She hadn't noticed the traffic light turn green. "Adopt?" The word sprang from Frank's mouth in such a manner that it surprised Brenda and caught her off guard. She hadn't anticipated this kind of reaction from her husband. He'd responded in a manner which suggested that she was crazy or somewhere near it. And although he'd said "Adopt?" in the form of a question, it was more like a statement. Their conversation turned silent—like a fly landing on cotton. He knew that look. He'd seen that look before on his wife's face. Frank realized that Brenda was sulking, but not like a spoiled child who couldn't have her way. More like a woman who'd so long wanted to have a child, but had constantly been disappointingly denied by Mother Nature. He didn't like seeing her this way. He loved her very much. He was disappointed, too. He wanted children just as much as she did, but he wanted their own children; not somebody else's. They had been trying to have children of their own. They'd tried damn-near everything but artificial insemination and invitro fertilization.

"Brenda, baby, I'm not saying that my mind is closed to adoption, but why this baby? A baby of a mixed race? I don't feel good about considering such a child. That is, if I were to consider adopting." The fact that Frank seemed opened to discussing adoption caused Brenda to sit up in the bed. "Why not a baby with mixed race? What does it matter? All children need to be loved." "But why this particular child?" "I told you, Frank; he's adorable. And I can feel that Baby Lim and I have bonded." "That was the first mistake." "What?" "That bonding stuff. The moment you held him in your arms, that motherly desire of yours surfaced. It didn't matter if it was this child or another child." Brenda smiled at Frank. She realized that he knew that holding a baby, any baby, stirred something inside of her and made her feel attached. But it was different with Baby Lim. The other babies she'd held belonged to someone. Baby Lim didn't belong to anyone. The mother had signed papers to place him up for adoption. He was all alone with no one to love him. She could love him. She could nurture and raise him. She could raise him to be a good person, someone to be proud of. She knew it. She felt it.

"Baby Lim is different, Frank. I simply adore him. He's just the sweetest little thing. And he has no one to love him. We could love him, Frank. We could give him a good home." "Brenda, I don't know. What about the man that fathered this child you call Baby Lim?" "What about the father?" Brenda asked. "No one knows who the father really is." "That's just my point. Now, what kinda person do you think would rape a woman? The father could be mentally ill; maybe mental illness is a family trait. This child could be predisposed to violence or something because of some inherited mental illness." "Oh Frank. You're pushing it. There's nothing wrong with Baby Lim." "How do you know? How can you be sure?" "I know Frank. I just know. Whatever may be wrong with Baby Lim, if anything, I don't think it's anything that love can't cure."

Brenda looked seductively at Frank and smiled. Those big brown eyes of hers were alluring. Frank mulled that her full breasts could surely nourish a baby. But right now he wanted to be her baby. He wanted to suckle her breasts. He was compelled to draw her close to him. He was obliged to insert his hand underneath the Delta Sigma Theta Sorority extra large T-shirt his wife was wearing. He kissed her lips and fondled her breast. One of his hands slid up and down her smooth inner thighs. His hand returned to her breasts, then slipped back between her legs. He continued kissing her. "Maybe we'll make a baby tonight," Frank whispered. "Maybe," Brenda murmured softly. "Maybe." The bedroom filled with the sound of their lovemaking, including the pounding of the head board against the wall.

Chapter Fifteen

His lawyer had tried. He recognized that. So he had nothin' bad to say 'bout his lawyer. And he really didn't have nothin' bad to say 'bout the prosecutor. "Guilty as sin!" is what the prosecutor said to the jury. Had said that he wuz "as guilty as sin." And he realized why the prosecutor would say that 'bout him, 'cause he wuz. He wuz as guilty as sin. It wuz a sin what he and Juice did to that poor white girl. They wuz guilty. He and Juice wuz guilty, Henry pondered. Ain't no other way of lookin' at it, 'cause they wuz guilty. And like that prosecutor said, "they wuz as guilty as sin."

But Juice wuzn't there to hear it. The police had already kilt him. Kilt him good. Heard that Juice's body looked like Swiss cheese wif so many bullet holes in it. Kilt him good. But can't say that he didn't deserve it. He wuz a mean and ornery son-of-bitch. He wuz that. For sho' that young boy wuz jest flat out mean and ornery; and don't rightfully know what made Juice that way. He hadn't really known that much 'bout him. He never talked 'bout his family. Didn't know if he had brothers or sisters or what. Didn't know too much at all 'bout that young boy. Didn't know if his motha and fatha wuz still livin' or what. Just didn't know. The young boy never talked to him much 'bout such thangs. Hell, all they talked 'bout wuz gittin' high and findin' some pussy. They found the wrong pussy that night they raped that white girl. Yeah, they wuz guilty; guilty as sin like the prosecutor said. Henry understood and appreciated that his court-appointed lawyer tried. And can't say that he didn't try. He tried; tried real good to get his sentence reduced. His lawyer told the jury that he wuz a Vietnam veteran who suffered from post-traumatic war syndrome. Said that PTWS had an impact on what he did that night he and Juice raped that white girl. His lawyer had said that his PTWS, along wif the drinkin' and pot smokin', had did somethin' to his mind and made him unable to tell right from wrong. But the jury didn't buy it; didn't buy it at all. Didn't buy it no more than an Eskimo would buy ice. Hell, he didn't buy it himself, but it sounded good to him anyway at the time, 'cause he wuzn't really a rapist. He wuz willin' to pay for his pussy. Would've paid that white girl, too, but Juice wanted to—how did he put it—"gangsta some pussy."

He knew it wuz wrong. It wuz wrong what he and Juice did to that white girl. And Juice would've kilt that white girl if he hadn't ran over some shit in the road that night. He would've kilt her for sho'; knew he would've. He wuz mean like that; mean as hell. And that young boy was gonna kill him, too. Just knew that he wuz before all those police showed up like a scene outta a James Cagney movie. And he loved him some ol' movies. But hardly would see anymore ol' movies again; not where they wuz sendin' him. The jury found him guilty of criminal sexual conduct in the first degree and sentenced him to life in prison. Sho' probably won't see no more of those good ol' movies again, Henry Cornwell thought from his jail cell.

Hugo was anxious about the special meeting the grand superior had called. He had called him personally, which normally the grand superior didn't do, because others generally did the calling, like Brother Rhine or Brother Volga. But hardly ever the grand superior. The grand superior told him that it was very important that he be there. "Very important," he'd repeated. He'd also said that whatever, if anything, he had planned to "deep six it" because it was urgent, very urgent that he be at the special meeting that had been called. And be on time he'd said; be on time he'd repeated.

Hugo showed up at the meeting on time. As a matter of fact he showed up twenty minutes early and practically all the Brothers of the Society were already there. Unusual. Unusual as hell, Hugo contemplated. Strange. Strange as hell. Probably another Code III situation. Probably some niggers, Jews, gooks, or wetbacks did something repulsive or despicable to one of the Brothers or a family member, Hugo pondered. He was hoping that it wasn't another Code III situation; not this soon. It would be crazy with the FBI already involved with the firebombing of the churches and the Metropolitan Anti-Violence Task Force investigating the murders

of those three black Muslims and the two blacks who got wiped out
on the Lodge Expressway. Too soon. The Brothers must know it.
The grand superior must know it. Too soon; much too soon for
revenge on account of a Code III. Sure hope no damn niggers,
Jews, gooks, or wetbacks have fucked up again so soon, Hugo
mused. Sure in the hell hope not. The Brothers' clamorous voices
echoed inside the barn as they congregated and greeted each other
with esoteric and ritualistic handshakes. Most of the Brothers
appeared to be at a loss in regard to why the special meeting was
called on such short notice. But they all knew it had to be important. Grand Superior Alps and the other members of the Grand
Board were huddled in front, talking in a whisper. The grand superior had a twisted countenance and he looked very irritated—like
someone swatting at mosquitoes. The grand superior called the
meeting to order. It took less than a minute for the Brothers to line
the benches facing the grand superior and Grand Board members.
Grand Superior Alps stood silent as he looked over the membership; taking time to look into the questioning faces of the Brothers
who were gathered in front of him.

The sound of rustling field mice and cooing pigeons filtered
through the otherwise silent barn. Upon the grand superior's command, the Brothers stood and cited the Society's pledge and sat
back down upon command. Brother Volga reported fifty-four members present, which was everyone. The grand superior looked the
Brothers over again. He removed the hat from his bald head and
wiped a handkerchief from his forehead to the back of his head in a
fluid motion. He did this twice. He placed his hat back on his head,
held onto the handkerchief and said, "Brothers, I know you all are
wondering what precipitated this meeting this evening. Well,
you're about to know. We have a grave matter before us this
evening. A very grave matter that I've prayed we would never have
to face. And since our inception we've never had to face a situation
like this." The grand superior halted as a noisy airplane flew directly overhead. Hugo contemplated that this must not be a Code III
situation if, as the grand superior said, it was a matter that had never
come before the Brothers before. Now he was profoundly perplexed, as were most the other Brothers, with the exception of the

Superior Board members. The grand superior continued, "It appears that one of our Brothers has gone off and taken revenge on his own and independent of the Society." All the Brothers seated before the grand superior looked around, wondering to themselves who would have done such a stupid deed and exactly what was it that this maverick Brother had done.

"God, help the Brother," Hugo mumbled. The grand superior went on. "Now, Brothers, don't we all know that as a member of this Society that revenge, retaliations, or reprisals are not...not to be taken under any condition or circumstance independent of the Society?" "Yes, Grand Superior!"   all the Brothers bellowed. "Haven't we all been informed of this?" "Yes, Grand Superior!" "Haven't we all been instructed of this?" "Yes, Grand Superior!" "Haven't we all been enlightened about such?" "Yes, Grand Superior!" "And, Brothers, haven't we all been constantly reminded and edified?" "Yes, Grand Superior!" "So, we all know this; am I right?" "Yes, Grand Superior!" "Then why, Brothers? Then why would any one of us go off and take matters into his own hands, which jeopardizes the Society? And that's exactly what one of our Brothers has done- jeopardized the Society and every single Brother here this evening. I know you're wondering who the Brother is and I'm gonna call his name out." Just like all the other Brothers, Hugo was holding his breath, wondering which Brother could do something, anything, that was harmful to the Society.

"Brother Elbe," the grand superior barked, calling out Hugo's code name like a drill sergeant to a recruit in boot camp. Hugo nearly fell from the bench. All eyes were on him. He realized everyone had to be looking at him, but it was a combination of paralysis and shock that prevented him from rotating his head. "Brother Elbe," the grand superior barked again,"did you have anything to do with the firebombing of the Home Estate Realty Company?" The question was easy enough for Hugo to answer. He was actually relieved. Enough oxygen and blood returned to his brain to allow him to assert with authority, "No, Brother Grand Superior; absolutely not!" "Okay," the grand superior responded, "I'll accept that as a true and accurate response." Hugo was relieved. The grand superior said, "Brother Elbe, I posed the question to you because I've been informed by a reliable source that the FBI has questioned some people and your name has surfaced as a suspect in that firebombing inasmuch as the FBI has discovered that Home Estate Realty had shown a black family a house across the street from you. But that's not all." The grand superior removed his hat again and wiped his brow and head with the handkerchief in his hand. Hugo removed a handkerchief from his back pocket and mopped the sweat on his forehead and the nape of his neck.

"No, that's not all, Brother Elbe. That's not the half of it. It seems that one night you got drunk at a local bar and in a room full of witnesses you stated that you were Brother Elbe, a member of the Euro-Brothers Defense Society. Do you remember that Brother Elbe?" Local bar? Drunk? Hugo's mind was spinning. He recalled. He recalled the occasion. He remembered being drunk; more like plastered. He remembered the faces in the bar, but not vividly. He just remembered the faces being white and all staring at him. He remembered saying something to them. He vaguely recalled telling them that some niggers had raped his daughter. He recollected saying something about the nigger baby he'd helped deliver; but nothing about him being Brother Elbe, a member of the Euro-Brothers Defense Society. He wouldn't say such a thing. Would he? Was he too drunk or plastered to remember? "Brother Elbe," the grand superior said, "there are witnesses. The FBI has learned this information. The FBI will be following up and investigating. This all makes you a liability to the Society." Hugo was numb. His heart was pacing. His mind was jumbled. He knew what this meant. But it couldn't be happening to him.

"Brothers," the grand superior evoked, "this is a serious and grave matter before us. Brother Elbe's conduct and actions have subjected the Society to outside scrutiny. And what is it we vow before we close out a meeting? We all vow in the name of God; in the name of Europe; and on behalf of the white race to be loyal to one another and not reveal anything directly or indirectly associated with the Society to others. Brother Elbe, you have forsaken this vow, so we have no other alternative than to disavow you from membership in the Society. I'll now ask Brother Rhine and Brother Volga to remove your cord and collect your ring. You have twenty-four hours to return other properties of the Society." Brother Rhine and Brother Volga headed toward Hugo. All eyes were intently on Hugo, who stood up and pleaded, "No, no, you can't do this to me. I'm a founder. I'm still one of you. I hate niggers, Jews, and the like just as much as any of you. Have you forgotten? I'm a founder; a founder, damnit! You can't do this to me. I beg you not to do this. I made a mistake; I admit it. But I was drunk. It wasn't intentional. I was drunk. I'd just buried my dear wife and then had to deliver a nigger baby because my daughter had been viciously raped. I was outta my mind. I would never do anything intention-ally to harm the Society. Never! Do you hear me? Never! So, please don't do this. I'm one of you. I'm a founder. Please! I beg your forgiveness. Please!"

They were taking Henry Cornwell to the state penitentiary in Jackson, Michigan, to serve his life sentence without parole for criminal sexual conduct in the first degree.

"Ain't really like that," Henry babbled in a muffled tone in the back seat of the police car. "Ain't really like that. Never meant to hurt nobody. Ain't really like that."

Henry had plenty of time to think about things since he'd been arrested. He couldn't get high off of anything while incarcerated, so his mind was clearer than it'd been since he could remember. His mind was getting clearer every day. He recalled how he ended up leaving Alabama at age seventeen to come to Michigan to live with his Aunt Flossie. He'd thought about that mean old white man they call Mr. Cheat who'd slapped him across the face. Slapped him hard, too. Slapped him dizzy. Slapped tears to his eyes and snot from his nose. Slapped him 'cause he asked why he had to pay seven cents fir the same candy that the white boy jest paid a nickel fir. That's when the mean ol' white man called him a stupid, dum' nigger and told him to either pay the seven cents or git the hell outta his store. That's when he told the mean ol' white man that he always cheated black people; and that's why his name was Mr. Cheat. That's when that white man turned red like a turnip and slapped him hard 'nough to make him go dizzy; made tears run down his face; and made snot pour from his nose. That's when he picked up Mr. Cheat's Louisville Slugger that he kept on the counter whenever more than two black boys wuz in his store. He cracked that mean ol' white man over the head wif that Louisville Slugger. Scared the livin' shit outta him; thought he kilt that mean ol' white man after seein' him lyin' on the floor wit blood oozin' from his head.

That's when him and his cousin Jerry ran outta that store like he remembered Laurel and Hardy doin' in a movie he saw. But it wuzn't funny like the movie. Wuzn't funny at all. Scared the livin' shit outta him. Scared the livin' shit outta his cousin Jerry, too. Scared the livin' shit outta everybody. Would've scared the livin' shit outta his daddy if he'd been livin'; but he died four years earlier when he got kicked in the head by a mule while sharecropping Mr. McKinley's farm. They told him to go off into the woods and hide and be on the east bank of Sunflower Lake come nightfall so his Uncle Jessie could pick him up in his truck and take him to Tuscaloosa to catch a bus north to Detroit to stay wit his Aunt Flossie. Two years later he wuz in Vietnam. Wuz goin' to make a career outta the army 'til he wuz sent to that fuckin' war. His mind wuz clearer; clearer for sho'; and clearer than it'd been since goin' to Vietnam. It'd been that long since he'd been this clear-minded. He stayed high in Vietnam; and stayed high since returnin' from Vietnam. He didn't wanna have a clear head and mind 'cause it made him remember too much: Remember plantin' that Louisville Slugger against Mr. Cheat's head, and remember the hundreds of twisted, mangled, and severed bodies in Vietnam that tormented his mind.

"Ain't really like that," Henry mumbled as the police vehicle progressed west on I-94 to Jackson. "Ain't really like that. Never meant to hurt nobody. Never meant to hurt Mr. Cheat. Never wanted to go to Vietnam and kill nobody. Never wanted to hurt that white girl. Ain't really like that. Swear to God I ain't. Ain't really like that. Swear to God I ain't." Henry looked up and saw the white officer in the front on the passenger side staring at him; more like glaring at him. Henry avoided his eyes by looking out the window. With a clear mind, clearer than it'd been in a long time, Henry settled back into his rumination. He'd heard that white girl had a baby. Never did understand why she didn't have an abortion.

Probably wonderin' who the fatha is: him or Juice, Henry mused.
Most likely Juice. Most likely Juice who'd done his business wif
her two times that night. And they both wuz outta their minds that
night—at least hisself wuz. Juice wuz always outta his mind; more
than hisself wuz 'cause the young boy did hard drugs—not like hisself. He didn't do hard drugs; jest smoked weed and drank hisself
silly. Not no needles. Juice didn't like needles. As big as that
young boy wuz he wuz scared of needles. But he enjoyed him some
crack. Sho' did. But Juice sho' didn't like nobody's needle. Sho'
didn't. He liked weed, too; jest like hisself. Liked him some cold
beer and whiskey, too. Sho' did. Juice is probably that baby's
fatha, Henry thought. Baby probably got big bones, big hands, and
big feet jest like Juice. Probably do. But hope that baby don't grow
up to be mean like him. Wonder what made Juice so mean?
Meaner than a junkyard dog, as they say. Meaner than a junkyard
dog. "You know, Henry, where you're going there are a lot of men
like you."
   Henry looked up. it was the white officer talking. A black officer was driving, and neither of the officers had said hardly a word
to the other. "What'cha mean?" Henry asked. "A bunch of low-
lifes. Low-lifes like yourself, Henry." Henry was thinking that the
white officer didn't have no business talkin' to him like he wuz. He
jest wuzn't like that. He wuzn't no low-life. He jest wuzn't like
that. He never in his life meant to hurt nobody and that's the God-
lovin' truth. "A bunch of low-lifes, Henry. Just like you. Men that
like to prey on other people. Men like you, Henry. Men like you."
Henry wanted to tell the white officer to kiss his black ass, but was
afraid. He wanted the black officer behind the wheel to intervene.
But he just kept driving and looking: looking at the highway, looking intermittently at the white officer, and occasionally looking in
his rearview mirror at him in the back seat. "Yeah, Henry, there's a
lot of low-lifes in Jackson like you. And you know what, Henry?
Do you know what? Just like you and your buddy preyed on that
lady, they're gonna prey on you. Somebody's gonna fuck you,
Henry. Fuck you in the ass. So are you gonna give it up willingly,
or are they gonna have to take it by raping you like you and your

buddy raped that lady? Ever thought about it, Henry? Have you? I know you probably haven't because your kind is too goddamn stupid to think beyond the moment. Right, Henry? Am I right?"

It was then that Henry heard the black officer speak. "Cut it, John! Man, that's enough. There's no need to harass the prisoner." "Cut it? You're protecting this low-life? Why do you care about him? Is this one of those black things?" "No, it ain't no black thing. Why you bring up race? It's not our job to harass a prisoner, plain and simple." "No, it ain't. Tell the truth. You're protecting him because he's black." "I'm not protecting anyone. I'm doing my goddamn job! And now that you wanna insert race, what in the hell did you really mean by that 'your kind' crack, anyway? Tell me that, John." The two officers were now in a heated argument. Henry was relieved that the black officer had spoken up, but now the driver wasn't hardly watching the road in front of him. He wasn't looking at where the car was heading. But Henry saw. He wanted to shout a warning, but fear froze his tongue. He folded over in the seat and braced himself.

"What happened?" the state trooper asked. The driver of the eighteen-wheel tractor trailer said while quivering,"The car just came into me. It collided with my front wheel on the driver's side, then bounced and rolled across the median in front of oncoming traffic. I saw the patrol car drifting into my lane, but I had no way of avoidin' the collision. The car just drifted into me."

"I'll need to get more information from you," the state trooper said. "We won't be able to get anything from any of them. They're all dead. Appeared to be two Detroit police officers transporting a prisoner." "Damn!" the truck driver said, "you would think a police officer would be more alert; more observant. Something must've distracted the driver." "I suppose we'll never know," the state trooper replied. "We'll never know."

Chapter Sixteen

Lieutenant Washington watched the black FBI agent smiling like the cat that ate the canary. He probably got something worthwhile to contribute today, Lieutenant Washington thought. Agent Courtney Lewis. He looked like a brother that somebody would name Courtney, with his brothers-avoidance-no-speaking-ass. His ass probably thought he was white. But all the brother had to do was look in the mirror so reality could smack the shit outta him and bring his dizzy ass back to reality. That's what Lieutenant Washington was thinking when Sheriff Wilson called the meeting to order.

"Gentlemen," the sheriff said with a hint of enthusiasm in his nasal voice, "it certainly appears that we're making progress in investigating the murders of the three black Muslims as well as the firebombings. I feel optimistic about all that we've discovered and pieced together at this time. I believe some arrests are imminent and that soon we'll be able to bring closure to these cases." "Sheriff, do we have enough to go to the media with, so we can get them and the black community off our backs?" a black task force member asked. "Good question. That's a decision we'll make here today. My personal recommendation is to call a press conference to announce that the task force has made significant progress and that it's just a matter of time before we solve the cases." "Well, we need to do something," a white task force member said, "Minister Louis Farrakhan has already accused us of-how he put it, 'aiding and abetting a climate of no consequence in regard to the racial genocide of African Americans'; whatever that means."

Lieutenant Washington mulled that Louis Farrakhan wasn't far off target. Maybe not in regard to these cases, but surely in reference to all the goddamn drugs this country had allowed to pour like a constant thunderstorm into black communities like Detroit. It sure wasn't black-owned planes and boats that brought all that shit into this country. And it sure wasn't black dollars that financed that shit and created a network of distribution. Sure in the hell ain't, Lieutenant Washington pondered. A conspiracy against the black community was all it was and honkies were behind it. And he knew damn well they were. Black racial genocide; that's all it was. And honkies getting filthy rich behind all the drugs. Farrakhan sure in the hell knows what he be talking about, Lieutenant Washington thought. Gotta respect a brother like that. Sure do. Honkies just don't like to hear the truth about their asses, especially when a black man speaks it. Sure don't, Lieutenant Washington mused. "Well," the sheriff said, "we're gonna prove Farrakhan wrong on this. Okay, let's see where we are and bring everybody up to speed. And I caution you all, you're sworn to hold all information in the deepest of confidentiality. To do otherwise is a breach of your office and sworn oath to serve as a member of this task force. Any member who violates his oath and/or places the investigations in jeopardy is subject to prosecution." The sheriff looked around the room at each of the task force members and asked, "Are we of the same understanding, gentlemen? Are there any questions?" Some heads shook in the negative to the question posed by the sheriff. Some member grunted: "Not me." "I understand." "Na'll. . ." Ullysis looked over at the black FBI agent. He was still smiling. Just sitting there smiling; more like grinning. He never gave a head motion. Never said a word. Just grinned like some anointed Uncle Tom, Lieutenant Washington was thinking.

"Captain Peters," the sheriff said, "let's hear your report." "Gladly, Sheriff," Captain Peters said as he pushed his chair away from the long, oakwood table, stood, and glanced at some written notes he had made. "In investigating this case in our jurisdiction," Captain Peters said, "two of our officers were called to a bar one evening to remove an intoxicated and unruly customer. We've since learned that this customer was ranting and raving about having just buried his wife and delivering a baby right after his wife's funeral. He bragged, maybe bragged is the wrong word, but he boasted that he was a member of a society that protects the rights of white people. He called himself Brother Elbe. At this point, I wanna turn it over to Agent Lewis, who will apprise you of more." Lieutenant Washington mumbled, "Oh, now he's gonna speak. Courtney, Mr. Charlie's boy, is gonna speak now. Wonder what his no-recognizing-another-brother-ass gotta say." Agent Lewis pushed away from the table and rose from his seat, smiling as far as everyone else was concerned but Lieutenant Washington who read it as a shit-eating grin on his face. Agent Lewis' facial expression turned more earnest as he spoke. "Captain Peters has given you basic information, the skeleton so to speak, but allow me to add flesh to the bones."

"This is gonna be good," Lieutenant Washington mumbled under his breath. Agent Louis continued,"The gentleman at the bar that night who referred to himself as Brother Elbe is a retired Detroit police officer by the name of Hugo Heiderberg." Lieutenant Washington started coughing. He had begun to drink from a glass of water when Special Agent Courtney Lewis stated the name Hugo Heiderberg. The water went down the wrong pipe. A couple of task force members slapped the lieutenant on the back. The lieutenant captured everybody's attention by his loud hacking, which generated tears that streamed from his eyes, down his cheeks. "Are yah okay?" the sheriff asked as he peered at the lieutenant with genuine concern. "I'll be okay," Lieutenant Washington sputtered as he regained his composure. His coughing subsided. He took a sip from his water glass. "I knew that psuedo-brother was gonna say somethin' to make me gag," Lieutenant Washington mumbled.

Agent Lewis continued, "Mr. Heiderberg came to the FBI's attention after the Home Estate Realty Company in Farmington was firebombed. Our initial efforts relative to the firebombing was to determine motive, then suspects. A caller to the agency had already determined a motive by making reference to the showing of homes in white areas to black families. So, a trace of where the agency had shown homes to black families in white areas led us to Mr.

Heiderberg, who lives directly across the street from a home that had recently been shown to a black family." Agent Lewis halted long enough to take a sip from his water glass. "Why Mr. Heiderberg, you may ask?" Agent Louis said. "Mr. Heiderberg was heard by witnesses saying that he was Brother Elbe who belonged to this society that Captain Peters mentioned. Well, we've learned in our investigation that Elbe is a code name derived from a river in Europe that flows into both Germany and central Europe. The society that Mr. Heiderberg belongs to is the Euro-Brothers Defense Society. We have some of their members under surveillance, but we don't know too much about them at the present time. But we do know that they wear uniforms, a special engraved ring, and they meet on a large farm near the Detroit Metropolitan Airport in a rural area in Romulus. Special Agent Fillmore will pass out a diagram of the ring the Society members wear."

Agent Lewis again picked up a glass of water from the table in front of him and said, "Captain Peters also informed you that Mr. Heiderberg stated in the bar that night that he'd delivered a baby right after his wife's funeral. That he did. He delivered his oldest daughter's baby. His daughter was raped while attending the Country and Western Jamboree last year in Detroit. She chose not to abort the baby because of her long-time anti-abortion stand. The baby was delivered on the back seat of the limousine that the family rode in for the funeral that day. The baby that Mr. Heiderberg delivered was black, or you could say mixed—half black, half white—but, in essence, the child will go through life considered black." "Holy shit!" one of the white task force members blurted, "I remember that story! I read it in the newspaper. You think the society that Mr. Heiderberg belongs to had something to do with the real estate agency's firebombing, the murders, and the firebombings of the churches?" "We do," Agent Lewis replied, as he reached for his glass of water. "Holy shit!" the white agent said again. Lieutenant Washington wondered why honkies always said "holy shit" when there wasn't a damn thing holy about shit. He never could figure it. But for sure, Special Agent Lewis had his mind churning. All that shit was adding up now. Hugo Heiderberg. He always knew his ass was a racist. And as for the diagram of the ring he was looking at in front of him, he had seen that ring before. He remembered having seen it on Hugo Heiderberg's finger the night his daughter was raped and the same night he came to the Beaubien Street Precinct. "I've seen this ring before," Lieutenant Washington asserted. "I saw it on Hugo Heiderberg's hand." "I've seen it, too," Assistant Chief Sprowl from the Detroit P.D. said, which even surprised Lieutenant Washington.

"Both you guys from the Detroit P.D. have seen these rings?" Agent Fillmore asked. "That's interesting. We understand the ring in Mr. Heiderberg's case because of his known association with the Euro-Brothers Defense Society, but we're interested in knowing where you've seen the ring, Sergeant Sprowls." "I saw it recently," Sergeant Sprowls said. "Two of our officers were transporting a prisoner to Jackson for rape. As a matter of fact, that prisoner was convicted for raping the Heiderberg girl. Anyway, the two officers transporting the prisoner both died in an automobile accident, along with the prisoner. When we went through the officers personal effects I saw this ring. I thought it was an unusual ring and it belonged to Sergeant VanBenschoten." "The Dirty Dozen!" Lieutenant Washington said with authority. "The Dirty Dozen!" "What?" the sheriff asked. "The Dirty Dozen," Lieutenant Washington repeataed, "a group of white Detroit P.D. officers who were put on trial for police brutality against black citizens. About four of 'em, as I recall, were found guilty; the others were acquitted. VanBenschoten was one of the ones acquitted, as was Hugo Heiderberg." A silence unfolded in the room. Sheriff Wilson lifted the silence. He said, "We're on to something here, men. We're definitely on to something big. I feel good about it. We're gonna bust this thing wide open." They all sat back in their chairs, savoring and devouring the information they had consumed like ravenous carnivores. Sheriff Wilson once again broke the silence. He said, "Gentlemen, I think we're due for a press conference."

Chapter Seventeen

Hugo sat on the bed staring at the nine millimeter revolver next to him. This is it, he contemplated. He didn't have any reason to go on. His life was more disheveled than the socks and underwear in his dresser drawer. When his wife, Freida, was alive she used to keep his drawer neat and tidy, as well as his life in order. She'd brought him so much happiness, contentment, and stability. Damn, he missed her; but he was gonna soon join her. He was gonna be with her, because he was ready to check out. His life wasn't worth a damn: kicked outta the Society; a black family had moved into the Callihans' house across the street; and the FBI was asking him all sorts of questions.

Then there were the frequent calls from the Society warning him of what would happen if he ever revealed any of the Society's secrets to law enforcement. He'd been told that he was actually a liability for the Society, considering the circumstances. And he knew what that meant. He knew damn well what it meant. It meant that his and his family's lives were in jeopardy. He'd been told that the only reason he'd been spared was because he was a founder of the Society; but yet he was considered a liability. A "heavy liability" is how it'd been put to him. So, he ruminated, it'd be best for his family if he checked out. No sense in putting his family in danger, because there was no telling when the Society might decide they needed to eradicate him. They'd already paid him a visit. And that was the evening he sent Emily and Johanna away from the house. He'd given them some money and told them to go out and be gone about four hours.

"Go where?" Johanna asked. "Anywhere," he'd said. "Go to a movie; go to the mall. Here, take my credit card, go shopping. But whatever you do, be gone for at least four hours," is what he'd instructed. It'd been obvious to Hugo that his daughters sensed it was something important that developed, so they left. They left right away and stayed gone for five hours, making sure he had enough time to discuss whatever it was with the men who showed up at their house wearing stern faces. He was glad Brian wasn't there. Brian would've asked more questions. But Brian wasn't around. He had left for the Navy two weeks after they buried his dear Freida.

When Emily and Johanna left the house, the men who visited him that evening, and the same men who used to be his brothers in the Society, discussed very little with him. They ordered him to listen. They talked; he listened. They didn't talk long, but they did stay long enough to search through the entire house to make sure he didn't have anything around that could be incriminating to the Society. It was the same thing they'd done at the Guardian Security Agency several hours before and the day after the special meeting that the grand superior called when he was debarred of his membership in the Society. When they left, he left. He went for a walk in the neighborhood. He needed to breathe fresh air. He hadn't walked far when he saw the dark colored car in which two strange men with suits and ties were sitting; just sitting there looking, watching. He right away suspected they were FBI agents. But who could he tell? He had to keep the information to himself. He couldn't tell the Society. If he had, his life wouldn't be worth a plug-nickel. He knew too much. If he informed the Society that he was being watched by the FBI, no telling what they might do. They'd searched his house and business high and low and found nothing incriminating that was tangible, but they couldn't search his brain where he had a wealth of information stored concerning the Society. But they knew it was stored there; that's why they'd referred to him as "a liability." So he kept the information about being watched to himself, because he had no one else to entrust it to.

Hugo felt like the world was closing in on him: like he was a holed up felon. It was time to end it all. No sense in endangering his family. He had to do it. He didn't see what other choice he was left with; no more than a blade of grass in the path of an approaching lawnmower.

Johanna was in the family room practicing on the piano. And that was something she was going to keep on doing. Practicing.

She was going to practice and get good, real good. Her mother wasn't around to encourage her anymore like she always did. She was going to practice on her own, her very own. She was going to get real good like her mother had encouraged her and took her to piano lessons twice a week since she was six years old. Her mother had wanted her to be good at playing the piano. Her mother loved the piano and played the piano, too. Sometimes she and her mother would play the piano together. She missed that. She missed sitting on the stool next to her mother playing the piano. But she was going to practice; practice for her mother. Practice until she got good, real good. Johanna stopped playing for awhile; long enough to wipe tears from her eyes. Then she started playing again. Practicing.

Emily had started running again. She knew she needed the exercise and the psychiatrist she'd been seeing had encouraged her to exercise and gradually resume her normal routines. She was even going to start classes again at Oakland University in the fall.

The late evening sun made a reddish-yellow hue in the grayish-blue sky as it flirted with straggly looking clouds and began its habitual descent. Emily looked at her watch and figured she could complete her five-mile run before the sun faded in the western horizon. Emily found it exhilarating to be running again. She was better able to sort through her thoughts as she ran. The evening was perfect for running. Not hot, but comfortably warm. The gentle eventide breeze was soothing to her exposed face, arms, and legs. She hardly broke a sweat after one mile. The third mile was when she generally began to really perspire.

Emily was into her second mile when she saw a black jogger running toward her in the opposite direction. He was about seventy-five yards away. She went into a panic. Beads of sweat leaped on her forehead. The palms of her hands perspired. She began to breathe rapidly and deeply from her abdomen. Emily turned around and ran as fast as her legs would carry her. She was sprinting and now sweating profusely. She was escaping; getting away from the black man who was behind her. She was afraid to look back for fear that she would lose speed and he would gain on her and catch up to her. She knew if he caught up with her what he was going to do:

rape her. She began to cry and ran faster. She made it to her house. She was safe. She came through the door in such a hurry that she tripped and stumbled against a table and knocked over a vase that fell to the floor and shattered. She fell to the floor sobbing and balled up into a fetal position. Johanna came running out of the family room. Hugo hurried from the bedroom. They saw Emily bawling, her hands covering her face. They dropped to the floor to comfort her. Hugo and Johanna embraced her. Emily continued her wailing. "What's wrong, Emee?" Hugo solicited. "What's wrong, sweetheart? What's wrong? Tell me what's wrong!" Johanna began to cry, figuring something bad had happened to her sister. She didn't want her sister to be sick again. Didn't want her lying in bed hour after hour. So, she cried, figuring Emily was sick again, thinking Emily was going to return to her bedroom and stay there like she'd done before. There Hugo was with both his daughters crying. He hugged both of them. He hadn't hugged either of them since Emily's rape. Emily said, "I want my life back! I want it back! I don't wanna go through life being afraid. I want my life back! Is that too much to ask? I wanna be myself again; not this person inside of me." "It's gonna be all right," Hugo said. "It's gonna be all right. We're family. We're gonna have to all pull together. Your mother would want it that way." They all cried and hugged each other; right there in the middle of the floor until their tears were exhausted. Hugo was fifteen minutes early for his appointment with the FBI agent. They'd agreed to meet on the Canadian side at a park in Windsor off the Detroit River.

Hugo went to the rail near the river and looked across at the Detroit skyline. He reminisced about his days on the Detroit police force. That's all he'd wanted to be was a policeman after he returned from Vietnam and served as a military policeman in the Army. Crime didn't seem to be so rampant in the old days, when he was a young man in his twenties and early thirties. Things changed as hard drugs became more prevalent and niggers started acting crazy and more lawless than they'd ever been. In the old days, when Cavanaugh was in office as mayor, policemen had more liberties when dealing with the low-lifes who broke the law. Hell, Detroit wasn't an easy city in which to enforce the law, Hugo mused. You had to always watch your back. You had to take command of situations and earn respect. In those days that's what a good ass-kicking would get from niggers, respect. Respect for the badge, uniform, and the person in the uniform. Police brutality his ass, Hugo thought. If anything, it was hostility against white police officers who'd been sworn to uphold the law. That's all they'd been doing is trying to uphold the law.

Then those damn trials of twelve white police officers and simply because they'd been trying to uphold the law; and that "Dirty Dozen" label that niggers in the black community put on them; that was just too damn much. That's when some of them had gotten the idea of creating an organization of white men who would work to protect their God-given rights in America. That's how it started. That's how the Euro-Brothers Defense Society began. Hugo still thought the Society was a good idea. They had no business throwing him out, though. Shouldn't have been treated like that, Hugo conjectured. He didn't appreciate them threatening him like an outsider and outcast. He didn't appreciate it worth a goddamn. Hell, he was a founder. "Hugo Heiderberg?" The calling of his name ended Hugo's rumination. He turned around and saw approaching him a slenderly built man, about six-foot-one, dressed in a dark suit. "Yes, I'm him," Hugo responded. The gentleman offered a hand of greeting to Hugo and said, "I'm Special Agent Prast." He flashed his ID on Hugo and said, "Mind if we sit on the bench?" He pointed to the bench he had in mind. They momentarily sized one another up before the agent asked, "So, what's the deal you wanna make, Mr. Heiderberg?" "I wanna make a deal to save my family," Hugo said. "How so, Mr. Heiderberg?" the agent asked. "I'm sure my life's in danger, as well as my family's." "Why do you think that?" "I'll tell you if I can be offered immunity from prosecution." "Prosecution from what. You haven't been arrested for anything. So what is it that you think you're guilty of?"

Hugo turned his head away from the agent in a manner that showed his annoyance. He wasn't in a mood to be volleying words back and forth. He looked back at the agent and said, "Let's not play games with each other. Let's cut to the chase. I know you're on to somethin' and I'm a suspect. That's why you've had surveillance on me. I think you guys still think I had somethin' to do with the firebombing of that real estate office, but like I told you before; I didn't have anything to do with it. I swear." "Yeah," the agent said, "you've stood pat on your statement of innocence, but there's a connection and we're going to find it. It's just a matter of time. So, tell me, Mr. Heiderberg, how do you like your new neighbors; your black neighbors? Have you met them? Have you spoken to them?" Hugo was of the mind to tell the agent to go screw himself, but the importance of why he'd requested this meeting in the first place forced him to retreat from such an injudicious consideration. "I know you're aware that I was a member of the Euro-Brothers Defense Society. I'm willing to give you information about the Society that can significantly help you with your investigations." "Was, did you say, Mr. Heiderberg? Was a member of the Society?" "Yeah. I'm no longer a member." "Did you resign?"

"No. I was thrown out. That's why I need to make a deal. I know my life's in danger and probably my girls' lives, too, because the Society knows I have information that can harm them. I'm not so concerned about myself, but it's my girls that I need to protect. So, I'm willing to make a deal. I'll give you information about the Society, but I'll need to be arrested along with the other members so that they won't suspect me as an informant. But I don't wanna be prosecuted. I swear to you that I haven't personally broken any laws, but the Society has as an organization. I'm willing to help you take down the Society, but I don't wanna be sent to prison." Hugo and the agent looked at each other intensely until the agent said, "If you have substantive information that would help us, then we probably could cut a deal." "Good!" Hugo responded like a man who'd had a large burden lifted off him. It'd been a long time since he felt this unburdened; a long time. And it felt good, real good. He had to hurry and return home. He had two daughters to hug.

Chapter Eighteen

PLAYERS' LOUNGE
HIGHLAND PARK, MICHIGAN

Blair grabbed another bottle of Truly Canadian from the cooler, opened it, and placed the bottle in front of Acholam, who had his attention focused on four young men sitting at a table in the middle of the lounge. He was irritated with them because they didn't have any respect: No respect at all; not for black people old enough to be their mothers and fathers; not for the sisters or anyone else. Didn't even have respect for themselves, is what Acholam was thinking. Just a damn shame, he thought, the young brothers couldn't use a sentence without "fuck" or "mothafucker" coming out of their mouths. A damn shame is what it is. The young brothers need some enlightenment, Acholam thought.

"A little more ice," Alcolam said to Blair. Blair took Acholam's glass, put more ice cubes in it, and placed it back in front of him. Acholam filled the glass, got off the barstool, and headed over to the table where the four young men were talking loudly and lacing their conversation with incessant profanity. Acholam left the bottle of Truly Canadian on the bar and asked Blair to watch it for him. As he approached the table, the guys at the table all looked up at Acholam when he said, "Good evening, my young brothers. How you brothers doing this evening?" "Hey man." "What's up, blood?" "Yo, bro." "Jest chillin'." "You brothers mind if I pull up a chair and rap to you for a moment? Would that be cool with you?" Alcholam asked. "Cool, brotha." "Deal, man." "Solid, bro." "Sho'." Acholam slid a chair from a near table to the table occupied by the four young men. He knew two of them—at least by their street names. He greeted the two he knew. "Diz here is Eholam," the guy named Little Bro said. "A-cho-lam," Acholam corrected. "I'm Bo Peep," one of the guys who was a stranger to Acholam said.

Acholam and Bo Peep greeted each other by joining their hands and twisting them in a cultural ritual that was intrinsic.

"Calls me Scooter," the other guy who was a stranger said. He and Acholam twisted hands. "What kinda name is Acholam?" Scooter asked. "Muslim," Bo Peep said. Ain't it, man?" "No. Actually it's a West African name which means Do not provoke me," Acholam answered. "Provoke? What's that, man?" Little Brother asked. "It means don't fuck wif me," Wise Guy, who was the young man who introduced Acholam said. "Echolam's a down brotha in the 'hood. He knows his fuckin' shit. He knew Malcolm X and useta be a Black Panther." "Kick some fuckin' honkies' asses when yah useta be a Black Panther didn't yah, bro?" Bo Peep asked. "We defended ourselves," Acholam said, "but it wasn't really about kicking white folks' asses. Remember brothers, the white man in America got more of an arsenal than black people; so in those days the Panthers weren't about looking for armed confrontations. It was about defending what was ours and speaking up for ourselves. You might say it was about respect. Do you brothers comprehend the notion of respect?" "Yeah," Scooter said, "that's when yah bus' a cap in a nigger's ass when he tries to fuck over yah."

"No, brother," Acholam said, "what you're talking about is killing another brother. Violence against your own. Black-on-black crime. In the days of the Panthers it wasn't about killing brothers. It was about loving your brother. It was about respecting your blackness. When you respect your blackness, then you learn to love yourself and love and respect all black people. There are redeeming elements in the person—the black person, brothers—who can be proud of his blackness, respect it, and respect all who are black." "Run it, brotha," Wise Guy said. "I told yah the brotha wuz down." "Somebody git that bitch's 'tention so we can git another drank," Scooter said. He was referring to one of the black waitresses. "See what you just did, brother?" Acholam said, addressing Scooter. "Wha?" Scooter asked. "Wha the fuck I do?" "You disrespected the sister by referring to her as a bitch," Acholam said. "The 'ho is a bitch!" Scooter said with indignation. "The bitch thanks she's cute wif her stuck-up ass. Won't give a brotha a play." "The sister is somebody's daughter, or maybe somebody's girlfriend or wife. She might be someone's mother. How would you like for someone to refer to your sister, girlfriend, wife, or mother as a bitch or a whore?" Acholam asked.

"Man, are yah dissin' me? Nobody invited yo' ass to this table in the first fuckin' place. Me and my boys wuz havin' a good conversation 'til yah brought yo' outdated ass over here. Fuck man, this is the nineties; that ol' shit yah talkin' 'bout is as outdated as dose clothes yah ass got on." All the guys at the table laughed. Duece, the guy sitting across the table from Acholam, hadn't said a word all along, but he was laughing, too, along with his home boys. Acholam stood up from the table and said, "That's what's wrong with you young brothers. Can't anyone tell you a damn thing. Think you know everything. Think you're down and got all the answers. But you're wrapped in stupidity. Killing one another like fools. Filling the white man's jails and prisons and creating a prison industry that strives on the stupidity of brothers like yourselves. Stupid fools!" "Fuck yah, man," Scooter said, "I'll show yo' ass who's stupid!" He stood up, reached under his shirt, and pulled a revolver from the waistband of his pants, hidden under his shirt. Patrons began screaming, ducking under tables, hitting the floor, and running to the bathrooms, behind the bar, and outside Players'. Tables and chairs were scattered all over the floor. Acholam launched at Scooter. A single shot was fired. Acholam fell to the floor. Scooter, Bo Peep, Wise Guy, and Duece bolted out the door. Acholam lay on the checkerboard linoleum floor bleeding, critically wounded by the malicious act of a young brother he cared about.

Chapter Nineteen

THE LANDMARK RESTAURANT
PLYMOUTH, MICHIGAN

He had been working long hours at Grace Memorial, so Dr. Danny Donnell really wasn't that keen about dressing up to go out for dinner. He was going to be the only person in his dinner party who was under the age of thirty. He could anticipate the conversation: his father and Mr. Stapleton discussing golf and the stock market; his mother and Mrs. Stapleton doing a play-by-play of last Thursday night's bridge party and comparing notes relative to their flower gardens. And at sometime during the course of dinner he could expect that often asked question: When are you going to find a nice girl to marry?

But, no matter, it was his parents' thirtieth wedding anniversary, so they had asked him to join them and the Stapletons for dinner. It was his day off, so he knew he couldn't say no. The Stapletons didn't have any children, so they treated him and his sister, Anna, like their children, too. It was as though he and his sister had two sets of parents, which he wasn't complaining about, because it did have its advantages.

His sister was away. She had gone to France this summer with some friends from college, so he was the only progeny there to be molly-coddled, which he had never been fond of, even when he was younger. But that's how his parents and the Stapletons were with him and his sister: solicitous and pampering. He accepted it and was going to make the best of this evening. He was hoping he wouldn't hear "My son, the doctor" eminating from his mother's mouth this evening. It always embarrassed him. After the appetizers, Danny's mind began to wonder. He thought about how happy Brenda Morgan was yesterday when she informed him that her husband, Frank, was willing to consider adopting Baby Lim, that is, with the proviso that they be able to check the father's background in order to determine whether or not the baby might be predisposed to mental illness. Brenda sounded so confident. She'd said, "Baby Lim is too bright-eyed, full of life, and alert to suggest that the precious thing has any kind of mental illness." But she was willing to check it out for Frank's peace of mind. She was so happy and so optimistic. Danny hoped that things would work out. He knew how much Brenda wanted that baby. She had fallen in love with Baby Lim. He had never seen anything like it. Never.

Danny looked up and there she was being seated at a table adjacent to theirs. She was with an older guy and a young girl. She looked beautiful. She was wearing a bit more make-up than when he first set eyes on her outside the hospital when he saw her getting in a car. He wondered who the guy she was with was. Could he be her husband? After all, he'd seen men the guy's age with wives that young before. But no way could the young girl be her daughter; not unless she'd had a baby when she was twelve or somewhere around there. Maybe they're sisters, Danny contemplated. He bet they were probably sisters. But the girl could be her step daughter or a niece or something. Somehow he was going to find out. No way was he going to leave this evening without finding out who she was. He just had to know. But how was the question. How was he going to meet her without appearing brash, is what Danny asked himself.

There are hundreds, if not thousands, of Williamses in Detroit, Brenda thought to herself as she pored through the Detroit telephone directory. Lieutenant Washington had been helpful. He had said something about she and Frank must be saints for wanting to adopt Baby Lim. And in reference to her quest to discover who actually fathered Baby Lim, Lieutenant Washington said that DNA tests eliminated one of the rapists, whose name was Henry Cornwell, so it had to be the other guy by the name of Tommy Williams. Frank had asked the lieutenant how much he knew about Tommy Williams. Lieutenant Washington said Tommy was a troubled young man who had been involved with the law nearly half his life. That truly bothered Frank. That's when he looked at Brenda as though she was loony to want to adopt Baby Lim. And that's when Brenda mentioned "environment." Told Frank that environment had a lot to do with a person's behavior. "Not gonna give up,

are you?" Frank asked. "Not easily," she replied. She convinced
Frank that they needed to contact Tommy Williams' relatives in
order to gather more information. Lieutenant Washington informed
them that he hadn't seen Tommy's parents since he was sixteen, so
he had no idea where his parents lived. He did know that they lived
in Detroit years ago, but there was no telling where they might live
now. "Could live outside Detroit in the suburbs with the other black
runaways," Lieutenant Washington said.

They contacted Freeman's Mortuary, the funeral home that
Lieutenant Washington said had handled Tommy Williams' body
and buried the poor soul. The people at the funeral home told them
that an unidentified lady paid for Tommy Williams' burial. The
funeral director informed them that other than the mortuary's staff
only a lone woman had attended Tommy's funeral. They'd said the
woman never identified herself, but she'd cried like she could've
been Tommy's mother, or at least someone who knew him well and
obviously loved him or cared about him a lot. That's what Brenda
and Frank had been told. They'd also been informed that the lady
who had been crying so left in a large black car that had one of those
bumper stickers that said clergy next to an encircled cross. That's
when she and Frank looked at each other with their eyes lit like
lanterns and their minds shouting "Eureka!" Had them both speculating that Tommy Williams' father might be a preacher, so all they
would need to do was maybe search the telephone directory for all
the Williams that had Rev. listed with their names. And it was she
who had to do it, because Frank had already said, "This is your
thing. You handle it." And that's exactly what she was doing: han-
dling it, with Baby Lim on her mind. It was the twenty-second call
(she had been counting them) when she mechanically stated, after a
woman answered the phone, "Hello, I'm Brenda Morgan and I'd
like to speak with a parent of Tommy Williams. Would this be the
right number?" There was a pause. The lady asked, "Who did you
say you were?" The fact that the lady asked the question excited
Brenda. After all, it was the best response she'd gotten to this point.
Better than: "No. Wrong number. Sorry. Tommy who?" This time
Brenda thought she might be on to something. "I'm Brenda
Morgan. Tommy Williams has a son that my husband and I are con-

sidering adopting." "Tommy has a son, did you say?" "Yes, do you
know Tommy Williams?" "I used to."

"Pardon me, you used to? I don't understand." "People change.
You think you know somebody, then they change, like Tommy. I
used to know him, but he changed. I didn't know the Tommy they
buried. He was somebody different. You say he has a baby?" "Yes,
ma'am. Are you some kin to Tommy?" "I'm Tommy's mother."
She said it with so much pain that Brenda shared it. "Mrs. Williams,
your son, Tommy, left behind a son. A beautiful baby. I just fell in
love with him. My husband and I may want to adopt Baby Lim.
That's the name I gave him. But if we adopt him we're going to call
him Limuel." "Tommy has a son?" "Yes, Mrs. Williams. He was
born June seventeenth." "Is it that white girl's baby that Tommy did
that terrible thing to?" "Yes, Mrs. Williams." "He's a beautiful baby,
did you say?" "Yes, he is. You should see him. You'd fall in love
with him." Brenda heard Mrs. Williams sobbing. She had broken
down. Tears came to Brenda's eyes; she was sharing Mrs.
Williams' pain and sorrow.

Mrs. Williams agreed to meet with Brenda and Frank in a couple of days. But she didn't want her husband, Reverend Nathaniel
Williams, to know anything about this, at least not yet. Danny kept
his eyes riveted on the table where the mystery woman was seated.
He was half-eating his medium T-bone. He saw the young girl with
the shoulder-length, platinum hair rise from her chair and began
walking in the direction that the waitress pointed. Danny excused
himself and left the table. He headed in the same direction as the
platinum-haired girl. He saw her enter the ladies restroom. He
waited in the vestibule. The young girl he followed came out of the
restroom. "That's a beautiful dress you have on," Danny said.
"Thank you." "Is it your birthday?" "No." "I bet it's somebody's
birthday at the table where you're sitting, which, so happens, is next
to the table where I'm sitting." "Well, you're wrong. It's no one's
birthday at my table." "Now how can that be? Two lovely ladies
sitting at one table and it's no one's birthday, that's got to be a mistake. I bet it's the other beautiful lady's birthday if it isn't yours."
"I bet you're wrong." "Think so, huh?" "I know so." "What's the
other lady's name at your table."

"That's my sister, Emily, and her birthday ain't until August."
"Your sister, huh?" "Yes, she's my sister and I know when her birthday is." "Okay. Maybe I was wrong. Nice talking to you." "Okay.
Bye." "What's your name?" "Johanna." "Bye Johanna." Danny
returned to his table and saw Johanna pointing at him, which caused
the other lady at the table, whom he now knew as Emily, to lower
Johanna's outreached arm with her hand. The three people at their
table all looked at him. He nodded to them. They simply looked at
him and continued to eat their meals. Danny wondered how his parents and the Stapletons could really make an event out of eating dinner out. To consume two and a half to three hours in a sitting was
standard. But this evening he was pleased with the amount of time
they were taking, because he didn't want to leave before the surprise. And it was going to be a surprise. He had seen to that. He
saw the waitress coming. She had recruited another waitress and a
waiter to assist her. One candle was aflame on the miniature cake
with a luscious chocolate topping. They sat the cake on the table
and began singing. They ended with: "Happy birthday dear Emily;
happy birthday to you."

Danny started clapping. Everybody at his table clapped along
with him. Others around them joined in with applause. The people
at the table with the birthday cake all looked at Danny. They were
all smiling; smiling at him because they knew full well who the cul-
prit was. It was him; no doubt about it. Johanna knew for certain
it was him. That's why she was pointing in his direction again. But
this time she was allowed to point without reproach. The gentleman
at the table rose from his chair and came over to their table. "I'm
Hugo Heiderberg," he introduced himself. "This young man is
quite a jokester, I see." Other than Danny, no one else at the table
knew what Hugo was referring to—that is, until Danny explained
what he had done. They all laughed. Hugo motioned for his daughters to come over to the table. They made introductions. They all
laughed. Hugo said, "Danny reminds me of my Emily here." He
wrapped an arm around her shoulders. "She's good for practical
jokes now and then, too." They laughed some more. Danny had
finally met her—the mystery woman. The Angelic One. Her name
was Emily. Emily Heiderberg.

Driving home, Hugo had a pleasant smile on his face. He had a lot to smile about because of the joy of watching Emily smile. He hadn't seen her smile since... He fought the thought and, instead, weighed the fact that Emily was still smiling and that she'd also laughed this evening. It'd been a long time since she laughed. It'd been a long time since she'd had something to laugh about, Hugo thought. And that Danny fellow, Hugo mused, he's a real nice guy. Like him. Nice fellow. Nice people. Been a good evening and damn near made me forget about my problems is what Hugo was thinking. It felt good to laugh again, Emily thought. There was something liberating about being able to laugh. It was strange how therapeutic laughter could be. It made her feel warm inside and had given her a reprieve from self-pity and anguish. Her psychiatrist had told her that if she wanted to reclaim her life and the person she once was that she had to rediscover and find joy, pleasure, and laughter. She discovered that this evening, simply because of a birthday cake; and it wasn't even her birthday. All those people applauding. It'd embarrassed her, but it was funny, she had to admit. It was the funniest thing that had happened to her in a long time. It was something she would've done at one time; like when she short-sheeted her parents' bed one night. It was the funniest thing seeing her father attempting to pull up the sheet. Man, was that funny. And after he discovered what'd happened, he knew she'd done it. He knew right off, because she was the practical joker in the family. Thinking about some of the practical jokes she'd played caused Emily to smile even more. Even made her laugh out loud and prompted her father to ask, "What's funny?" "Nothing. Just thinking about some things," Emily said.

"Must've been awfully funny," Hugo replied. "They were," Emily answered. They both went back to smiling. Emily's thoughts turned to Danny. He'd asked if he could call her. She gave him her telephone number, but was uneasy about it. He really seemed to be a real neat guy, but she wasn't sure if she was ready to get involved with anyone. She still had baggage; heavy baggage. But she wasn't going to be concerned about it right now. Danny had made her laugh, so that was good enough for now.

Chapter Twenty

Brenda knew she'd laid some good loving on Frank night before last. Some real good loving. She always knew when their lovemaking was extra good and immensely satisfying to Frank, because he would hold her all night with his arms wrapped around her as though he was protecting something more precious than gold. She needed to caress Frank tonight. Earlier that evening she had caressed Mrs. Williams—that is, emotionally, while speaking with her over the phone. She had felt Mrs. Williams' pain. After she hung up the phone—around eight o'clock or so—she went straight to the bedroom where Frank was. She didn't say a word. She crawled next to him on the bed and caressed him. He felt her need. He was good like that. He could always feel her need; so he opened up his arms and let her fold into them like a pea in a pod. She felt sexually feverish and transmitted her feelings of sultriness, arousal, and desire to Frank, which caused his libido to surge. It was after they made love that she told him of the conversation she'd had with Mrs. Williams. By then, Frank was docile and amenable to anything she suggested. Brenda was eager. Frank possessed considerably less trepidation. Brenda was anxious to meet with Mrs. Williams. They had agreed to meet at seven o'clock this evening at her home. Brenda thought Mrs. Williams had been quick to let her know that her husband would be in Nashville at a conference. Frank's anxiety had diminished because from the information Brenda had shared with him, the parents of the fellow who fathered Baby Lim seemed to be good people. And it certainly surprised him when Brenda said the guy's father was a minister. She had also said that Mrs. Williams spoke like an educated woman. And they lived in the Rosedale Park area of Detroit; a real nice area where a lot of affluent and influential black people lived. Frank was impressed. They found the address Mrs. Williams had given Brenda. They pulled their Olds 98 into the driveway, alongside a late model, black

Lincoln Continental that had a sticker on the back bumper on which the word clergy and a circled white cross were prominent. The house was a tri-level ranch style with flowers bordering the walkway. The lawn was green, lush, and manicured.

Mrs. Williams, a tall, attractive middle-aged woman with a walnut-colored complexion, greeted Brenda and Frank at the door with a smile. Mrs. Williams was wearing a blue Liz Claiborne dress with a white pearl necklace around her neck. Her medium length, dark hair was perfectly coifed. Brenda and Frank were glad they had dressed up. When Frank asked Brenda what should they wear, she had reasoned that they perhaps should dress as though they were attending Sunday church service. Mrs. Williams led them into the family room. The room was tastefully decorated, as were the other sections of the house that they could see. Religious artifacts were conspicuous. There were several photos in the room that grabbed both Brenda's and Frank's attention. Brenda paid particular attention to a family picture that captured Mrs. Williams when she was perhaps twenty years younger and enviously beautiful, and there was a handsome gentleman in the photo with pearly white teeth. Sandwiched between the two of them was a bright-eyed, smiling, young boy about age eight or nine. Frank focused his attention on a picture of a good-looking boy probably age eleven or twelve who was posed in a football uniform, wearing a wide smile. Brenda was impressed by Mrs. Williams' grace and charm and also moved by the undaunted inner strength she obviously had to possess, considering the circumstances involving her son. From what little Brenda knew about Mrs. Williams' son, it was enough to grieve about, burden over, or maybe even break any mother's heart. She didn't really know this woman, but for a strange and unexplainable reason, Brenda felt a kinship with her.

Mrs. Williams invited the Morgans to sit down on a green and tan sofa as she sat daintily on the edge of a matching chair, squeezing a white handkerchief in her hand. After a few stilted pleasantries, Mrs. Williams said, "Please tell me more about this child my son supposedly fathered." "DNA results substantiate that Tommy's the father. My husband and I wanted to find out something about the father before we moved to adopt him," said Brenda. "I see," Mrs. Williams responded. "You want to do your homework—so to speak—and be sure the baby had good lineage." "We weren't necessarily. . . Well, not at all interested in the baby's lineage, but wanted to know. . . Well, how can I put it?" Brenda stammered. Frank spoke up, "Simply put, Mrs. Williams, because of the nature of the crime, I thought it'd be a good idea if we knew something about the father's mental state." "You want to know if my son, Tommy, was crazy, demented, psychotic, or something? Is that what you want to know? Well maybe he was." Tears dribbled from her eyes. Brenda said,"Mrs. Williams, we don't mean to upset you. We didn't come here for that purpose. Please forgive us." "You don't have to apologize, Mrs. Morgan." "Please call me Brenda."

"You don't have to apologize, Brenda. I'm Tommy's mother. I know what kind a person he was. What hurts is that I know what kind of person he could've been. Running with the wrong crowd and fooling with those devilish drugs are what claimed my Tommy. Tommy came from a good home. He was a good boy until he changed. When he got to be thirteen or fourteen—don't rightfully remember now—he began to change, almost over night. I looked up one day and presto, just like that, Tommy was getting into trouble and the police were coming by or calling our home." Mrs. Williams placed the handkerchief to her face and blotted her tears. Brenda and Frank sat close to each other with somber expressions on their faces. Mrs. Williams continued, "Of course, with my husband being a minister, a well-respected man in the community, and, at the time, an assistant pastor in the church, he resented Tommy's behavior. He said it was just the Devil that had gotten into Tommy. Tommy started to rebel when he became a teenager. When he was little, he went to church often: twice on Sunday, choir rehearsal on Thursdays, and Bible study on Wednesdays. He never could do the things he wanted to do as a child, things most other children did. His father said Tommy wasn't like the other children: children half-raised by single mothers, alcoholic parents, cheating spouses and the like. So, he wouldn't allow Tommy to do much outside the church. He did let him join a little league football team when he was small. I think he allowed Tommy to play football because he, himself, had been a pretty good football player in college. He made All-American." That really caught Frank's attention. "Your husband was an All-American football player?" he asked.

Mrs. Williams nodded her head and continued. "Rebellious. That's what he'd become. Tommy became rebellious and his father became tougher on him. They grew apart; like they were enemies and not father and son. So the first time they sent Tommy to the juvenile home, his father refused to go and see him. Never then or after. It seemed like Tommy lived at the juvenile home more than his own home. I don't think he wanted to be around his father. Now, don't get me wrong because my husband's a good man, a decent man, but he just didn't understand Tommy and Tommy didn't understand the kind of man his father really was. Then Tommy got older and started running around with people who didn't go to school or have jobs. None of them cared about school or a job; not a real job. Tommy became the same way—noncaring. Noncaring about everything except getting high. He dropped out of school when he turned sixteen. His father put him out of the house. Told him to leave if he couldn't follow the rules under his roof. So, Tommy left and a large part of me left with him." Mrs. Williams began to cry softly. Brenda got up from the sofa to comfort her and gently patted Mrs. Williams on her back as she stood by her. Frank said, "What is it about so many of our young black men? What is it? What's happening to 'em? Why can't they see the light and the path of self-destruction so many of 'em are headed down? Why? Why? Why?" Frank pounded a fist into his hand each time he asked why.

Franks's comment was more or less a monologue, for no one acknowledged him, but they heard him just the same. Mrs. Williams dried her tears and said, "Tommy started getting heavily into drugs and stealing from people. He even got a girl pregnant when he was seventeen. We never saw the baby. All we know is that Tommy had a baby girl. Now here you come letting me know he has a son. Lord Jesus knows I never wanted to have grandchildren under these conditions. Lord Jesus knows I didn't!" Mrs. Williams began to cry again. Brenda wiped tears from her own eyes as she continued to pat Mrs. Williams on her back. Frank took out his handkerchief and blew his nose. His eyes were moist. A chorus of sniffling filtered through the room. Mrs. Williams said, "And every time Tommy went to court or jail, his father refused to go, but I had to when I knew about his troubles. But a lot of times I didn't. Do you know how hard it is to see your son in handcuffs before a judge? Everybody in the room told the bad things the son you gave life to has done, and to hear the judge's sentencing? I bled each time I experienced that. I hope this child, my grandson, you're thinking about adopting doesn't cause you such pain. I pray that he doesn't. I pray to God that this child turns out to be a good man some day. If I can live to see him become a good man, then I'll go to my grave with some peace. Bless me, Lord, I would!" Brenda and Frank were silent as they drove back home. Their minds were full and their hearts were heavy. Mrs. Williams had given them a lot to think about—like the awesome responsibility of becoming parents. They wondered how a person like Tommy Williams, who came from a good home, could turn out to be the person he had been. His father a respected minister, and his mother an elementary school teacher. They were satisfied that Baby Lim's biological father hadn't been mentally debilitated. They had been enlightened this evening. Now they had a monumental decision to make.

Chapter Twenty-one

Hugo expelled a freight train-sounding yawn as he pulled the key from the lock at the Guardian Security Agency. It was at that precise moment that an octopus grabbed him. At least it felt like an octopus, but it was three men wearing masks, dressed in black from one extremity to the other. Their arms were wrapped firmly around his neck and upper torso. He knew right away what was happening and who these men were. They were abducting him; carrying him away to some place where he knew he didn't want to go—especially under such unpromising circumstances. And they were men whom he once had an affinity with. They had been brothers; brethren in the Society. He had been one of them. They had made him an outcast and now they wanted him for something. And it was something that couldn't be pleasant and never was when men came stealing behind you in darkness the way they had and dressed like they were: not one of them speaking a word—just breathing hard and struggling with him. He could feel their hot breath on his face and neck. There were too many of them, so his tussling was as futile as a fly attempting to free itself from a spiderweb. Hugo was shoved into the back seat of a dark colored car with a hood over his head that was secured at the base of his sweaty neck by a rope. The car began moving; headed some place, but Hugo didn't know where. All he knew was that it wasn't a joy ride they were on and it wasn't April Fool's Day. Hugo couldn't see, but his hearing was keen. He could hear his abductors' breathing, the car engine whirring, cars passing, the rubber wheels of the car humming against the asphalt, the pinging sound of gravel against the car's underpinning, and then the sound of crickets chirping. It seemed like they had been riding for hours, but it had only been a matter of minutes. Hugo heard, "We're being followed!" "It's a sheriff's car," the man with the rough voiced announced. "What do we do?" asked a man with a quiver in his voice. "Don't know. We gotta do something." "The car stopped." "What do you think they're doing?" "Don't know."

"Drive slowly." "I am. The car's moving again. It's tailing us again." "Do you think they suspect something?" "Don't know. Something's up. Be prepared." Hugo heard their bodies twisting and squirming, then a sound he was familiar with, the sound of a safety being taken off a gun. "There are two more police cars and an unmarked car behind us now." "What do we do?" "Get prepared!" The men in the car grew silent, then Hugo heard over a speaker-mike, "This is the Wayne County sheriff. Pull over! I repeat, this is the Wayne County sheriff. Pull over, now!" "They're on to us," said the man with the rough voice who seemed to be in charge. "So, now what?" "We fight! This is it! We fight! When I stop, on the count of three we get out and commence firing." It was the man with the rough voice giving the orders.

The car pulled over and stopped. Hugo heard, "One, two, three!" He heard the car doors open, then all hell broke lose. It sounded like a fire fight in Vietnam. Hugo fell to the floor of the car and took off the hood. But he didn't look. He didn't open his eyes. He didn't want to see. But he could certainly hear the noise: firearms blasting and some screams of pain, like in Vietnam when bullets tore through a man's flesh. The shooting stopped. Hugo could hear the car's engine running, moans of pain, and the sound of intrepid crickets. "Hugo are you all right?" Hugo rose from the floor and found himself looking into the face of Special Agent Prast. "Wha, wha, what's all this?" Hugo asked. "Law enforcement at work," Agent Prast said. We figured sooner or later the Society would have to make a move on you because you knew too much and we've been putting heat on some of their members. We figured they would think we were doing the same to you and that they wouldn't feel comfortable about it and would want to silence you. You gave us good information, but we knew the members weren't stupid. We figured they would remove some things and destroy some key evidence, so we've had you under tight surveillance. We had your back." "You mean you used me as bait? Put my life in danger?" "Hugo, your life was already in danger. It's a good thing

you came to us when you did. Besides, the information you gave
us, though as good as it was, wasn't enough for sweeping indict-
ments or convictions without your direct testimony, which you did-
n't want to give as part of our deal, so we needed to gather more
solid evidence. Now we've got probable cause all over the place
and can issue some critical search warrants. I'll see that you get
home to your family. Things are peaceful on the homefront. We've
had your house watched. The girls are fine."

     Members of the Euro-Brothers Defense Society were herded
into court at the Patrick V. McNamara Federal Building in Detroit
two weeks later for their arraignments. Hugo was part of the herd,
but was more like a maverick because he wasn't officially one of
them anymore. But it was part of the deal; part of the affront; and
part of the appearance of being treated like the other brethren as
Hugo had requested. That's the deal he had sought. But things
weren't that simple or cut and dry. He still was going to be exposed
to the public and known to be a member of the Euro-Brothers
Defense Society. He had never let his family know about the
Society, not really. When they had asked about his club membership (that's what he had referred to it as, just a club), he had simply
said that it was a men's political group that was concerned about the
direction the country was going in. His family didn't need to know
all the details of the Society. Besides, he had been sworn to secre-
cy and couldn't divulge anything to them anyway. But now they'd
know. The press was going to print it and the media were going to
milk it. So he had had to come clean with Emily and Johanna. He
told them the truth about the Society and swore to them that he had
never killed anyone. Nor did he plant any firebombs. But it was-
n't because he wouldn't have; he hadn't because he had never
drawn the assignment. For sure he had hated enough to kill, to fire-
bomb, and to do whatever else the Society would have asked or
requested of him. He never anticipated that he would ever place
any of his family members' lives in danger, nor his own. This was-
n't how it was designed and how things were supposed to work out.
And now the mayor, police chief, city council, the task force, you

name it, were having a field day with press conferences and press releases, Hugo entertained. Things had changed.   And Hugo realized how much things had changed when he turned red watching his daughter, Johanna, play with that little colored girl whose family moved into the house across the street.   He had called Johanna's name, getting ready to order her to come home and demand that she never play with that colored girl.   But when Emily saw how upset he was, she came up behind him, hugged him, and said, "Father, please leave it alone.   Get it out of your system.   That little girl isn't hurting anyone.   They're having fun.   They're kids.   Please let it go, Father."   He had nothing else to say.   So, he just told Johanna, "That's okay, sweetheart.   Enjoy yourself.   Have fun."   And that's when Emily hugged him again, kissed him on the cheek and said, "It's going to be okay, Father.   It's going to be okay."   And Hugo wanted things to be okay because he was tired and not as young as he used to be.   But he was wiser.   Wiser for a number of reasons.

Chapter Twenty-two

It was a warm July evening as Lieutenant Ullysis Washington strolled through the park that adjoined the neighborhood of Palmer Park, where he and his family lived. He had a lot on his mind. He contemplated that it was the second time Hugo Heiderberg had gotten his lucky ass out of something that should've sent him to prison. Ullysis considered Hugo to be one lucky honkie, though he was pleased that this time Hugo didn't get away scot-free, believing that media coverage had managed to somewhat taint him as a result of his affiliation with the Euro-Brothers Defense Society. "Ain't that some shit?" Ullysis mumbled to himself. "Eight of the Dirty Dozen belonged to the Society, along with some other white boys who were professional people and businessmen. A defense society! What the fuck were they defendin'? Probably defendin' against black folks makin' any progress; just wanna keep their feet on black folks' necks. That's what it was."

Ullysis forced a change in his train of thought. He felt good about his neighborhood that was inhabited by whom he characterized to be progressive upper crust black people that had nice homes and kept them up. His English Tudor-styled home was comfortable and good enough for him and his family, though there were bigger and more expensive homes in Palmer Park. Ullysis reflected that white-flight had carved the composition of his neighborhood and thought that no other area in Detroit, nor hardly any other black community or neighborhood in America would contain a park that had tennis courts, a pool, a walking path, baseball and softball fields, and a golf course—no matter that it was only nine holes. The damnedest thing, too, Ullysis thought, with so many black people playing golf: Some of them acting like they're Calvin Pete—at least the ones who didn't compromise their blackness. He figured some other black folks didn't even consider Pete because he was a brother and ebony in color; so the compromising, so much wanna please the white man blacks related more to white guys like Arnold Palmer, Sam Snead, and some of those other honkies. As Ullysis continued to walk, he thought about how some of his neighbors, friends, and associates had been trying to encourage him to start golfing and saying stuff about "It's challenging. You'll make contacts. A good way to socialize. It's relaxing..."   And so on.

Ullysis felt that he had all the damn challenges he needed; too many in fact. Didn't need any more contacts; had enough of those and, as a matter of fact, there were a few he'd like to lose or forget about. He could think of better ways to socialize than on a damn golf course chasing a little white ball. And then, too, he couldn't see anything relaxing about the sport—especially when he saw some of them cursing and throwing their golf clubs out of anger or frustration. "Screw some damn golf," Ullysis uttered to himself. "Got better things to do with my time." Ullysis made it back to the house and sat on the top step of the porch. Gloria came to the door and said, "You need to call Candy. Something happened to Kevin." "To Kevin? What happened?" "He's in the hospital. He got beat up." "In the hospital? Got beat up? Who beat him up?" "Ullysis, come in and call Candy. She'll give you all the details." After talking with Candy, Ullysis booked a plane for early the next morning to fly to Scranton, Pennsylvania, where his son, Kevin, was in the hospital in guarded condition. Candy had informed him that when she and Kevin were visiting friends in Scranton, they went to a park where about six white guys accosted them and started beating Kevin. She said she thought they were Skinheads because they all had their heads shaved.

While on the flight to Scranton, all Ullysis could think about was that Candy was going to get his son killed and it was a wonder that those Skinhead fuckers hadn't killed Kevin. Why couldn't Kevin find a nice black girl? Why did he have to find him a white girl? And he wants to marry her, Ullysis thought, and figuring all it was going to be is trouble if his son married Candy. Ullysis arrived by cab about nine o'clock Sunday morning at Mercy Hospital in Scranton, where Kevin had been taken. When he entered the hospital room, Candy was sitting in a chair next to Kevin's bed, holding both of Kevin's hands. She looked as though she had hardly had any sleep. "Hi, Mr. Washington," Candy dragged out of her mouth as she let go of Kevin's hands and stretched her arms out to her sides, and yawned. Ullysis didn't return the salutation. He simply asked, "How's Kevin doin?" "About the same. He's still unconscious. He's been unconscious since the incident."

Seeing his son all bandaged up, bruised, and with puffy eyes and lips made Ullysis angry. He was sure enough angry at those Skinhead fucking cowards who did this to his son and also angry at Candy for putting his son in danger. He could see them now, probably in the park kissing like they always did whenever they went anywhere. They just didn't give a damn where they might be. It didn't matter who or how many people were around, they would have to kiss at some time—like their damn lips had timing devices inside them. And he knew full well that they were in that damn park holding hands. That's why those Skinhead bastards beat his son, because of Candy. She was probably all over Kevin because that's how white girls were. They be all over their men; not like the sisters, Ullysis thought. Black girls don't do shit like that—at least not in public. So, it was her fault; he knew it. Candy saw the way Ullysis was looking at her and said, "And?" "And what?" Ullysis countered. "Why are you looking at me like that? Sort of suspicious." "You really wanna know? Do you really?" "I know. You think it's my fault that those bastards beat up on Kevin, don't you?" "Yeah, I do." "Why?" Because I'm white and Kevin's black and it was because of me that those bastards did this to Kevin. Is that what you think, Mr. Washington? Is it?" "You're damn right that's what I think?" Candy started crying and said, "You don't have to swear at me. I love Kevin." "Ah, shit! Now don't go cryin' on me. Somebody will probably try to hang my ass up in here in this room with you cryin'; thinkin' that I did somethin' to you."

Candy continued to cry. Ullysis grabbed a handful of tissues out of a box on the nightstand and handed them to her. "Come on, Candy, now stop that cryin'. Come on now," Ullysis pleaded. Candy dried her tears and halted her sobbing. Mascara was smudged underneath her eyes; eyes that registered hurt. She sat back down in the chair. Ullysis pulled a chair to the opposite side

of the bed and sat down. They looked at each other; neither one
speaking for a while. Ullysis said, "Candy, I don't have anything
against you as a person; it's just this interracial thing. If you and
Kevin get married it's only gonna be trouble. Don't you see that
what happened to Kevin is simply an indication of what can happen?" "Mr. Washington, I'm awfully sorry as to what happened to
Kevin, but I don't see it as being either of our fault. Kevin nor I can
be held accountable for others' hatred and bigotry. And for you to
say that you don't have anything against me as a person, that's not
true. It isn't true at all. If I were black, you wouldn't have a problem with me; but I'm not black. I'm white. And white is what I am
and what makes me who I am. So, you do have a problem with me
as a person, a white person who fell in love with your son who's a
wonderful man. And I can make him happy. He is happy. He's
happy with me and I'm certainly happy with him." "Candy, you're
gettin' this whole thing all confused. You ain't black, so I don't
know how to make you understand." "And you're not white, so why
do you think you understand me so well."

"Because I've had to deal with your kind all my life. That's
why." "My kind? My kind did you say? And what kind am I? I
suppose all white people are alike; so does that also make all black
people alike? I think not!" "Candy, Candy, Candy," Ullysis said as
he shook his head, pressed the palm of his hand to his forehead, and
swept his hand down his face like a squeegee. He looked away
from Candy and at Kevin, who was lying there motionless. "Mr.
Washington," Candy said. "Yeah?" Ullysis said without looking at
Candy. "I want you to know that not only do I love your son, but
I'm also his friend. You know, there's a song that goes, 'in good
times or bad times, I'll be by your side, for that's what friends are
for.' This is a bad time and I'm here by Kevin's side. And whether
it's good times or bad times, I'll always be by his side. Always."
Candy reached for one of Kevin's hands and held onto it. Ullysis
reached for Kevin's other hand. He squeezed it gently. Candy
reached across Kevin with her free hand and offered it to Ullysis.
He accepted it. They were two people, holding hands, who both
loved Kevin. That they both had in common.

Chapter Twenty-three

Late last night Brian had returned home on leave from the Navy. Hugo had served in the Army—joined in 1962 out of high school like his son had done. He had to admit that Brian looked good in his uniform. He looked mighty handsome. Brian reminded Hugo of himself when he was younger. Brian even appeared more mature, Hugo thought. He was real proud of his son; a chip off the old block. Hugo had awakened Emily and Johanna last night to welcome their brother. They'd talk for a while, but since it was so late, they'd said good night and promised to resume in the morning where they'd left off.

Hugo had coffee brewing. The aroma of the perculating coffee filled the air and filtered through the house. Brian awoke to the smell of the brew. It was a scent that reminded him of how his family used to sit down to breakfast together and discuss all kinds of subjects. Those were good times when his mother was still living. The aroma brought back a lot of fond memories. Brian pulled the covers off of him. He was wearing only his Navy-issued briefs and dog tags. He slipped on a pair of jeans and a white undershirt and went to the bathroom. The time on his watch showed eight-fifteen. The coffee's aroma worked its way into Emily's room. The scent brought back memories, which she didn't particularly want her mind to be encumbered with this morning. She'd been awake since seven o'clock. She was thinking about resuming her studies at Oakland University in September. She felt ready to return to college. But what she wasn't ready for was a relationship with Danny Donnell. She thought he was a nice enough guy and all of that, but she wasn't whole yet. She was better, but not whole. Danny had been calling; calling a lot. She even agreed to go out with him once. They'd taken in a movie, but she felt uncomfortable the whole evening. She didn't think she was good enough for Danny or any other man, as far as that went.

Emily recalled that evening that Danny had touched her: not like a lover, but like a friend. She saw the expression on his face when her body jerked and recoiled. She knew she'd acted weird. And it'd only been a simple touch—a benign touch—but yet it'd made her feel unnerved. She'd wanted to explain, but she couldn't. She couldn't be frank or straightforward with him and come out and say, "I'm a victim of rape, so this is how I react. This is how I behave." If she had told him, then he'd have known that she was a polluted woman and he'd had left her alone right away and not waited until later when he found out about her. Emily contemplated that by Danny working at Grace Memorial, he'd probably heard about her and knew her secret. But it was apparent that he hadn't discovered the skeleton in her closet—at least not yet—because he still called and asked her out. And she kept making excuses about being tied up and busy with something; trying her best to discourage Danny in order to spare him the disappointment down the road. And suppose she started developing strong emotional feelings for him, Emily thought. All that would happen would be her getting hurt because once Danny learned about her—the real her—then he wouldn't come around anymore. He'll stop calling. Then he'd be the one with the phony excuses about being tied up and busy. So, there was no way that she was going to open herself up to the sure disappointment, hurt, and pain. She'd had enough to last a lifetime. Brian was sitting at the kitchen table drinking coffee while Hugo prepared eggs to go along with the fried ham. They'd been sharing military experiences. Hugo said, "Let's go to the lake today and catch a few. We haven't done that in a long time. I hear they're catchin' some good size perch." "Sounds good, Dad. It'll be fun." "Well, good. We'll leave soon after breakfast and return early this evening so you can spend some time with your sisters and get out to visit your friends."

Hugo and Brian entered the house laughing. Laughing loudly and heartily, like two good buddies who'd had a very good time together. They'd laughed and talked; talked and laughed. And in between they'd caught some fish. Hugo had heard right. The fish were biting at the lake; biting real good, damn good, in fact. And they'd caught their share of perch, bluegills, and crappies. Hugo caught more than Brian, but he always did. The contest was part of the fun, trying to see who would catch the most fish. Emily was very pleased to hear her father and brother laughing. It sounded like old times to her, when there used to be laughter in the Heiderbergs' home. Lots of laughter. But the laughter had vanished; it was more like it'd been stolen and as though thieves had come into their home and robbed their joy. Her father's and brother's laughter sure sounded good and made Emily smile as she sat at the kitchen table talking to Danny on the telephone. He'd called her, entreating her to have dinner with him tomorrow evening. She finally agreed. But tomorrow she was going to open her closet to him and let her skeleton out. He'd be gone after that, Emily was convinced, then she would continue her healing. She would continue seeing her psychiatrist and continue trying to make herself whole again. She said good-bye and hung up the phone.

They certainly smelled like they'd been fishing, Emily thought as she hugged her father and brother. "Had a good time?" Emily asked. "Sure did," Hugo said. "Just like old times." "It was great," Brian added as he headed to the bedroom to get out of his smelly clothes and take a shower. Brian suddenly returned to the kitchen where Emily and Hugo were talking. He asked with anger in his voice and with a look of infuriation on his face, "Who's that little nigger girl in the family room with Johanna? When did we start inviting niggers into the house?" Emily beseeched Brian to lower his voice. He got louder and said, "I can't believe it. We're allowing niggers to visit now? When did all this happen?" Hugo was dumbfounded; lost for words. He sat down at the kitchen table. Emily said, "A black family bought the Callihans' house across the street after you went off to the Navy. They're nice people." "Bought the house across the street? They must be either some brave or stupid-ass niggers to wanna move into the Callihans' house after I . . ." "After you what, Brian?" Emily asked. "After you what? What did you do?" "Never mind about me! What about that little nigger girl in there with Johanna? Tell that nigger to get outta our house. Somebody tell her to go home. In fact, I'll tell her."

"No, Brian!" Emily said. She reached for him and grabbed his arm. Brian turned around and said, "Emily how can you stand up for a nigger after what they did to you?" "It was two of them, Brian! It wasn't every black person who . . ." She began crying. Johanna ran to the kitchen crying. She said, "We heard you, Brian. Charlene heard you and ran home crying." "Oh, shit!" Hugo said as he stood up from the table. "All this crap has got to stop!" "Crap? What crap? When did you change?" Brian asked. "Things are different, Brian. Things have changed and we must accept it." "Father, are yah saying that it's now all right to have niggers come visiting? When did you change? What about your membership in the Euro-Brothers Defense Society? What about that?" "It's over, Brian. It's all in the past. We need to get on with our lives. We're better off that way," Hugo said. The doorbell rang. Johanna stopped crying and ran to the front door, thinking that Charlene had returned and they could commence playing together again. She hurriedly returned and said, "Father, it's Charlene's dad. He wants to talk to you." "That little nigger's father is on our doorstep?" Brian asked. "Be quiet, Brian!" Johanna shouted and commenced bawling again.

Emily hugged Johanna and they both cried together. Hugo left to talk to Jessie Campbell, Charlene's father. He knew what he wanted. He knew what he was going to ask him, but he didn't have any answers. What was he going to tell Mr. Campbell? Hugo mused. Was he going to tell him that his son, Brian, was a racist and he got it naturally from his father? Brian walked behind Hugo. Hugo stopped in his tracks and said, "No, Brian, I'll handle this! I'll handle this! Please!" Emily and Johanna rushed away, crying. Brian had a bewildered look on his flushed face, not understanding any of it. It was late. The house was quiet. Emily and Johanna were sleeping in the same bed tonight. Brian left and went somewhere. It'd been one of the toughest things Hugo had had to do: attempt to explain to an upset father about his little girl being referred to as a "little nigger." He explained it as best he could and in the process he'd learned that Jessie Campbell had read the newspapers and had known that he was a member of a white supremist group. "Used to be," he'd informed Jessie Campbell, who also told him that he was reluctant for his daughter, Charlene, to play with Johanna; but she kept coming over to play with Charlene, so he let it go, as long as there wasn't a problem. He apologized to Mr.Campbell and assured him that it'd never happen again. He also told Mr.Campbell that he wasn't the same person who used to belong to the Society and that he now saw things differently and he hoped that his son, Brian, would too. A nice guy, that Mr.Campbell, and seemed nicer than a lot of white people he knew, Hugo deliberated. Hugo was perplexed about what Brian meant when he mentioned that the Campbells had to be either brave or stupid for purchasing the Callihans' house after something he'd done. Hugo was hoping that Brian wouldn't do something stupid tonight. The thought forced him off the sofa to look through the Venetian blinds at the house across the street where the Campbells lived.

Chapter Twenty-four

The waitress brought Emily's artichoke pasta paulette to the table. Danny had ordered fettucine alfredo. Figgerro's was an upscale Italian restaurant in Dearborn. It was the first time Emily had been there, though she'd heard of it before. But Emily wasn't at all surprised that Danny had selected a place like Figgerro's inasmuch as she'd earlier on found him to be a romantic and a person of very good taste. And he'd brought her long-stemmed, red roses when he picked her up this evening. But she didn't want to be romanced. Not that she didn't desire romance or never wanted to be romanced, but not now. The time wasn't right. She felt she wasn't whole yet and still had some healing to do. So, this evening she was going to expose her secret to Danny; the secret that was going to, for certain, drive him away. She knew it.

Emily wanted to find the right time to tell Danny what she'd rehearsed in her mind numerous times. She knew exactly what she was going to say to him and how she was going to say it. She'd already chosen the words to say: measured words; thorny words that would prick her and cause her pain; and Houdini words that would prompt Danny's escape. Danny broke the ephemeral silence. "Do you shop at the Fairlane Mall?" he asked. "Occasionally," Emily said. She rotated her aqua-colored eyes away from Danny and said,"I haven't gone to a shopping mall in quite awhile. I haven't had the desire." "I thought most women enjoy shopping. I know my mother and sister do." "How old is your sister?" Emily asked. "Seventeen. She'll graduate from high school next year." "It's just the two of you?" "Yes. It's just Anna and me.

Have you heard about the NAACP threatening to boycott in Dearborn?" Danny asked. "No. I don't recall hearing or reading anything about it. I guess I haven't chosen to read the papers for awhile. I suppose I'm afraid of what I might read." "Afraid?" "Yes, but that's another story," Emily said and looked away from Danny.

"Anyway," Danny said, "the NAACP has threatened a boycott of Fairlane Mall and other stores in Dearborn because they claim that black people who come into Dearborn to shop are harassed about using the city's public parks. I guess the parks are only to be used by residents. You probably can count the black people who live in Dearborn on one hand; so I suppose when the police see black people in the parks, they assume they're non residents and ask them to leave. The NAACP says that the police only question black people. They say if black people are barred from using public parks in Dearborn, then black people shouldn't shop in Dearborn. This lady who I work with says that she and her husband would support such a boycott. I don't blame her." "Is the lady you work with black?" Emily asked. "Yeah. She is. Her name is Brenda Morgan. She's a nurse and a real nice person. Her husband, Frank, is a good man. Too bad society isn't colorblind. I won't come to Dearborn to shop or eat if a boycott is called. It just isn't right. There's just too much racial division and hostility in this country. What's need-ed is a giant magic wand that could make all the hate and bigotry disappear." "That would be nice," Emily said. "It would be nice if things could be that simple, but they aren't. I could use a magic wand myself at this stage in my life." Emily looked off as her mind imagined her statement. "And what would you make vanish if you had a magic wand? And please don't say me," Danny responded. They both smiled. Emily said, "It's part of the past that I'd make disappear."

Danny playfully wiped his hand across his forehead and said, "Whew. That saves me." They smiled at each other again before a somber expression graced Emily's face. She said, "Danny, you read the papers. You must know that my father was linked with a white supremist organization. I've known my father to be a racist ever since I can remember. Since the trial I see a noticeable change in him, so I think he's a different person now. We even have a black family that lives across the street and I find it amazing how my father has gotten along with Mr.Campbell." "Is Mr.Campbell black? "Danny asked. "Yes. There was a time my father would've gone lit-erally crazy having a black family in the neighborhood, yet alone across the street." "I'm happy to hear your father has changed. Yeah. I read the papers. I've read about the Euro-Brothers Defense Society and your father's association. I haven't judged your father. Actually, I find him to be a very likeable person. Not quite as likeable as the daughter he calls Emeè (Danny smiled), but still likeable. Can I call you Emee, too? I like Emee on you." Emily nodded her approval. Danny asked, "How do you feel about black people and other minorities?"

That was a loaded question for Emily, but she was going to handle it. This evening she was going to be open and honest with Danny. She'd vowed as much. She was going to let him know truly who she was or, at least, who she'd become since. . . She abandoned the thought. Emily said, "I am my father's child. Growing up, listening to my father talk, I thought blacks were the lowest form of humanity. I learned to fear blacks, thinking that they all would do something bad or harmful to me and as though they had some kind of plague; so I avoided them as much as I could until I went off to college. In college I met some real nice black people, but I never would tell my father because I knew how he was. I knew he would get upset if I ever told him that I had some black friends, so I never mentioned it to him. But I mentioned it to my mother." Emily stopped talking when she mentioned her mother. Anytime she mentioned her mother she could visualize her and it made her sad and lonely not to have her mother around anymore. "And what did your mother say about you having black friends?" Danny asked. "First my mother hugged me. She liked to hug. Then she told me that there wasn't any harm in it and that she, herself, had adopted a young inner-city black woman with a child as a part of our church's Reach Out and Love Someone program. She said she never told Father and that it would be our secret. Father would've simply died if he'd known about what Mother was doing. I suppose it was her way of trying to compensate for her husband." "Your mother sounds like a saint."

"She was." Emily fought tears as she said it. She used the corner of the plum-colored cloth napkin in her lap to wipe the tears forming in the corners of her eyes. Danny reflexively reached for

Emily's hand and held it. She didn't reject his empathic gesture.
Emily continued. "That was a secret that Mother and I shared. Then
one day not very long ago, something very painful happened to me.
. ." Emily looked Danny solidly and unflinchingly in the eyes. This
was the time to tell him and let him know her other secret. The
secret that he didn't know about. The secret that would drive him
away as soon as he discovered it. "I was raped." There, she'd said
it. This was the first time she'd said it, because she'd never had to
say it to anyone before. She hadn't had to say those three brutal and
painful words to anyone because others already knew what had happened to her or they told others what had happened to her; so this
was the first time she'd said it herself. And it hurt. It hurt her
deeply, as though something was chiseling the lining of her stomach and making it raw. She reclaimed her hand that Danny was still
holding and used the napkin again to dab her tears. Danny said, "I
know, Emee. I know all about it." "You know?" "Yes. I've known
for weeks. I know about the baby." "How did you find out? You
never said anything. So, since you know, what is it that you want
from me? What purpose do I serve for you? I don't understand it."
    "Whoa!" Danny said. "You've asked a lot of questions." He
took a sip from his water glass as he saw the waitress approaching.
"How you doin' over here?" the waitress asked. "Would you like
to see the dessert tray?" They both declined dessert. Danny asked
for the dinner check. "How I found out isn't important, Emee. I
didn't inquire, if that's what you want to know. I never said anything about it because I didn't have a need to discuss it. I realize the
whole ordeal had to be very painful; so if you care about someone
you don't need to dredge up hurt and pain. On the contrary, when
you care about someone you need to be understanding of their pain
and suffering and be there for them. I understand your pain and suffering, Emee. Understanding pain and suffering is what I do as a
doctor. And I'm here for you, Emee. I want to be here for you if
you let me. I care about you, Emee." Emily's eyes filled with more
tears as she wiped them with the napkin. "Why do you care about
me? I'm no good for you," Emily rejoined.
    "I care about you because you're beautiful; both inside and out.

But it's your inner beauty that I love. You're a good person, Emee. A real decent and caring person. When I first laid eyes on you, I thought there was something angelic about you. You've got a lot to give and offer. If you can go through what you've gone through and still have compassion for all people, then I place you in the same category as your mother." "How's that?" Emily asked. "You're a saint. Just like your mother, I consider you a saint." "But I'm not a saint. I used the N-word after my rape. I used it several times and started to believe what my father always said about black people was true; so I'm no saint." "You are, Emee. That was temporary rage that you experienced, which is to be expected under such circumstances. It was a coping mechanism. You were violated and hurt, so you were unconsciously fighting back. And the only way at the time you could fight back and strike a blow was to vent your anger. You hated the guys who did that to you. You don't hate all black people, now, do you?" "No, I don't." "And you feel remorseful about having used the N-word as you did, don't you?" "Yes I do." "Then you're a saint, Emee. At least I think you're a saint and I think the Big Man upstairs would agree." Danny smiled at Emily. She returned the smile. She was smiling as a result of the three things Danny had given her this evening: kindness, understanding, and friendship.

Danny parked his BMW in the driveway. Emily waited, allowing him to be chivalrous. Danny floated to the passenger side of his car and opened the door for Emily. He escorted her to the front door. They stood facing each other and gazed into each other's eyes without speaking. He kissed her. They said good night to each other. Emily felt she was getting much better and arriving at the person she desperately wanted to be because she'd actually kissed Danny back without cringing or feeling unnerved. What she felt was warmth—a deep warm feeling inside. It was a feeling she hadn't felt in so very long. It felt therapeutic. She went into the house and straight to her bedroom, smiling.

They had had Hugo down at the FBI office a few times, asking him questions concerning the Home Real Estate Company fire-bombing. Hugo had told them a zillion times that he'd had nothing to do with it; nothing at all. He told them that he had been home that night and at the time of the firebombing. They asked him who could verify where he was and the time. He didn't have to think much about it because it had been he, Emily, Johanna, and Brian at home together that night. He remembered it well; real well, because Brian left for the Navy the next day.

"Convenient. . .," the special agent said—like he figured Hugo was lying and that his children would take up for his lie because he was their father. That's when he became somewhat indignant and told the worrisome-ass special agent to let him take a polygraph exam. That's what he had asked. That's what they gave him and he passed it. Sure did. He passed it. But that wasn't good enough. They then wanted to know how he could know for certain where his son was that early in the morning when the real estate office was firebombed. They wanted to know if he could say for sure that Brian was in his bedroom asleep at the time. He had told them no because he was asleep at that time of the morning. The agent then asserted that it was possible that Brian could have left the house without him knowing it. They just tried to confuse him, is what Hugo thought. They tried to baffle him and make him say something that would make it look like Brian might have had something to do with the firebombing. Then one of the agents asked, "How does your son feel about black people? Does he care for them? Does he hate them? Does he have any black friends?" They were asking him all those damn questions, Hugo remembered, which were none of their goddamn business, but he didn't tell them that. He just said, "I don't know" to those questions. The agents made it apparent that they believed he was lying. And so fuckin' what if he was lying. It wasn't any of their goddamn business anyway about how Brian felt about black people. He was happy Brian left that morning to go to the Navy before they'd had a chance to question him is what Hugo was thinking.

Now they're in that room questioning Brian, Hugo mused. And it worried him, because he wasn't sure what Brian meant by the Campbells being either brave or stupid on account of something he'd done. Hugo contemplated that they'd had Brian in there for more than three hours, grilling the shit outta him. Poor Brian. Hugo heard the door open. He looked up and saw Brian coming out of the room, along with the two FBI agents who had been questioning him. "How'd it go?" Hugo asked. Brian looked at his father pitifully. The special agents didn't acknowledge Hugo's question. To Brian they said, "We're arresting you on suspicion of firebombing the Home Real Estate Company. You have the right to remain silent. . . " They led Brian away in handcuffs with him looking back at Hugo with Help! signaled on his shock-ridden face.

Chapter Twenty-five

The new year ushered in lots of love, joy, and happiness for Brenda and Frank Morgan. On January 2, 1994, they stood before the church congregation teary-eyed, as were the baby's godparents and paternal grandparents: Hazel Williams and her husband, Reverend Nathaniel Williams. Hardly an eye was dry in the church for the christening. Practically everyone had heard the story surrounding Baby Lim, who was about to be christened in the name of Limuel Justin Morgan.

Dr. Danny Donnell was there, too, as he'd promised. But he had come alone. He and Brenda had made a pact with one another after she learned that Danny was dating Baby Lim's biological mother. They had both agreed that it would be awkward. Brenda had said to Danny that Emily didn't need to know that someone he knew and worked with had adopted the baby she delivered. "That's too close to home. . .," she'd said. They had both agreed that it wouldn't be healthy for Danny's and Emily's relationship for Emily to know that Danny was in constant contact with the person who adopted Baby Lim. "Trust me," Brenda had said, "a woman knows about such things. Emily probably couldn't handle it emotionally or psychologically." Danny agreed. It'd made sense; a lot of sense. So, they made a pact: He agreed to never let Emily know who had adopted Baby Lim. But it wasn't as though she was going to ask. Brenda agreed never to bring up the word adoption whenever she might be around Emily. And if ever there was an occasion for Emily to ask questions about Limuel Justin, then she would simply tell her that she was raising Limuel for a deceased relative. That was the pact they had agreed on, knowing full well that Danny didn't want to do anything to jeopardize his and Emily's relationship. He was in love with Emily and hoped to marry her, but Emily wasn't ready for such a commitment. She had improved, but she still had some emotional healing that needed to occur. Brenda and

Danny understood as much. Danny was very happy for Brenda and Frank. They were going to make excellent parents. Limuel Justin was going to receive plenty of love, no doubt about it. Plenty of love. Ironic though, Danny ruminated. It's ironic as to how that baby almost destroyed Emily, but yet has brought so much joy to Brenda and Frank. And on top of everything else the godparents are actually the mother and father of the guy who fathered the baby. He thought things like this only happened in books or movies. "But what is it they say?" Danny muddled, "truth is sometimes stranger than fiction."

Chapter Twenty-six

The rain had been as relentless as the chatter in the news room. On this morning of May 16, 1995, Emily was anxious about doing the story, even though it had been her suggestion to the editor. She had only worked at the Metropolitan Daily News for a year after graduating and had grown jaded, for the most part, to her suburban law enforcement beat. The news had been pretty much commonplace and routine: break-ins, theft, arson, battery, robbery, etcetera. Occasional homicides and carjackings were the most engaging things she had covered while "paying her dues" as a novice reporter. But what she had read on the Oak Park Police blotter had really piqued her interest: The brutal rape of a model at the Greenfield Mall.

"It's just a rape case," the editor said. But it was more than a routine rape case to Emily. It was lots more. There was the victim, a person with feelings. She had a strong desire to tell the victim's story. She wanted to report the story from the victim's perspective so that the readers could have an enlightened understanding as to how dehumanizing rape is for the victim. And though the story would be emotionally taxing for her to cover, she, nevertheless, felt compelled to do it. Danny thought it was a "dreadful idea" because of what she, herself, had experienced. She'd made significant progress dealing with her own rape, but Danny was fearful of her dredging up pain, unnecessarily. Her father agreed. Emily had reconsidered doing the story, but it was just something powerful inside of her convincing her to cover the rape and bring the victim's pain and suffering to the forefront. The editor had bought her idea after seeing her point. "Go ahead," he'd said. "Go ahead and cover it; it may be an interesting read. . ." The rain was still pouring when Emily entered the Dresden Apartments complex in Oak Park around nine-thirty that evening. She was searching for Building H. She was suppose to make a quick left as soon as she turned right into the complex. That's what she had remembered after writing down the directions. The windshield wipers were working at maximum; nevertheless, she found it difficult to make out the letters on the buildings in the rain.

She wasn't particularly pleased about having to come out at night to do the interview with Rita Dawkins, but the time was best for both of their schedules. Her editor had admonished her to be careful. He'd said, "That area ain't Drizberry Estes," which meant that the area where she was going in Oak Park wasn't inhabited by upscale white people, but she had known that all along. It was the story that was important to her. But she had to admit that the area, along with the darkness and rain, had summoned some uneasiness in her, bordering on some trepidation. Even Danny had said,"I hesitate to say it for fear it may sound racist, but, Emee, please be careful sweetheart." She had assured Danny, her editor, and her father that she would be careful. After leaving work, Emily had time to go home, eat, shower, and change clothes. She had changed out of the two-piece pantsuit she'd worn to work and put on a pastel-blue skirt along with a pastel, floral blouse. She traded her heels for pumps. She let her hair down, and it fell to her shoulders, the way Danny loved it.

Emily contemplated about how skeptical Rita Dawkins had been when she spoke to her over the phone. Rita had been quite leery of discussing her rape with anyone other than the police. Rita had said that even discussing it with the police was an ordeal that made her feel as though she had been responsible in some way for what had happened to her. Rita wanted to know why should she talk to a reporter? What good it would do? She'd said, "I don't want the world knowing my business." Emily realized that all of Rita's questions were reasonable and her concerns were legitimate. She understood Rita's reluctance. She definitely understood. She had promised Rita that her name wouldn't be used and her identity would be protected. She told Rita that she wanted people to understand the viciousness of rape and have a better understanding of what a rape victim goes through. She also told Rita that she could help other rape victims by telling her story, and perhaps her story would bring more resources, empathy, and support for victims of rape. Rita listened. What she had said was fairly convincing to Rita, but she was still hesitant; still not quite sure. Rita asked, "How do I know I can trust you?" Another good question. That's when Emily told Rita that she, herself, had been a rape victim. That revelation convinced Rita to do the story. Emily found Building H and parked her blue Pontiac Firebird in front of the building. She didn't remember the exact apartment number, so she looked inside her purse and checked the small, black address book. She turned on the dome light and checked her hair and lipstick. Her lipstick was fine. She combed her hair back out of her face. She picked up the umbrella that was on the floor on the passenger side of her car, then opened the door to dash to Building H.

A dark-colored van pulled up behind her with its headlights on as Emily was into her third or fourth stride. A man exited the van and shouted, "Lady, you dropped something!" Emily turned around and saw the man, a black man, wearing a cap. She saw the van behind him. She panicked. She was seeing and experiencing it again: The falling rain; the black man wearing a baseball cap; a hard object being pressed into her ribs; being forced into the van; the smell of beer and marijuana; her eyes and mouth taped closed; the van moving; her clothes removed; strangers between her legs; the threat of death. Emily turned back around. Fear had a vice-like grip on her. She ran fast. But he was running faster. He was about to catch up to her. She reached the door of the apartment building, but she couldn't open the door. It was locked. She had forgotten that the building had a security lock and that she needed to press the button to apartment H-12 in order to be let in. But there wasn't enough time. He was upon her. Her arm froze. She dropped her umbrella and cringed against the door—frozen in fear. She was about to scream in panic, then heard him say, "Lady, I didn't mean to scare you. Here. You dropped this." He handed her a small, black address book. It was wet. She figured it must have fallen from her lap when she got out of the car. She looked into his face, then at the blue, short-sleeved shirt he was wearing that had Richard & Son's Plumbing embroidered on the left pocket. His pants matched the color of his shirt. His cap had the same embroidered words. He was wet from head to toe. "Have a good evening," he said and then darted back to his van.

Emily picked up the fallen umbrella and extended it above her head as she watched the van leave. Her breathing was less labored. She pressed the buzzer to apartment H-12. She had a rape victim to interview.

Chapter Twenty-seven

Rita Dawkins was a very attractive woman, age twenty-four, five-eight, short hair, a cinnamon-colored complexion, nice slender legs, and, for sure, she had a model's physique. Rita had been candid with Emily. She told of having modeled at Hudson's at the Greenfield Mall the evening she was abducted, beaten, and raped. She was heading to her car around nine o'clock when a van pulled up behind her. She'd said a man on the passenger side got out of the van, approached her, and stuck a knife to her stomach and told her to get in the van. "That's when fear struck her like a lightening bolt," Rita said. She said her legs felt like they weighed a ton and that her breathing had become fast and deep and that she felt as though any moment she would faint. She said she had wanted to scream, but couldn't. She was afraid to scream. Afraid that if she screamed her attacker would plunge the large knife in her or slit her throat. And it had been two of them, she said. But it had been Emily's assumption that the two guys who raped Rita were black. "No," Rita said, "they weren't black, they were two white guys." She apologized to Rita, who was herself black. Rita told how the guys beat her when she attempted to fight off the first guy who tried to enter her. He struck her in the stomach with his fist, then he backhanded her in the face and said something about "Bitch, I'll kill you if you don't stop." He then pressed the tip of the knife to her throat and she felt warm liquid running down her neck. That's when she stopped resisting. Then they tore her clothes off and took turns raping and sodomizing her. She said that she had wanted to die as soon as the first guy entered her. She said she felt worthless and less than dirt. She spoke of her frequent showers and never feeling that she was clean enough. Emily recalled that several times during the course of the interview they'd had to pause. It was painful for Rita to tell her story. It was equally painful for Emily to hear her story. So, they both cried a lot. They hugged one another as Rita told her story. She could relate to Rita's pain and all she had gone through and would continue to go

through. It had been that same evening that Emily's mind summoned all the nauseating details encompassing her own rape over
two and a half years ago. And, God, she hoped Rita wasn't pregnant or HIV infected. That's one thing she, herself, was happy
about; happy that she hadn't been tested HIV positive. But there
was a period of time when it didn't matter, because she would have
welcomed death. But not now. She had found some happiness.
Danny made her happy.

Emily had begun writing the story last night after she returned
home. She had thought about getting a good start on it and then fin-
ishing it the next morning at work. But she couldn't stop writing.
She couldn't pull herself away from the computer keyboard in the
den-like area of the basement where she worked on the story until
two o'clock this morning. Her editor liked it. It was going to be
published in today's edition of the Metropolitan Daily News, on the
front page of section A. Rita Dawkins laid across her bed that
evening and began reading the Metropolitan Daily News. Her
attention was focused on the article titled "Anatomy of a Rape,"
written by Emily Heiderberg. Tears from Rita eyes soaked into the
newspaper. The article continued on page six of section A. She
used a lot of tissue as she read the article. Rita was pleased that
she'd agreed to do the interview. It had helped her emotionally to
vent her anger and release her emotions. She dried her eyes and
called Emily Heiderberg, whom she thanked. They thanked each
other and both cried over the phone. Within two days of the article
first appearing, hundreds of letters regarding "An Anatomy of a
Rape" poured into the Metropolitan Daily News to appear in the
People Speak section of the newspaper. There were far too many
letters to be published. There were letters from rape victims;
friends, relatives and acquaintances of rape victims; sympathetic
readers; law enforcement agencies; women's groups and organiza-
tions; as well as state officials, which included several lawmakers
and a U.S. senator from Michigan. The article was clipped by hundreds and discussed in classes at schools, colleges, and universities.
Emily had now made up her mind. She felt that she could do it now.
She felt as though she had crossed the last hurdle to her recovery.
She was going to call Danny to accept his proposal of marriage.

Chapter Twenty-eight

On August 8, 1996, Brian Heiderberg won an appeal to his conviction for firebombing the Home Real Estate Company. His attorney had successfully raised the issue that some of the evidence against Brian had been illegally obtained and shouldn't have been entered into evidence during the criminal trial. Brian had served better than two years in prison. He would be facing at least another eight years in prison if his conviction wasn't overturned. He was anxiously awaiting the jury's return to render its verdict. Brian nervously rubbed his hands together. The surface of his left hand had a swastika tattooed on it, which he had acquired while incarcerated at the Milan Federal Correctional Institution in Milan, Michigan.

Brian was dressed in a navy blue double-breasted suit and white shirt and tie. His hair was cut military style, which was the manner all the members of the Anglo Brotherhood wore their hair. He looked behind him and caught the eyes of his father and sisters, who all sat together in the front row of the benches. No one smiled. Somber expressions graced their faces. Brian appeared to have aged ten years. Hugo sat there blaming himself for Brian's woes and the deep trouble he had gotten into. After all, Hugo contemplated, hadn't it been himself who taught his son to harbor the hatred that had sent him to prison? Now he regretted it. It wasn't worth it. But it'd been too late to save his son. Hugo never anticipated that anything like this would ever happen. Brian had pleaded not guilty to the firebombing, but he never could explain his whereabouts at the time. He had gotten caught in lie after lie, while attempting to explain where he was the morning of the firebombing. At first he said he was home in bed, but a neighbor had seen Hugo's Chevrolet Impala returning home around four-twenty that very morning. Brian hadn't known that, so he changed his story and admitted that he had taken his father's car that morning. He said he had been restless as well as excited about going to the Navy and that he had at first lied because he was afraid they might try to pin the firebombing on him. Hugo wanted to believe Brian wasn't guilty and had nothing to do with the firebombing, but they had caught Brian in so many fabrications. And Brian's comment about the Campbells' being either brave or stupid after something he'd done still weighed a ton in Hugo's mind.

Emily felt anesthetized by it all and as though she were sleepwalking. Her heart was heavy. None of this should've happened, she thought. None of this. Emily knew that Brian still had hatred in his heart: he wore a swastika and spewed venomous words laced with racial abhorrence and loathing. Emily felt the hatred was destroying her brother. If only she could reach him. She had tried, but had been unsuccessful. And Brian still couldn't understand how she could be so pardonable after, as Brian said, "what those jungle bunnies" had done to her. He had picked up the words "jungle bunnies" while in prison. He had never used such words before, Emily mused. She was obliged to tell Brian of a story she'd done regarding the rape of a black woman by two white men. "That's different because she was probably a prostitute to begin with," Emily recalled Brian saying. Sad. So very sad, Emily thought. She likened Brain's hatred to cancer. Emily attempted to suppress her pending tears.

Johanna didn't like being in the courtroom. She didn't like being in the same room where they brought bad people, which her brother Brian was. She had thought initially that Mr.Campbell had Brian arrested for calling her friend Charlene a little nigger. Deserves him right, Johanna thought at the time. But then it had been explained to her that Brian hadn't been arrested for the name he had called Charlene. She was told that the police had arrested Brian for something else: for setting a building on fire. She couldn't understand why Brian would do such an awful thing. She figured he must have done it because they kept him in jail. Now he was trying to get out. If he does get out, Johanna thought, I hope he becomes nicer and doesn't call Charlene a bad name anymore. Johanna considered that it certainly wasn't nice of Brian to make

Charlene cry, and to make herself and Emily cry as well. She just didn't want Brian to be mean anymore, that's all. The jury filed back into the courtroom and took their seats. Twelve people were going to determine Brian's fate by deciding if there was sufficient evidence to acquit him. The fact that four of the jurors were black didn't go unnoticed by Brian. He absolutely hated the fact that his destiny was in the hands of some jungle bunnies. They certainly weren't his peers, Brian mulled. He had never had the least thing in common with niggers. The judge, an elderly white man with a full head of gray hair, asked Brian and his attorney to stand as the jury's foreman read the verdict. Brian dropped his head, closed his eyes, clenched his hands together in front of him, and held his breath. The foreman held a single sheet of paper in front of him and said, "We, the members of the jury, find the defendant guilty as charged."

Brian couldn't contain his feet, which received a sudden impulse from his brain. He bolted from behind the table, knocking over the chair behind him. He ran toward the exit. A black law enforcement officer stood in his path. Brian's right foot went into action, kicking the officer in the groin, which made the officer fold over in pain like a severely deformed hunchback. Brian removed the officer's service revolver from his holster. He pointed the gun in every direction while he continued to move to the exit. The judge and the jurors made a hasty retreat to the back rooms. Instantaneous shock filled the room. Some spectators gasped loudly. Those who could stampeded out the courtroom ahead of Brian. "Stop being mean, Brian! Stop it!" "Shut up, Johanna!" Brian snarled as he backed out of the courtroom into the hall. He pointed the revolver menacingly, swinging it left and right. People in the hall scattered, seeking protection from the deranged gunman. Brian backed into the closest restroom, a women's restroom. He heard shrieks of fright. The door to the restroom crashed opened and about eight women stormed out. Hugo came to the closed bathroom door, stood outside of it, and pleaded in a sorrowful voice, "Brian, please don't do this, son. Please, Brian. Put the gun away, Brian, and come on out. Please son! Please! I love you, Brian. I'm sorry about everything. Come on out, Brian. Please!" "No, Dad. I don't wanna go back to prison. I'll kill myself first." "No, Brian. Please don't say that, son. You don't need to harm yourself anymore. Come on out, Brian. Please son!" "I hate prison, Dad. I don't wanna go back to that fuckin' place. I'm gonna do it, Dad. I'm gonna kill myself. It's better this way," Brian shouted. "No, no, Brian! It ain't! You're still young, son. You can get through this. We'll get through it together."

"Dad, I just wanted to be like you. I always wanted to be like you." Tears streamed down Hugo's face. He said, "Son, I've made a lot of mistakes in my life. I've done things and said things that have hurt the people I dearly love. And I love you, Brian. I do, son. Please Brian, don't let your blood be on my hands. If you kill yourself it'll be as though I pulled the trigger. Please, Brian, in God's name, in your mother's name, please don't do it, son!" In about forty minutes a platoon of police officers moved through the chaos in the hallway, taking control of the crisis, ordering people to leave the floor as they steadfastly yet cautiously approached the restroom door. They carried shotguns and arrived with revolvers drawn. Hugo was at the bathroom door still pleading to Brian when they arrived. Two officers grabbed Hugo and pulled him away. "No, that's my son in there," Hugo begged as they dragged him off. "Brian, can you hear me?" the officer in charge asked. "I hear yah!" Brian answered. "We're S.W.A.T. officers, Brian. Come on out. It's over. Give it up. Crawl over to the door and slide the gun out the door. Do it, Brian. It's over. Nobody needs to get hurt. Come on, Brian. Do it." "No! I'm gonna end it here!" "Don't do it, Brian! Think about your family, Brian."

No answer. It was quiet on the other side of the restroom door. Brian was in a state of confusion, pacing, thinking, and intently watching the restroom door. He heard faint sniveling coming from a stall. "Come on out!" Brian commanded. The door to the stall opened; out came a young lady who looked to be in her mid to late twenties. She was smartly dressed, like the female lawyers he'd seen in the courtroom. "I've got a hostage!" Brian bellowed. "What's your name?" "Kathy," she said trembling. "Her name is

Kathy," Brian shouted toward the closed bathroom door. Now things had changed for the officers. It was a different situation. There was a hostage involved. The officers huddled momentarily. One of them left to get Hugo Heiderberg. He needed to be made part of the equation.

It was four hours later when Brian Heiderberg came to the realization that he didn't want to kill himself. His father's fervent, relentless, and heart-wrenching pleas got to him; but it was his youngest sister Johanna pleading that really touched him. Her entreaty for him to stop being mean played in his head during the standoff. He never thought of himself as really being mean. In fact, he'd been forthright righteous in regard to his attitude in life and disposition toward others. He never considered himslef as mean. To the contrary, he'd considered himself as upright and virtuous; just like his father. But his father had changed. Emily had changed. Why? Brian didn't have any answers for the self-imposed question. Brian put down the gun and surrendered because he really wasn't ready to die. He wanted to go on living. As they handcuffed him and lead him back to jail, Johanna's callow plea for Brian to stop being mean had softened his heart and was resonating in his head.

Chapter Twenty-nine

It was Limuel Justin Morgan's tenth birthday. "Just look at how Limuel has grown," Hazel Williams marvelled. "It sure doesn't seem like nearly ten years since his christening." "Sure doesn't," Brenda agreed. "I tell you, the years sure have flown by." Limuel Justin's godmother and mother were observing him with pride spread across their faces. They were sitting together on a padded bench on the lower level of Brenda's and Frank's tri level home in Southfield. They were having a party and had invited a few neighborhood kids to come over. And, as well, Brenda had sent an invitation for Dr.Donnell and his wife, Emily, to bring their two children to the party.

Brenda hadn't seen Dr.Donnell in quite a while. They both were no longer at Grace Memorial. They had moved on to bigger and better things: Brenda had left to become a head nurse at Wayne Community Hospital four years ago, and Dr. Donnell was in his sixth year as an anesthesiologist at the University of Detroit Mercy and also an instructor at the university. They still kept in touch with each other. Their pact to keep Limuel Justin's original identy secret from Emily was still intact, but that didn't prevent Brenda from being somewhat anxious about Emily coming to the party. Brenda saw Danny, Emily, and their two girls, ages five and three, entering the room. The girls were dressed in short dresses, and patent leather shoes. Strips of colorful ribbons adorned their hair. Her husband, Frank, was escorting them. Brenda asked Hazel to excuse her as she walked over to greet the Donnells. "I was just thinking about you all," said Brenda as she walked toward Danny, who was carrying a large, gift-wrapped box. Brenda hugged Danny, then Emily and the girls. Frank said,"Let me take the package off your hand, Danny. "Danny handed the gift to Frank and said, "I hope Limuel likes it." "He will," said Brenda. "He isn't a child who's hard to please. I'm sure whatever it is he'll enjoy it." "I can't believe how he's grown," said Emily. "Good genes, huh?"

Brenda and Danny gave each other an if only she knew glance. It was strange how Emily took to Limuel and Limuel took to her. Even Danny's and Emily's two children took to Limuel. It was like an extended family, Brenda contemplated. Brenda was mindful that only Frank, she, and Danny knew that Limuel was a half-brother to the two lovely children to whom Emily had given birth. Brenda admired how Emily had kept the weight off and stayed so fit and trim. Emily still looked good after having those two children—really three, but Brenda wasn't counting Limuel. Emily was still running five miles, four days a week. More power to her, Brenda thought. The best Brenda was doing was thirty minutes a day, three times a week on her Health Rider. She had gained ten pounds since giving birth to Lenora four years ago. Ten pounds she couldn't shed, it seemed, no matter how much she tried, but as far as she and Frank were concerned she still was shapely. She even thought Frank preferred the extra weight on her. He had told her more than once that she had the weight in all the right places, and she knew what places he was referring to.

This was the fifth time that Brenda and Frank celebrated Limuel's birthday with people beyond Limuel's godparents. They had intended it that way. Brenda knew she would have felt badly if she invited others and did not invite Danny and Emily—even though she knew Danny would have understood. But even after she and Frank started inviting others to celebrate Limuel's birthday, commencing when he was six, Brenda had felt a bit uneasy about inviting Danny and Emily inasmuch as she was concerned about giving remembrance to June 17—the day Emily had actually given birth to Limuel. Brenda had been concerned about stirring up unhappy and painful memories. But things appeared to have worked out. Emily never showed any signs of distress with the date. Danny had said that he thought Emily had discarded the date from her mind as a way of coping with the whole ordeal. Emily looked happy and acted as though she was happy. And Danny was really in love with her, Brenda observed. "Angelic," Brenda recalled as to how Danny had referred to Emily when he first laid eyes on her. He had described her as having an angelic appearance. Now who would've ever thought all this would happen the way it did? Brenda pondered. She still couldn't get over it. It amazed her every time she thought about it. But she was happy: happy to have adopted Limuel; happy to have conceived a child on her own after years of trying; happy to have friends and godparents for Limuel like the Williamses; and happy to have a good man and husband like Frank. She contemplated that she couldn't be any happier. So, she must be doing something right for the Almighty to have blessed her the way he had, she thought. Everyone appeared to be having an enjoyable time, which pleased Brenda. Frank had the children engaged in some games and was being assisted by a couple of the other fathers. Several of the mothers were visiting with one another. Danny was talking with one of the other fathers.

"Oh, no," Brenda said to herself as she saw Hazel walk over to Emily, who was talking to Limuel. She was afraid of this. She didn't need Hazel and Emily talking to each other for any period of time. There was no telling what Hazel might say. She might start talking about her godchild and sharing with Emily how Limuel had been adopted. She might also tell Emily that a white woman had given birth to Limuel and placed him up for adoption. Then that's when Emily would figure it out. That's when the date June 17 would flash in her mind like a beacon. Then she'd know: She'd know who Limuel Justin Morgan really was. Emily's mind would then register back to ten years and she'd remember her mother's funeral and the baby she delivered in the back seat of the limousine on this date ten years ago. She'd remember and she'd know. She'd know that Limuel Justin Morgan was her biological son. Then her tears would flow. And then Emily would turn to Danny and ask if he knew. Then Emily would feel betrayed after discovering that Danny had known all along who Limuel was. Then there was no telling what would happen after that, which Brenda didn't want to think about it. Brenda remembered her grandmother telling her, "Honey girl, when life gives yah a lotta sunshine, yah best start lookin' fir rain."

Brenda wasn't going to wait around for the storm, she hurried toward Hazel and Emily. She needed to interrupt them. She didn't want them getting chummy with one another because that would loosen their tongues, and then no telling what they might talk about and reveal to each other; just no telling. For sure, Brenda didn't want Emily to know the truth about Limuel and, as well, she didn't want Hazel to realize that she was face-to-face and conversing with the very woman her son, Tommy, had raped more than ten years ago. It wouldn't be good for anyone, Brenda thought, not anyone. She remembered her grandmother telling her, "Honey girl, when yah see trouble brewin', cut off the fire." Brenda approached Hazel and said, "How about giving me a hand with the food?" "Sure, honey," Hazel replied. "I can help, too," Emily volunteered. "Thanks, but we can manage. Just enjoy yourself," Brenda insisted. Brenda and Hazel left to go upstairs to the kitchen.

The birthday party was finally over. Hazel had just left after helping Brenda and Frank clean up the mess and put their house back in order. Both Limuel and Lenora were in their bedrooms asleep—simply exhausted. Brenda was tired herself. It had been a long day. She had worked hardest at keeping Hazel and Emily apart. She kept her eyes on the two of them all the time. No way was she going to allow Hazel to let the cat out of the bag; not if she could help it. She had to keep them separated, which made her feel like the railroad tracks in the place she lived when she was younger. The tracks kept black folks and white folks separated. That certainly was the thought that had come to her mind: those railroad tracks.

Brenda realized that she had neglected some of the other mothers at the party because she talked to Emily most of the time—but for a good reason. Both Frank and Danny knew why she kept bending Emily's ear all evening. She just had to keep Hazel and Emily apart; just had to. Brenda thought it was best; best for all concerned. Brenda had asked Emily all kinds of questions. She had asked about her father and discovered that he was suffering from aplastic anemia and needed a bone marrow transplantation. She had told Emily that she was sorry about her father's condition. Emily told her that her father needed to find a suitable donor rather soon

and that she, Brian, Johanna, and some other relatives had been tested and were awaiting the results to see if any of their marrow was
compatible. Brenda also asked Emily about her brother Brian.
Emily said that Brian was getting his life together and that he had
joined the ministry at the church he attended and was working as a
counselor at a home for wayward boys. Finally, Brenda inquired
about Emily's sister Johanna. Emily replied that Johanna was a junior at Central Michigan University, majoring in music education.

Brenda was surprised when she learned that the Donnells were
moving to Arizona. Danny had said that it was a good opportunity
for him and that he had landed a job at the Good Samaritan
Regional Medical Center outside Phoenix. Emily was going to join
him later because she didn't want to leave her father alone in his
condition. She was hoping that they would first find a donor for her
father. Brenda had talked incessantly to Emily at Limuel Justin's
birthday party. She didn't want Emily to know the truth about
Limuel. She needed to hide from Emily the fact that Limuel was
the halfbrother of her two children. It wouldn't have served any
purpose for Emily to find out; so Brenda played like the railroad
tracks where she used to live when she was younger and when she
could hardly wait to be grown. Things sure were simpler then—
railroad tracks or not. Not better; just simpler, Brenda considered.

Chapter Thirty

Brenda Morgan contemplated that the time was quickly approaching when they would need to tell Limuel. They had put it off all this time, but he was growing like a weed. They never told him that he had been adopted. They hadn't had a reason to inform him, nor the gumption. But time was progressing and he was getting older. Brenda and Frank knew in their hearts that they needed to inform Limuel that he'd been adopted. They both were uneasy about what they would tell him. They thought it might upset Limuel if they told him that his biological mother was white. And if he asked, "Why didn't she want me?", or something of that order, what would they tell him? Were they going to tell him that a black man raped his biological mother and thus was the reason she put him up for adoption? There was no way they could tell Limuel that. No way. But they had to tell him something. The questions in Brenda's mind were troublesome. The house was quiet. Limuel and Lenora had been picked up by the Williamses. They had gone to the Shrine Circus at Joe Louis Arena in Detroit.

Brenda's encumbered heart and mind brought her a sudden yearning to talk to Frank about what she was pondering. She considered that Frank had to have thought about it, too; but they had never discussed it. They had been going on with their lives like a Sunday drive on a pleasant day; but she understood that it was time to assess the situation and apply the brakes before they arrived at the intersection of the crossroads. Brenda placed the last of the dishes in the dishwasher, wiped her damp hands on the floral apron wrapped around her waist, removed it, and went into the living room where Frank was sitting in his favorite chair: a black, leather La-Z-Boy recliner. Mounted on the wall behind him was a framed print of Summer Serenade, which she loved when she first saw it. It was a painting of two lovers in a canoe, both wearing large straw hats; the woman reclining on pillows and wearing a white, cotton dress, and the man also reclining on a pillow playing a banjo and serenading the woman. She had also been impressed that the painting was the work of a local artist who resided in Ann Arbor. Brenda sat on the sofa near Frank and crossed her shapely legs, which didn't go unnoticed by Frank. After sixteen years of marriage he still admired Brenda's legs, but her legs weren't the only part of her anatomy Frank regarded. Frank rested the newspaper he was reading in his lap. He knew Brenda wanted to discuss something with him. She had that look. And he'd been married to her long enough to ably decipher her countenance.

"Frank, we need to talk," said Brenda. "So I gathered," Frank responded. "Frank, have you thought about when we're going to tell Limuel that he was adopted?" "Yes, I've thought about it some." "So when do you think we should tell him? He's growing up." "Yeah. I know. Do you think it's time to tell him that he was adopted?" Brenda leaned back against the sofa and closed her eyes for a moment and then said, "I don't know. I'm afraid." Even though Frank thought he already knew the answer, he asked anyway,"Afraid of what?" "I'm afraid of revealing that his biological mother is white and then have to explain why she'd put him up for adoption." "Brenda, you're assuming that we have to give Limuel a reason." "What do you mean? Why shouldn't we give him an explanation? I'm sure he'll ask." "Do we have to tell him the truth? Do you really want Limuel to know that his biological mother was raped?" "Not really. But what do we tell him? I just know he'll ask." "So what is all this now? Are we into the problem part of adopting Limuel? Remember, it was all your idea to begin with. You hadn't foreseen all of this, had you?"

"So, what's that comment suppose to mean?" Brenda asked with an unmistakable hint of indignation. "Are you saying that you're sorry we adopted Limuel?" Frank saw the look of dismay and disappointment on Brenda's face. He rose from the La-Z-Boy and sat next to her on the sofa. He gathered her into his arms and said, "No, Brenda, I'm not sorry. I'm not sorry at all. I'm scared, though. And I admit it." "Scared? Scared about letting Limuel know that he was adopted?" "No. That gives me concern. But what

I'm really afraid of is his teenage years. I see so many young men who, because of peer pressure, or what have you, go astray when they become adolescents. And some of 'em come from good homes. Look at the Williamses' son, Tommy. They're good people who gave their son a good home, but look at how he turned out. He ended up being shot down by the police like some crazed animal. How could that be?" Brenda looked up at Frank. She surveyed the disturbed look on his face. She kissed the corner of his mouth and said, "Reverend Williams admitted making mistakes with his son. He said he loved Tommy, but thought he had been too confining with him. Remember Hazel saying that she thought Tommy became rebellious because of so many limitations her husband placed on their son? I think the reason Reverend Williams spends so much time with Limuel is because he's trying to atone for the mistakes he'd made with his own son." "It's hard being a parent. Ain't it?" Frank asked. "Yes it is, but I wouldn't trade anything for it."

"Me either," Frank said. "Do you think we're good parents?" "Yes, I do. And not only do I think you're a good father, but you're a good husband, too." "Thank you, baby. And I, too, think you're a good mother and wife." They kissed. "I think everything is gonna be all right," Frank said. "We'll work things out together and we'll figure out what to tell Limuel. But do we need to figure it out this evening? Can we think about it a little longer?" "Sure," Brenda said. "And you know what, Frank? You know what else you are?" "What, baby?" "You're also a mighty good lover." That was good enough for Frank. He didn't need to be hit upside the head. He rose from the sofa with a wide smile on his face. He offered his hands to Brenda and led her to the bedroom. Brenda said, "We have two hours before the kids return." "We'll both be smiling by the time they get home," Frank said. "No doubt about it," Brenda replied as she slapped Frank seductively on his butt.

Chapter Thirty-one

Limuel Justin Morgan recently had his eleventh birthday. It was different than the years before. Danny, Emily and their two girls didn't attend. They were living in Phoenix. Brenda learned that the Donnells had moved Emily's father to Arizona with them and that he was getting worse and had yet to find a suitable bone marrow donor. Danny said that if Emily's father didn't find a donor match within six months that it was unlikely that Emily's father would survive much longer. Brenda found out that Emily was working as a reporter at The Phoenix Plain newspaper. So, other than Emily's father's condition, everything was fine with Danny and his family, Brenda learned when she last spoke to Danny on the phone. Brenda stayed in touch with the Donnells—particularly with Danny. She told Danny that everything was going well with her family and that both Limuel and Lenora were doing quite well in school. She told Danny with pride that Limuel had never missed being on the honor roll. Brenda also informed him that Limuel's football team had won a championship and that Limuel had scored three touchdowns in the championship game, which caused Frank and Limuel's godfather to grin from ear to ear like Limuel's team had won the Super Bowl. Brenda pondered that she and Danny had shared lots of laughs since they've known one another. They had managed to keep the pact they made with each other, though it'd been tenuous. Nevertheless they'd done it for more than a decade.

From what Danny told her, it really sounded like his father-in-law was in bad shape. Brenda hoped Mr. Heiderberg would find a donor soon, which reminded her that she needed to call her own father. She hadn't spoken to her father in quite a while. The only times her father called her was when he was having a problem with his second wife. He always would say, "I sure wish your mother was alive. Your mother was the best woman a man could have."

Brenda could detect the pain in his voice every time her father talked about missing her mother. The words he spoke were like thumbtacks piercing his tongue. Then she would get teary- eyed. She also missed her mother. She remembered how sick her mother was and that she'd been sick for a long time. She tried to help her mother as best she could. She helped feed her mother, combed her hair, and did as much as she could to help make her mother as comfortable as possible. But it wasn't enough. Her mother died when she was twelve. She often wished she could have done more to help her mother in order to make her well. Her father told her that she shouldn't blame herself, because she wasn't a doctor or a nurse. That's when she knew that she wanted to become a nurse.

Then right after her mother died, her father got so depressed and despondent that she had to go and live with her father's mother—her grandmother, Sadie. Her grandmother showed her plenty of love, which helped ease the pain associated with her mother's death. She learned a lot from her grandmother. For a woman who didn't get beyond the eighth grade, her grandmother sure knew a lot. She read a lot, too. It seemed like her grandmother was always reading something besides the Bible that she read every day. She remembered her grandmother saying, "Honey girl, yah cain't always 'pend on the words of man; but yah sho' can 'pend on God's words. Always remember dat, honey girl. Always remember dat. Yah listenin' to wha' I'm tellin' yah?"

"Yes, ma'am," she'd always say to her grandmother. Brenda remembered those days in Monroe, Louisiana, when she was growing up and where her father and grandmother still lived. Other than her father having his problems with his second wife, he was at least in good health, which Brenda was pleased about. She could imagine what poor Emily was going through having to watch her ailing father.   Brenda knew how difficult that must be because she remembered how it was with her own mother. Both Brenda and Frank were relaxed on their king-size bed. Frank was reading one of his education journals that had been piling up. Brenda had her head turned toward the television on the stand at foot of the bed, but her mind was inattentive as to what was on. She could have just as

well been looking at the wall beyond the tube. Brenda, Frank, and
their children hadn't been long returned from the Fourth of July cel-
ebration in Detroit. The phone rang. It was on Frank's side of the
bed. He answered and placed the phone on the bed between himself
and Brenda. He handed Brenda the receiver and said,"It's Danny."

"Danny!" Brenda said. "I was lying here thinking about you
all. So, how's it going?" After about ten minutes of exchanging
pleasantries and engaging in inconsequential conversation, Danny
said, "You know, Brenda, I've been thinking." Then there was a
lull. "I've been thinking that though it's a remote chance, but yet
it's possible that Limuel could be a bone marrow match for Emee's
father. What do you think?" What did she think? Brenda thought
She was thinking that maybe she hadn't heard Danny correctly. He
lowered a bombshell and then asked what she thought. Her mind
was too congested. He very well could have asked her what she
thought about nuclear fission or Beethoven's Sonata in C-sharp
Minor. Her response would've been the same: None. Her reaction
would've been comparable: Shocked. Her mind would've been
equal: Dumbfounded. The expression on her face would've been
similar: Stunned. Brenda lowered the phone from her ear. She
became clear-headed enough to place the receiver back to her ear.
She heard Danny saying,"Brenda are you still there?" "Yes, I'm
here." Frank lowered the journal he was reading and gave Brenda a
puzzled look. She saw the what's up expression on Frank's face.
She ignored it and said,"How remote of a chance is it?" "Probably
very remote. I can't really say, but it's probably very remote."

"If it's so remote, Danny, then I don't know if it's worth the
risk." Their conversation was far too serious; so this wasn't the time
to refer to him as Danny D. Brenda had reserved that name for
Danny for light moments, which wasn't now—not by a longshot.
"Brenda, anytime a person's life's at stake, it's a worthwhile consideration," Danny said. Now he had played his trump card, Brenda
thought. She was a nurse and comforting and healing was her business. But now it was her son who they were discussing. They had-
n't yet told him that he had been adopted. They would be forced to
tell Limuel the truth if he was a match for Emily's father. But it

wasn't that they had lied to Limuel; they just hadn't gotten around to letting him know that he had been adopted. Brenda's mind was overwhelmed. Her heart was troubled. But Danny was right, a man's life was at stake. She was a nurse and knew lots about life and death. "Brenda?" she heard Danny saying. "Yeah, Danny. Sorry. I was just thinking." Frank was no longer reading his journal. He suddenly became attentive to the conversation Brenda and Danny were having. "What about our pact, Danny? What about Emily? How will she handle it?" "That's down the road. First we need to determine if Limuel's a match. And if he is, then I'll explain it all to Emily."

"But if I tell my son that he's adopted, you know full well he's going to ask questions. Limuel's an inquisitive child. He'll probably want to know something about the mother and father who gave him life. So, what do I tell him, Danny? Do I tell him who his biological mother is? Do I tell him that his godparents are the parents of the man that fathered him as a result of having raped your—" "My wife?" said Danny. "I didn't mean to say that, Danny." "I know, Brenda. I know you didn't intend to say anything to hurt me. And, besides, it wasn't my wife who was raped. We weren't married at the time. Emee and I have both gotten beyond what happened to her before we married. I love Emee and wouldn't do anything to intentionally hurt her. The same with Limuel. I love him, too. But I am a doctor and a man's life hangs in the balance. Regardless of the fact that he's my father-in-law." "It's more like it's our duty, huh, Danny D.?" It relieved them both for Brenda to have called him Danny D. "Let me discuss it with Frank, then I'll call you back in a couple of days. I promise," Brenda said. They said their good-byes and Brenda placed the telephone receiver in its cradle. Frank said,"Danny's asking us to have Limuel tested to see if his bone marrow is a match for his father-in-law?" "Yes," Brenda said softly as her tender brown eyes searched Frank's face.

"Do you think it's a good idea?" Frank asked. "Saving a person's life is never a bad idea," Brenda responded. "Limuel might not be a match," Frank said. "But suppose he is?" Brenda countered. "What are the chances that he's a suitable donor." "The chance is remote. It's very slim, I would suppose. Frank, you know what my grandmother used to say?" "A lot of things according to you." "Yeah, she did. My grandmother told me and taught me a lot of things. My grandmother taught me about compassion and caring. One of the many things I remember her telling me, it was a long time ago; it was right after my mother died. My grandmother took me into her arms. . ." Tears trickled down Brenda's face. She wiped them with her bare hand. Frank removed the telephone from the bed and placed it back on the nightstand. He moved close to Brenda, wiped her tears with a tissue, caressed her in his arms, and laid his head against the side of her face. They allowed silence its sovereignty for awhile. Brenda continued, "My grandmother held me in her arms and said,'Honey girl, it ain't yo' fault yo' mama passed. Yah did what yah could and wha' yah knowed to do. Whenever yah do the best fir people, den dat's all yah can do.' Frank, I wouldn't be doing my best if I sat and did nothing while a man died. I would always wonder if Emily's father could've been saved if Limuel had been tested. I don't want that burden on me, Frank. Do you?"

Chapter Thirty-two

The limbs of Brenda's body were twisting and jerking like a marionette. Her facial muscles produced contorted and surreal images on her face. She was having a bad dream. She could hear Limuel screaming,"No, I'm not. I ain't no bastard. I ain't no white woman's child. I ain't! I ain't! I ain't!" "Are you okay, baby?" Frank asked as he shook Brenda to awaken her from her tormented sleep. Brenda's eyes opened wide as saucers. Her breathing was rapid and shallow. Her hands gripped the comforter on the bed. "I, I was dreaming," Brenda stammered. "I gathered as much," Frank asserted. "What were you dreaming?" Without going into detail, Brenda said,"I was dreaming that Limuel didn't take too well to being told that he was adopted. I hope this isn't a premonition of what we can expect later today." "I hope not, baby," Frank agreed. "I hope not." Brenda was anxious about what they were about to do. Frank was as fidgety as a novice on a tightrope. Limuel was taking it all in stride, excited about having an adult conversation with his parents. As a matter of fact he felt a bit grownup, but certainly he didn't feel like a child. After all, he figured the real child in the family, his sister Lenora, had left with his godmother just moments ago. They assembled in the family room; no one smiling except Limuel, whose pearly whites were conspicuous. Frank had a "you lead I'll follow" expression on his face, which didn't go unnoticed by Brenda, who had "we're going down this road together" thoughts in her mind. Brenda and Frank sat together on the futon sofa, across from a padded bench that Limuel occupied. Brenda's eyes quickly surveyed the room. She thought even the green potted plants were eagerly anticipating whatever it was she had to say. The July sun was bright. Its afternoon position in the sky cast a shadow on the western side of the house, which Brenda could see through the patio door that had vertical blinds pulled and folded to its flanks. Brenda had occupied herself by cleaning the house while she rehearsed in her mind what she was going to say to Limuel and how she was going to say it. She had also anticipated Limuel's questions, but could only hope that his reaction would be contrary to what she'd dreamed. Limuel was looking admiringly at his parents, still smiling, eager to discuss whatever it was in regard to their "powwow", as his mother had put it.

Brenda cleared her throat and said, "Limuel, you know your father and I love you, don't you?" "That's right, son," Frank added. "We love you very much." "I love y'all, too." said Limuel. "And you know your godparents love you too, right?" Brenda queried. "Yeah. And I love 'em too." "Okay," Brenda said, "so you know we all love you, right?" "Yeah." Brenda cleared her throat again. Frank was now smiling; he thought they had a good beginning in regard to their discussion. "Do you understand what happens when a child is adopted?" Brenda asked. Now Frank wasn't smiling. His wife had cut to the chase and now the discussion was becoming more serious and he was itching to hear his son's response. From the expression on his wife's face, he could discern her anxiety. Limuel didn't answer the question right away. He took time to ponder the question and rejoined, "When a mother or father doesn't want their boy or girl, they give 'em away." Brenda and Frank looked at each other. It wasn't the answer they were probing for. Brenda gave a slight bob of her head to Frank and looked at him in a manner that suggested that he say something and pick it up from here. Frank took her queue and said, "Limuel, mothers and fathers don't always give their children up for adoption because they don't want 'em. There are other reasons."

"Like what?" Limuel asked. "If they loved 'em and wanted 'em, why would they give 'em to somebody else?" Brenda thought it was time for her to intercede. She said, "Sweetheart, sometimes it's because a mother or father loves their child that they sometimes choose to place them for adoption. It's not necessarily that they don't love their child. Sometimes mothers and fathers think a child could have a better home and a better life someplace else; so then it's out of love and caring that they let someone else adopt their child. Can you understand that?" "Yeah, I can. But I still think that it's best to be with your real parents. I'm glad I'm with my real parents." Limuel's response elicited startled expressions on both Brenda's and Frank's faces. But it was too late to retreat. They both realized that Limuel needed to know the truth. They had put it off long enough. Today he was going to know the truth, then they would handle the aftermath with plenty of love for the son they adored. "Limuel, suppose you were adopted? Suppose your father and I adopted you? Would you feel any less loved than if we were your biological or real parents? Would you?" Limuel studied his parents' faces. Their expressions were sending him a message, along with the questions his mother just asked. He asked in a soft voice, "Was I adopted?"

Frank looked at Brenda. Brenda had her eyes focused on the face of her son. She rose from the futon and walked over to Limuel. She sat next to him and pulled him in her arms and said, "Yes, sweetheart; your father and I adopted you when you were just a little baby. We've always loved you, sweetheart, and we are your real parents, so never forget that. Okay?" "Okay, Mama. But why didn't my real mother, er, I mean my other mother want me?" "Let me ask you first, sweetheart, are you disappointed that your father and I adopted you?" "No. I just wonder about it. Was somethin' wrong with me? Was I a bad baby or somethin'?" "No, sweetheart. Nothing was wrong with you. You were a good baby, a beautiful baby, and you hardly cried. Nothing was wrong with you; nothing at all." "Then why was I given away?" "There would've been problems for the lady who gave you birth if she had kept you. And under the circumstances she couldn't keep you." "What circumstances?" Limuel asked. "Your biological or birth mother was white." "White? How could she be white? I'm not white!" "No, you're not, sweetheart. But you aren't all black, either." "Yes I am. I'm black. If I ain't white I gotta be black." "Limuel, sweetheart, some people have mixed blood in them, because one of their parents is black and the other's white." "So did my black blood come from a black man?"

"Yes, Limuel. It did." "So, where is he?" "He's no longer

alive," Brenda rejoined. "What happened to him?" Limuel asked. "Limuel, sweetheart, that isn't important. What's important is that your father and I love you, son. We're your parents and we've been your parents since soon after you were born. You said you weren't disappointed. So, do you really mean that, sweetheart? Do you really mean it? And if you don't, it'll be okay to say that you're disappointed. Your father and I will understand and will still love you no less." "Mama, I'm not disappointed. I love you and Daddy. I love you with all my heart. I do." That brought tears to both Brenda's and Frank's eyes. Their sniffling was obvious in the otherwise silence of the room. After gaining her composure, Brenda said, "There's another related matter that your father and I want to discuss with you. It concerns a man who's dying from a disease, but he can probably be saved if the doctors find the right person who matches something he needs, which is called bone marrow. Do you know what bone marrow is?" "No. I know what bones are, but I don't know about any marrow stuff."

"Okay, then we'll pull it up on the Internet and you'll understand what it is. But, anyway, there may be a longshot possibility that your bone marrow can match the bone marrow of the man who's dying. The only way we can find out that your bone marrow is like his is to have you tested. Would you mind being tested if it's possible that you can save a man's life?" "No, I don't mind. The angels would cry if I didn't, and I don't want the angels to cry." "Sweetheart, who told you that. I never heard you say that before. Why do you think the angels would cry?" "Because God-daddy told me that whenever people do wrong and they know they're doing wrong, or when people don't help other people who need help, then the angels cry." "Well, sweetheart, we certainly don't want to make the angels cry, do we?" "No, Mama. I know I don't."

Chapter Thirty-three

Danny Donnell contemplated that there were indeed "defining moments" in people's lives and this was to be one of them for sure. He needed to tell his wife that Limuel Justin Morgan was a compatible bone marrow match for her father; knowing full well that the revelation would summon inevitable angst for Emily. Danny realized that he'd come off sounding self-assured when he'd spoken to Brenda over the phone, but revealing to Emily who Limuel Justin was in regard to her past would be no easy task. In fact, it was going to be more daunting than he'd let on. And for that reason he thought the two of them should be home alone this evening; just him and Emily, no one else. Emily had dropped off the girls at the baby-sitter's as Danny requested, and her father had been picked up by a friend of the family whom they'd met at First Presbyterian Church, where they all were members. Danny had made the arrangements, in fact, he'd made all the arrangements, which was a thought Emily was entertaining as she took a soothing bubble bath upstairs in their spacious, four bedroom home that had a southwestern American style and flair about it. Danny had requested that they arrange to have some time alone, which Emily didn't have a problem with. She remembered Danny sounding so serious, but she didn't press him for an explanation, after all, it'd been a while since they'd spent some quality quiet time alone outside of their bedroom. They'd both been so busy with their jobs, raising their daughters, and caring for her father; so they needed some time alone. In fact, Emily was looking very much forward to their special time together this evening. She had the dress in mind that she would wear. Danny always liked her in it. Emily smiled as she thought about their evening together. Just the two of them. She settled back in the tub with her eyes closed, encircled by jeweled bubbles. Emily applied the sponge to her body. "Hmm."

Dr. Danny Donnell anesthetized his last patient in the trauma

ward at Memorial Hospital. Consulting his match, it was 5:39 P.M.
After showering he would call the East Wind Restaurant and order
a cuisine of Chinese that he would pick up on the way home. He
figured he would be home by seven o'clock, earlier than usual for a
Saturday. He and Emily would have a quiet dinner at home and then
they would talk. He was a bit nervous; that he'd admit. But they
needed to talk about it. It needed discussion. There was no way
around it. He just didn't know how Emily would take the news.

Candlelights. The works. Danny thought Emily had done a
superb job setting the dining room table, and told her as much and
followed up with a long, passionate kiss. Emily smiled as she sat
graciously at the table with the aid of her husband's chivalrous
assistance. She was enjoying every moment of it. She especially
adored the manner in which Danny was looking at her. It made her
feel special and loved. Danny's nose detected that Emily was wearing Pleasant cologne; his favorite. And he always loved seeing her
in the dress she was wearing. It fitted the contours of her body well,
which was always a turn on for him, like now, he was thinking. But
he had to refocus his thoughts because this wasn't really one of
those kinds of dinners, and it couldn't be on account of what he was
going to share and discuss with his wife this evening. They both had
had their fill. They'd more than adequately indulged themselves of
the scrumptious meal. Chinese was a favorite of theirs, second to
Italian. They'd both had a taste for Eastern fare this evening. It'd
been a good choice. They both cracked open Chinese cookies.
Emily read from the small piece of paper inside:"Your life will be
filled with love." She smiled and waited for Danny to read his for-
tune:"Someone you love will forgive you." Emily laughed and
asked,"Is there someone who needs to forgive you?"

Danny smiled and said, "Not now, but one never knows what
the future might hold." "True,"Emily said, "but if I had to forgive
you for something, I would." She flashed Danny a reassuring smile,
then said, I love you, Danny." "I love you, Emee." They exchanged
smiles across the table through the flames of the candles. Danny's
mood turned somber. He said, "Emee, there's something you need
to know." The earnest expression on Danny's face didn't go unno-

ticed by Emily. "What is it?" she asked. Danny leaned forward, rested his forearms on the table, looked Emily straight yet compassionately in her eyes and said, "Limuel Morgan was tested to determine if he might be a bone marrow match for your father." Emily kept her eyes trained on Danny's face. She was confused. "Why?" is what she asked. "Whose idea was it?" "Mine," said Danny. "But why? How could Limuel possibly be a match for my father?" Danny got up from his chair, walked around the table, stood behind Emily with his hands on her shoulders and said, "Emily, you gave birth to Limuel." Emily didn't respond. She sat like a stone in her chair, anchored by heavy emotions.

Chapter Thirty-four

When Brenda and Frank informed Limuel that he was a compatible match as a bone marrow donor for Hugo Heiderberg, he simply smiled. The smile on their son's face told Brenda and Frank that Limuel was going to be okay. He had brought them so much joy. But not only them; he had also brought other people joy. And they knew he had brought no less joy to his godparents who loved him dearly. He had become the kind of son that the Williamses always wanted, but somehow their own son, Tommy, had gone astray and gotten caught up in a venomous street-life that had warped his mind, disfigured his morality, and taken his life is what Barenda was thinking. Brenda knew they didn't have to worry about Limuel. He wasn't going to turn out like Tommy Williams. God rest his soul. She considered Limuel was the kind of child that got joy in making angels smile, which pleased not only Brenda and Frank, but his godparents as well.

The Williamses had clung to their faith in God; although they admitted that their faith had been seriously tested after Satan claimed their son. But after they agreed to become Limuel's godparents, they could see Tommy living through Limuel, which they considered to be a blessing. Limuel was indeed a blessing, Brenda contemplated. Brenda, Frank, Lenora, and the Williamses waited in the hospital's lounge while Limuel underwent the allogenic transplant procedure. Danny and Emily were also there in the lounge, sitting a distance apart from the Morgans. The Donnells had come from Arizona for the operation. Brian and Johanna were there as well. The atmosphere in the lounge was strained and uncomfortable for them all; but it was apparent that Emily was struggling the most, which was understandable under the circumstances. The turn of events had uncovered a lot—much like Richard Nixon's Watergate. Emily now knew who Limuel actually was, and Hazel and NathanielWilliams learned of Emily's relationship to Limuel and their son, Tommy. It was an atmosphere charged with powerful emotions that were deep-seated, melancholy, introspective, and lacerated. But yet, in spite of it all, a man's life was being saved. And it was being saved by a child, who, by no fault of his own, came into the world misbegotten. Dr. Thorndike, who performed the transplant, came into the lounge wearing O.R. scrubs. He appeared to be between forty-five to fifty years in age. He got right to the point. He said, "It went well, folks. Both Mr. Heiderberg and Limuel are recovering. You'll be able to speak to them very shortly."

Words of thanks and appreciation came from Brenda, Frank, Danny, Brian, and Johanna. Emily acted reserved and was reticent, though a sense of relief could be detected on her face. Dr. Thorndike flashed a smile of assurance, then left. Danny walked over to where Brenda and Frank were standing. Emily remained where she was—aloft, taciturn, and immersed in her own thoughts. "How's it going, Danny D.?" Brenda asked. Danny responded with a feeble smile and said, "Can we talk privately?" "Sure," Brenda said. "Do you mind, Frank?" "No, Danny. You two go ahead." Danny and Brenda left the lounge and walked slowly down the corridor side by side in silence for several paces before Danny spoke. "Brenda, I want to thank you, Frank, and Limuel for what you've done. And please don't read Emee wrong. She's appreciative, too. It's just that all this has been overwhelming for her. She's not her normal self. She's a bit withdrawn right now and confused." "I understand, Danny. Do you think she'll be all right. Is she going to be able to handle knowing who Limuel really is?" "I think she will. Emee's a fighter. She'll eventually come to terms with all of this. I'm confident." "I hope so, Danny. I hope so." "Limuel saved her father's life, so she can't be disappointed about that. I think she'll eventually see that a greater good came from all of this."

"It did; didn't it?" Brenda responded. "I think it did," Danny said. "I want you and Emily to be all right, Danny D." "We will. I promise you." "Then good. And please do something for me." "What is it?" "Stay in touch and let me know how things are going. I consider y'all family." "We are family aren't we?" Danny said, as he smiled at Brenda. They smiled at each other and hugged. On the way home from the hospital, Limuel saw a long, white, stretch limousine traveling the expressway just ahead of them. He said, "Wow, look at that. It must be somebody important in that car. One day I'm gonna be somebody important and ride in a car like that." Brenda and Frank looked at each other and smiled. Brenda turned around in the front seat of the car and said, "You are important, sweetheart. You are important. You're important to a lot of people. A lot of people love you." Limuel basked in his mother's words and looked back at the long limousine as they passed it.

Brenda turned back around and looked at the traffic on the road. She mused that anyone who was born in the back seat of a limousine had to be important and was destined for greatness. She recalled her grandmother saying, "Honey girl, gre'tness is in the heart. Yah jest don't stumble up on it. It's in the heart." Brenda knew their son had the heart to become a great man, a loving man; and a caring man. She was happy. She couldn't be happier.

Emily needed some quiet time to unburden her heart and mind. Danny understood as much and the reason he had insisted that Freidella, the oldest, and Heidi sit next to him. Danny reminded the girls that their mother was tired: the same thing he had been telling them since Emily discovered who Limuel Justin Morgan really was. Danny sat between Emily and their daughters. Emily occupied the seat next to the window on the jumbo 747 that was in flight to Phoenix. Danny reached for Emily's hand and held it. Emily's gaze was on the glistening clouds outside the window of the airplane. Emily had a lot to think about. The revelation of knowing that she'd given birth to Limuel Justin Morgan was still a shock for Emily, but she wasn't angry. She wasn't angry at Danny, Brenda, or anyone. But being shocked was another matter. The disclosure of who Limuel actually was had unquestionably shocked her. There was no doubt about it. It was jolting news that rattled Emily's brain and brought on an avalanche of emotions. But she wasn't angry. She wasn't angry at anyone. Nor was she forgiving. She had never forgiven the men who raped her. And even though her father's life had been saved by the unwanted child she'd given birth to, she still couldn't forgive her rapists, which, in a way, seemed discrepant to

Emily.

Emily realized that she had acted distant with Brenda and Frank at the hospital, but in time she knew she would come to terms with all that she had discovered in such a narrow space of time. But she wasn't angry. She wasn't angry at anyone. And she sure wasn't angry at Limuel Justin Morgan. Her mother would have loved him. The thought was comforting to Emily. In fact, she loved Limuel, too. There was no denying it. Her mind suddenly affixed to the irony of the fact that it had been her father who had delivered Limuel into the world. And, at the time, it was the last thing her father wanted to do. Emily recalled how her mother often said, "...God works in mysterious ways." This had to be one of those ways, Emily thought.

Chapter Thirty-five

Retirement was fitting Ullysis Washington well; much like the pricey, tailored suit he had purchased for the retirement party his family, co-workers, and friends had thrown for him last week at the Double Tree Hotel in downtown Detroit. After thirty-two years working, and working what he considered his ass off for the Detroit Police Department, he was thoroughly enjoying his emancipation. Gloria, his wife of twenty-five years, had constantly accused him of having been a slave to his job, working long hours and all. But it was simply dedication, along with his desire to help do whatever it took to make Detroit a safer place for its citizens. He also was goaded by the bad reputation which he thought Detroit unfairly got by outsiders: people who didn't live in the city but constantly bad-mouthed the denizens who lived there and worked damn hard. He loved Detroit. He was born and raised in The Motor City. And although he was retired, he wasn't about to abandon his beloved city for some suburb like some other turncoats he knew. But things had changed in Detroit.

Ullysis Washington smiled at the thought of having witnessed the Second Migration—at least that's how he saw it. And it all happened after they developed the riverfront casino district and brought the Detroit Tigers and Detroit Lions to stadiums downtown where they belonged is how Ullysis figured it. Then hotels, midrise office buildings, shops, clubs, and restaurants sprang up like dandelions in early spring. Humanity began crowding Detroit like hadn't been seen in decades and people were living downtown in newly built homes, condominiums, and highrise apartments.

The Second Migration is what it was, all right, Ullysis thought, with more people living in Detroit than in years, and swelling the city's population to over a million people after struggling for years to prevent falling under a million citizens in order to not lose considerable federal dollars and clout. Jobs a plenty. People all over the place: day and night, night and day.   And like his daughter Nwanaka said, "Detroit got it going on!"   But Ullysis didn't want to think about all this now, so he deserted his rumination as he relaxed with a glass of Scotch on the rocks. He was sitting at a table inside the dimly lit, nautically decorated Windjammer Lounge aboard the S. S. Norway as it cruised the calm waters of the western Caribbean. The cruise was his retirement gift to himself after thirty-five years in law enforcement, with thirty of them spent in employment with the Detroit Police Department.   Friends were still trying to get him to take up golfing, a sport he detested.   He'd thought about writing a book.   After over three decades of law enforcement work, he had seen a lot.   Hell, he figured if those lawyer-turned-author guys could write books and make millions, then he could do the same. Ullysis contemplated that maybe he could make enough money on a book to buy a bigger boat; certainly a lot bigger than the thirty-four foot Bayliner he'd purchased five years ago, which was moored at Harbor Hill Marina off the Detroit River.   The size boat he had in mind would really be in the category of a yacht.   The thought of owning such a watercraft was pleasureable and produced a smile on Ullysis' vintage face. Ullysis consulted his watch.   It was half past five in the afternoon.   Gloria had gone to their suite to freshen up after they'd returned from duty-free shopping on St. Thomas Island.   He looked for the waitress.   His glass was nearly empty.   Outside of the Windjammer he saw people reclining in chaise lounges, basking in the warm rays of the Caribbean sun, tanning their pale bodies. The sight caused him to chuckle. He looked down at his dark arms, rubbed one of his arms with delight and mumbled, "This is the real deal; a natural born tan.   No Copper Tone here." Ullysis smiled and chuckled to himself.   In fact, he'd had reasons to smile a lot on the cruise, which had four days left of its seven-day itinerary.   He wasn't missing police work.   He was having too much fun in retirement.

Ullysis caught the waitress's attention and ordered another Scotch.   He took out his wallet and examined the photos of his grandchildren: a young boy and girl.   He loved his grandchildren and he love to hear them call him "Grandpa."   Sweet kids they were, is what Ullysis thought as he beamed with joy. The very thought of his grandchildren always gave him a cheerful glow.   He would be the first to admit that he hadn't wanted his son Kevin to marry that white girl. He had wanted Kevin to marry a black woman. He had wanted black grandchildren, not "half-breeds" or "Oreos", like he had normally put it, referring to the cookies: dark on the outside and white on the inside. He figured that all had worked out well: Kevin and Candy were in love and had two beautiful children whom he loved just as much as his own children.   And now that his two daughters, Nwanaka and Binta, had graduated from college and were on their own with good jobs, he now had his two grandchildren to fawn over, and to the point that his wife was constantly chiding him about spoiling their grandchildren rotten.

Ullysis folded the photos back into his wallet and thought more about writing a book. People were always asking him to share accounts of his life while employed with the Detroit PD. Some of the things he would share were so mind-boggling that sometimes he got the impression that people thought he was telling them something less than literal. And people wanted to know his most memorable case. An easy question. For certain, it had been the investigation of the murders and wanton crimes orchestrated by the Euro-Brothers Defense Society more than a decade ago. No question about it. Solving that case had given him more satisfaction than anything he was a part of in police work. Ullysis sipped from the glass, savoring the taste of the twelve-year-old Scotch. His forehead furrowed—like it did anytime Hugo Heiderberg surfaced in his mind. He wished they had never cut a deal with the bastard. He wanted to see that honkie go to prison with the rest of those racist scums. As far as Ullysis was concerned, Hugo Heiderberg was just as guilty; the same as when he was charged with dereliction of duty and abuse of power as part of the Dirty Dozen case from which he escaped unscathed. He got off scot-free then. One luck-blessed honkie; probably living a charmed and peaceful life is what Ullysis thought. He figured Heiderberg to be luckier than that Teflon-ass Ronald Reagan when he was president, to whom no measure of wrongdoing would stick while he occupied the White House.

Gloria sat down at the table and ended Ullysis' meditation. He ordered Gloria a drink and another for himself. He and Gloria lifted their etched glasses in a nonverbal toast as they beamed solicitous gazes at each other while the keyboardist played Moon River. Tomorrow they were going to spend the day on the white sand beach of Stirrup Cay. But after one more drink, they were going back to their spacious suite on the starboard side of the upper deck and make love before attending a cocktail party in the captain's quarters and having a late dinner. Retirement was suiting Ullysis Washington quite well. He was loving it.

Chapter Thirty-six

Hugo Heiderberg strolled outside the towering structure of the Renaissance Center in downtown Detroit. The building had really changed since General Motors purchased the facility more than a decade ago and made the complex its global headquarters. The improvements were very impressive. Hugo figured that GM had spent a king's ransom to renovate the former Westin Hotel and make all the other physical enhancements in and around the center. Impressive indeed, Hugo mulled. Very impressive. He needed this sojourn. This is where it had all happened. Things had changed over the years. This was the weekend when the Country and Western Jamboree would have been held, but it was no longer held in downtown Detroit. Organizers had changed the format as well as the venue. The new promoters now referred to it as the Country and Western Extravaganza, which they'd held at the Palace in Auburn Hills for the last eight or nine years.

Hugo walked over to the concrete restraining wall and looked down into the dark water. The waves were dancing and leaping rhythmically into the warm night air. There had been many changes in Detroit over the past few years, but they had not physically changed the Detroit River. Hugo found pleasure in contemplating that God and Mother Nature still had control and dominion over some things. Tears clouded his eyes. It had been on this side of the Renaissance Center that his daughter, Emily, had gotten abducted years ago. He remembered that rainy night and all the agony. He allowed the tears to fall unabated. He thought he would die that night when he discovered that Emily had been raped. He blamed himself. He never should've let her go to the car that night alone. He should've gone instead. He figured it had been his fault that Emily was raped. He recalled all the hate. He looked up into the sky and saw the clouds revealing the presence of the half-crescent moon that God had sovereignty over. He had promised God and himself that he would never question God again. He had denounced God when Emily was raped. He questioned why God would let something so horrible happen to Emily, whom had never in her life harmed a soul. Then his wife was suddenly taken from him. He had had no use for God, because he was convinced that God wasn't in existence, and if He was, then God had abandoned and forsaken him and his family. So he figured, who needed a god whom you couldn't count on and who wasn't there when you needed Him?

Hugo took out his handkerchief and wiped the tears that had run down his face and settled into his gray beard. He reflected on how he seemed to be looking at himself in the mirror when his son Brian had returned home on leave from the Navy. All the hate. The hate was eating Brian alive. After they left the courthouse the day Brian was holed up in the bathroom, he decided to give God one more try. He prayed for Brian, Emily, Johanna, and himself. He prayed for God's forgiveness and mercy. He figured God had answered him when he was diagnosed with aplastic anemia and needed a bone marrow transplant. He figured that God was telling him that he wasn't worthy of His mercy and that God hadn't forgiven him. Then there was Limuel Justin Morgan, a child who was his biological grandson; a child he never wanted to see come into the world, the child he hated because of how he was conceived. Limuel Justin Morgan. A perfect donor. A child who saved his life. It was a reality that he woke up with and took to bed every day, and a rumination that was as routine as putting on clothes. It was all still overwhelming. It had been over a decade since his operation and he was feeling fine. The doctor had told him that he was doing quite well. He felt strong. Hugo felt that in spite of it all, things hadn't turned out too badly. He had two lovely granddaughters and a wonderful son-in-law who truly loved his daughter Emily. He was good for her. And Brian had turned his life around. And his daughter Johanna was doing well at the Julliard School of Music—studying the piano. All those years of practicing and dedication had paid off. The dedication had been in loving memory of her mother. Hugo felt blessed to have lived to see it all.

Hugo was immersed in thought, so the man's sudden appear-

ance startled him. He seemed to have come from nowhere—like
the sudden burst of wind that felt chilly against his crinkled face.
The man's appearance was untidy and as though he had slept in the
same clothes for at least a week. Hugo guessed that the man hadn't
shaved in several days by the appearance of the stubby hair on his
hollowed face. As their eyes met, the man looked remotely familiar. He seemed to have gazed into those steely blue eyes at some
point or time. No time recently, but some time in the past. But he
couldn't put it all together. And the man's appearance suggested
that he was no one whom Hugo figured he would've associated
himself with. Nonetheless, the man's eyes and now his facial features looked oddly familiar to Hugo. "You, Hugo Heiderberg?"
Hugo looked at the man with a bit of surprise, wondering how the
stranger knew his name. Hugo was now convinced that the two of
them must have met at some time. "Yes, I am," Hugo responded.
He stared at the man, attempting to bring him in clearer focus and
absent of his bedraggled appearance. "Don't recognize me, do
you?" "No. Not really. But you look somewhat familiar." "Yeah,
prison and hard times can change a man's appearance. Ever been
to prison, Mr. Heiderberg?" The sudden formality of the man's tone
confounded Hugo. And the man's intonation sounded familiar.
"Ever been to prison, Mr. Heiderberg?" the slenderly built man
repeated.

    "No I haven't." "Didn't think so." "Who are you? Where do
you know me from?" "Does Brother Volga register with you?" The
man clicked his heels together and came to attention like a soldier
readying inspection. Hugo couldn't believe his eyes. Now he knew
whom the person was. He had joined the Euro-Brothers Defense
Society two years after its origin. Hugo remembered him being a
gung-ho member: one of those Brothers that you could truly count
on and was willing to do anything for the brotherhood. The man
assumed a more casual and less of a soldierly posture and said,
"They arrested you along with the rest of the Brotherhood; so, why
were you the only one who didn't get any prison time?" The words
were harsh in tone and laden with accusation. He stared into Hugo's
stunned face. "I lost everything, Mr.Heiderberg. Everything. My

businesses, my wife, and my family. The question still begs an answer. How come they never sent you to prison along with the rest?" Hugo was no longer conversing with a disheveled stranger, but rather, a ghost of the past. He figured that he didn't owe him an explanation. The Society was a thing of the past. It was history. Hugo had come to this setting to reflect and hopefully come to terms with his life. He hadn't expected to encounter the apparition in his midst. He figured he would simply turn and walk away.

"Mr. Heiderberg!" The man called Hugo's name so loud that the waves in the river seemed startled. Hugo turned to face his tormentor. "You never turn your back on the Brotherhood. One can never be injurious to the Brotherhood without retribution." The man rushed toward Hugo. Hugo saw the glimmer of steel in the air at the end of the raised arm of the sinewy person who was attacking him. The object descended until it was thrust and buried deep into Hugo's chest by the strength that came from having pumped iron daily in prison for a dozen years. Hugo felt life draining from him as his life flashed before him like frames in a carousel projector. The last frame was of him and Limuel Justin Morgan in the operating room. The instrument of death was wrenched from Hugo Heiderberg's lifeless body and thrown into the Detroit River. The man had completed the mission. He was the first of the Society to be released from prison. Hugo Heiderberg's name had been on the top of the list for retribution.

Chapter Thirty-seven

He exited the long, white limousine that was provided compliments of the United Auto Workers. He and his entourage were ushered into the Marriot Hotel and up to the fourth floor. A boisterous throng of campaign workers and supporters greeted them as they paraded out the elevator into the capacious ballroom. He shared the stage with those who were most close to him: his family, confidantes, and those who had spearheaded his campaign for mayor of Detroit. It was a proud moment for him. He had literally been beseeched to run for mayor; lots of people saying that he was definitely the man for the job. "The man of the people" is how they had put it to him. This convinced him to run for the office after he talked it over with his family, who gave him their blessing, support, and much love, as did so many citizens of Detroit.

The polls had closed nearly two hours ago, and early returns projected him the winner. In fact, his rival had already publicly conceded the election. He looked proudly out into the large crowd of humanity; many of them holding placards with his photo, waving pennants, and throwing confetti. The room was lavishly adorned with red, white, and blue balloons and streamers. A bountiful and appreciative smile graced his handsome face as he observed all the gala and unabated excitement. Joseph Underwood, Limuel Justin Morgan's campaign manager, stepped to the podium. "Ladies and gentlemen." He paused. "Ladies and gentlemen, may I have your attention? Ladies and gentlemen. Ladies and gentlemen. May I have your attention?" A hush reigned. "Ladies and gentlemen, it's my distinct pleasure to introduce my very dear and personal friend, a person I've known for fifteen years, and make no mistake about it, the next great mayor of the city of Detroit: Limuel Justin Morgan."

Limuel Justin Morgan was surely a man of the people. The people of Detroit loved him—at least the vast majority did, which the voters demonstrated at the polls throughout the city. "A lop-sided victory" is what the media had proclaimed. Limuel Justin Morgan had mounted a commanding lead in the early poll counts. Early in his campaign, he opined that he was running to "Bring the good people of Detroit together." The citizens of Detroit loved him as their prosecutor: tough on crime, but fair. The criminal types both respected and feared Limuel Justin Morgan. They knew they were in trouble if Morgan was prosecuting them in the courtroom. The word in the street by those with the propensity to engage in criminal behavior was that you don't want to be Morgancuted, because if you were, you were as likely to be found guilty and sent to prison as seeing a light pole on Woodward Avenue. Limuel Justin Morgan had been the youngest person elected as the city's prosecu-tor. He had zero tolerance for crime and all the criminal-minded souls knew as much; and, subsequently, crime in Detroit dropped considerably. Most citizens gave credit for this to Prosecutor Morgan's office. He was a man of the people, for sure. He had a lot of backing. Money was no object. Campaign funds poured in from practically every nook and cranny in the city and, as a cam-paign worker had put it, swelled his campaign chest like a pair of spandex breeches on a Sumo wrestler. One couldn't walk or ride down a city street or turn a corner without seeing Limuel Justin Morgan's picture and campaign posters plastered practically every-where and as ubiquitous as street signs. His campaign committee had plenty of bucks, so they soaked big dollars into radio and tele-vision campaign ads that were heard and seen more often than McDonald's restaurant commercials. The people loved him and they loved him enough to make him mayor and give him a margin of victory that the pundits were projecting to be unprecedented. The people surely loved him, but no more than he loved them. Limuel Justin Morgan had lived his life believing that all people were significant—no matter their color, race, religion, gender or socio-economic status. It was a conviction he never wavered from. It was a conviction that was his driving force and that fueled his behavior and guided his conduct. Limuel Justin Morgan was a lover of people and life.

Success was nothing new to him. He had achieved much success in his life of thirty-six years. He had gone on to the University of Michigan with both an academic and athletic scholarship. They loved him at Michigan, where he became an All-American running back in his junior year. No one doubted that he would have been successful in the National Football League if he hadn't torn up his knee in his senior year. People said they hadn't seen anybody run with a football like Limuel "The Man" Morgan since that guy named Barry Sanders who played for the Detroit Lions back in the nineties. And a busted knee couldn't stop Limuel Justin Morgan, no more than man could stop the rain. They elected him student body president in his senior year. He graduated with honors, went on to law school and finished number two in his class. The big law firms were after him like prospectors discovering gold. They loved him at the Bradford, Goldberg and Smith law firm in New York City. They paid him handsomely. But though the money was good—damn near outrageously good—after five years he was missing his parents, who were getting up in age, so he left New York and came back home to Michigan, where he met the woman of his dreams one month after returning. Before he had been introduced to her, he had heard people—lots of people—describe Sheila Brooks as "smart and beautiful." He discovered that she was all that and more. She was a local TV personality with charm and sophistication personified. He knew right away that Sheila was the woman he was going to marry and he wasn't wrong about that.

Limuel Justin Morgan was a man who wasn't wrong about too? many things—especially about people. He was good at sizing people up. It was a talent he had come by naturally. And when he decided to forego the big money offers from law firms in Michigan to run for prosecutor in Detroit, he knew his decision was the right one. In his heart he knew it. He had a longing. He wanted to work in the trenches, along with the ordinary people who weren't well-connected to the powerbrokers or who didn't rub elbows with the city's socialites. His desire was to make a difference in the lives of everyday citizens. It was his calling. He promised the people that if they worked with him he would get the criminals and recidivists

off the streets of Detroit and find them addresses at jails and peni-
tentiaries. The people loved it. They loved him. They gave him
their support. He didn't disappoint them. He did just as he promised: He got a lot of felons, Mafiosos, and scofflaws off the streets
and into lockups. The criminals both feared and respected the man
Limuel Justin Morgan, who used the prosecutor's office for a bully
pulpit on behalf of the citizens of Detroit. Now they had elected
him mayor. And the moniker they had bestowed on him in college
during his days on the gridiron followed him: "The Man." He was
the youngest person to be elected mayor of Detroit.

Limuel stood at the podium as the crowd in the ballroom
cheered thunderously. The noise could be heard on the first floor at
the hotel's registration desk. His body was as trim as it was when
he tortured opposing teams on the gridiron in college. He looked
like he just stepped off the cover of Gentleman Quarterly Magazine
in the blue, Italian-cut, double-breasted suit that bedecked his six-
two frame. He leaned on the podium and savored the booming
applause and lavish adoration. It was a crowning moment for him.
He had a lot of people to thank and no less Sheila, his wife of eight
years, who had been very supportive and had given him the son he
wanted. Then there was his adoring parents: Brenda and Frank
Morgan. He felt their love right there on the stage in front of hundreds of people who were showering him with love. His godparents
had passed and gone to glory some years ago, but he felt they were
smiling down on him. There was enough love in the room to last
Limuel Justin Morgan a lifetime. As Limuel Justin Morgan, his
family, and others in his entourage left the hotel and got into the
waiting limousine, someone in the crowd was heard saying "Rumor
has it that Limuel Morgan was born in the back seat of a limousine."
Another person laughed at the remark, which was thought to be far-
fetched. "The things people come up with," the skeptical person
rejoined, shaking his head with a sign of disbelief.

Joseph Underwood was introspective as he leaned back against
the plush leather seat as the limousine drove off. The sides of his
mouth curled up. He was a man of vision. He knew Limuel Justin
Morgan well and was constantly telling him that his successes

always had a capital S. He had been the first to appeal to Limuel to run for mayor, but he hadn't shared with Limuel his more foresighted vision. It was a vision that went beyond Limuel being major of Detroit. For sure, Joseph Underwood's vision was greater. Much greater. And he wasn't going to be satisfied until he got his pal Limuel into the governor's mansion in Lansing and then residency at 1600 Pennsylvania Avenue in Washington D.C. President Limuel Justin Morgan had a nice ring. Joseph Underwood had long been convinced that the world became a better place the day Limuel Justin Morgan was born. And he knew a lot of people thought as he did. Lots of people. Limuel Justin Morgan was "The Man".

THE END